The copyright © to this book is held by John Edward Wright 2021
It Is a work of fiction and the people in this book bear no resemblance to people living or dead.

I dedicate this book to my wonderful wife Christine who has been my rock through my hard times

About the author

My name is John Edward Wright, I was born in Yorkshire but brought up in Bletchley, Buckinghamshire Home of the world war two code breakers. After leaving school at sixteen I worked as a butcher before taking my heavy goods driving licence, but after 37 years on the road I had to give that up after being diagnosed with Fibromyalgia, I now spend my time looking after my handicapped sister, going out with my camera, and sketching. This is my first try at writing a book and I hope you enjoyed it.

THE UNDERPASS KILLER
CHAPTER ONE

Dai Rees rolled over in his bed god had he really drank that much his head was thumping, this was the first real drink he had had since the lockdown had finished and it was a celebration his team had won its first rugby match against their oldest rivals Brackley and to top it all he had scored the winning try.
His phone was ringing and drumming in his head he picked up

"Ey up boss we've got a body" the unmistakeable tone of Detective Inspector Dave Parker a down and out Yorkshire man who got straight to the point no "good morning sir how are you" from him.

Dai sighed that is all he needed this morning he could do with a good shower and load of coffee to put him right,

"Where are you?"

"Underpass between Fishermead and Springfield the roundabout that joins the V8 Marlborough Street and H7 Chaffron way"

"I'll be there in 15"

Dai quickly showered, dressed made himself a thermal cup of coffee and shot out the door.

Dai lived in Milton Keynes the town that calls itself a city although it had never been given a city status known for its roundabouts and concrete cows and home to the Open University. Dai had moved here four years ago and given up his life in the valleys with his wife and daughter that he had already lost because of the job, for a life with what he thought was the real love of his life Steph a career woman who had moved for her job to the company head office here, they had brought a house together but that had only lasted a year and a half before she had buggered off with a younger man from her company. Dai loved the history of it a town made up of 4 towns and all the villages in between taking its name taken from the smallest "Milton Keynes" that over the years the council had had to put up signs calling its old doomsday book name of Middleton Keynes as lorries delivering to the main shopping area got

confused and ended up in the village. The four towns being Stony Stratford made famous in the fact in was an old town set on the A5 Watling Street main route from London to Holyhead where coach and horses would stop at the two hotels in the town and stories would be told each hotel trying to outdo the other the two hotels were the Cock and the Bull so this is where world now gets a Cock and bull story.

The next was Wolverton a town that had grown up around the railways and built coaches for it and at one time home to the royal train used by the queen, the Grand union canal also ran through here and the middle of the city.

Then there was Newport Pagnell home to one of the most iconic British sports cars ever built the Aston Martin made famous by one of the world's most favourite spy James Bond.

Then the last was Bletchley, and Bletchley Park home of the W.W.2 code breakers. At one time it had been home to large brick fields that helped rebuild the UK after the war but these had now gone and all that was left the large lakes that had been made by filling the clay pits, at one point it had been the centre of the rail link called the Varsity line connecting Oxford and Cambridge this had been closed by the Beeching cuts of the sixties but now work was on to reopen it and maybe by 2035 it will be open , Marshall amplification had its factory here also MK Dons had there stadium on the edge of Bletchley.

When Dai had moved here when he was asked what street he lived in he was told "oh you live in Bletchley" then after talking to the neighbours they confirmed he lived in Fenny Stratford again a village that had in the past been joined to villages Bletchley and Water Eaton to make the town of Bletchley.

Fenny Stratford itself was also on the Watling Street and the canal and it was in fact older than any of the towns being a roman settlement called Magiovinium.

Dai had found out also that although most people know a heavy oil engine is called a diesel engine after seeing a plague on the side of a shop round the corner to his house to a guy called Herbert Akroyed -Stuart that he in fact had patented a heavy oil engine in 1890 some three years before Diesel.

Dai got his keys out and opened the door of his car no fancy central locking for him his car was a 1974 Triumph Dolomite, again a thing Dai loved old cars this one was now the love of his life he had brought it five years ago from a guy who had looked after it well, it had been an ex-police car serving with the Nottinghamshire force as a traffic car and the guy had planned to make it so again but due to ill health he never got round to it. He had it when he was serving with the police in Cardiff as a DI but since moving to TVP one of the guys in the motor work shop had taken a liking to the car and with permission from the guys on high had done some work on it for him, some of the work Dai was not too sure about as he had fitted a DAB radio with hands free blue tooth so he could take calls while on the move the last thing he needed was to be pulled by his colleagues in traffic for using the phone, so the old radio had to go. He had souped up the engine fitted new better disc brakes and shocks all round and had gone mad on the light's, blues had been fitted in the grill and at the rear, a visor police sign that he could pull down had been fitted and finally they had allowed the only thing that was kept from the Nottingham car was the two tones. This now gets the comment of "right guv time to fire up the Dolomite" every time they are going to a job after a certain DCI Gene Hunt off the telly use to say.

It took Dai less than ten minutes to reach the scene the great thing with Milton Keynes was there was rarely traffic jams thanks to the fact if there was a road closed you simply went to the next roundabout and turned whichever way you needed and end up where you need to go. He parked up on the grass verge and walked down to the underpass showing his ID to the young PC guarding the tape that had been put up, he was given a white over suit and shoe covers that he put on before ducking under the tape, He saw the pathologist had arrived before him Doctor Ruth Pickford she was young she looked too young to be doing the job, but she was particularly good at it and nearly always spot on. Dave Parker saw him and waved him over

"ey up boss sorry if I woke you" it was funny how Dave attitude changed when he was around Ruth he was always polite and nice Dai knew that Dave had feelings for on her and Dai would great pride in winding him up about it although he always got the same answer "no boss not me" he was keeping himself to himself until the right time came up but he also knew Ruth liked Dave and had often asked Dai about him but he felt he was not the person to play cupid with his track record.

"Right, what we got" Dai asked to Dave

"Young Black male about 18 to 20 found this morning by a lady walking her dog"

"Any ID"

"No, no wallet mobile phone nothing"

"Mugging gone wrong maybe?"

"I don't think so take a look at this" it was Ruth talking

Dai and Dave looked and pinned to the man's shirt under his coat was a piece of paper written on it in big letters "HE WHO SINS WILL PAY THE PRICE".

it looked now like they had got them self a murder.

"Any idea of time of death?" Dai asked

"Not really rigger has set in but it was cold last night so I can't give a real time I'd say around ten or eleven last night" Ruth took out a thermometer and placed it on the body "I'll know better when I get him to the lab"

"Cause of death" Dave asked

"Well, there's a blunt force trauma to the back of the head but not much blood I'd say this knocked him unconscious then as you see from these marks around the neck looks like some sort of cord has been used to strangle the victim"

"What time was the body found"

"About eight this morning as I said by that lady over there walking her dog"

Dai and Dave walked over to where the lady stood with a PC.

"Morning Mrs?"

"Henshaw, Mrs Violet Henshaw"

"Right Mrs Henshaw I'm DCI Rees and this is DI Parker I'd like to ask you a few questions if you don't mind then you can be on your way, my colleague says you was out walking your dog when you found the young man"

"yes that's right I don't normally take him it's my husband's job but he's not been well so I said I would take Lucky out this morning I was going through to the shops on Springfield for the morning paper and milk all though we live on Fishermead they are closer to us, any way I had Lucky on the long lead and it was her that made me notice the young man she ran up to him before I could stop her, when she started to lick him I thought he would move and tell her to get away"

"Then what did you do when he didn't" asked Dave

"Well, I went over thought he might be asleep with a hangover but when I saw the blood, I knew something was wrong, so I checked for a pulse and there wasn't one, I use to be a nurse so it didn't bother me I have a mobile phone, but I left it a home"

"Then what" Dai asked

"Well, there was a young man walking up he asked if everything was ok, and I asked him to phone the police he did, but I don't know where he went from there, I don't think he wanted to be involved"

"that's ok Mrs Henshaw we'll have his records on the call log" Dave reassured her

"You can go now but we will have to arrange for someone to come and take some samples as you touched the body for elimination only no other reason PC Grace will take you home"

"But I haven't got my paper and milk, yet my Burt will be most upset"

"I'll tell you what Mrs Henshaw PC Grace here will take you to the shop and get your things for you then take you home and make you a nice cuppa each how's that? then we'll be in touch"

WPC Grace looked at Dai with the look of "thank you sir that's all I need" but Dai just smiled back.

"Ok thank you" Mrs Henshaw followed Grace to the car and off they went

"Right Dave let's get house to house set up see if we can find anyone who knows what's going on and get on to the call handlers see if they can point us in the direction of the lad that made the 999 call"

He turned and saw Ruth was just bagging the body to be moved to the examination room at Milton Keynes University Hospital he went over.

She looked up as he approached "right I'm finished here I should be able to do a post-mortem almost straight away do you want to be there"

"Yes, I better what time I'll make sure Dave is with me I know he love's a post-mortem" the truth was Dave hated them and would go all green at the gills, but he knew he would come and put up with it just to see Ruth.

"Shall we say 15.30"

"Ok see you then if you need me in the time, you've got my number or give me a call at the office"

Dai saw Dave and shouted over that he would meet him back at the office and made his way back to the car stripping off the over suit as he went the CSI lads where there now doing a fingertip search of the area, he saw Colin Mathews the lead man and told him to keep him up to speed on anything they found and that he would be back at the office.

He got back to the car and took a swig of his coffee it was almost cold he would have to get himself a proper Thermus flask these cups never kept the coffee hot.

Chapter Two

DCI Dafydd (Dai) Rees was 45 years of age he had grown up in the ex-mining village of Pontycymer in the Garw valley seven miles from Bridgend it was a happy childhood, his father and his grandfather (grancha) and those before them had been miners, his mother was a shop assistant who tried to spend as much time at home as she could with Dai and his sister Bronwen. By the time Dai had left school the mines had closed throwing hundreds of men on to the dole those that where young enough manged to get jobs elsewhere like the Ford plant in Bridgend or at one of the new hi-tech companies in Pencoed or the furniture factories in Brynmenyn but the older men had nothing his father had been lucky he was good with his hands and managed to find himself a job as a caretaker at the local school.

Dai didn't know what he wanted to do when he left school he'd had a Saturday job as a butchers boy and thought about that but the shop closed so he had to rethink his best mate Billy Williams had like most of the lads from the village had signed up for the forces but he didn't fancy that, so after a while he was the only one out of his little gang of mates that had not got a job that is until he got chatting to the local beat bobby who was investigating a series of car break ins in the valley it was then that he decided that was the job for him.

He applied found he had all the qualifications that was needed so not long after he turned 19 Dai joined Heddlu De Cymru the Wales Police, he did his two year probation period then decided after a time on the beat that he would try traffic He spent two and a half years in traffic but due to an injury playing rugby that at the time made driving awkward he decided he would give CID a go he moved over to CID in Bridgend made his way up to DS after a couple of years then by the time he was 35 he tried for Detective inspector he passed, there was an opening in vice in Cardiff for a DI and he was offered it so he moved over. Dai had married his childhood sweetheart Sian not long after he joined the force, she was training to be a teacher about a year later they were blessed with a baby girl Bethan and all seemed rosy but when he moved to vice things started to fall apart he was working all hours Sian was a headmistress at a local primary school in Bridgend, Bethan had turned 15 and like most teenagers of that age had started to rebel against her parents Sian kept blaming him as he was never home Bethan blamed them both as they never took any notice of her they were both wrapped up in their jobs to much and this may have been true after about a year it was decided that maybe a split would do them good so Dai found himself a flat in Cardiff to be closer to work and it was agreed that Bethan would stay with mum and see dad at weekends but that had not lasted it seemed that every weekend Bethan was due to stay he had ended up working till in the end Bethan had stopped coming and what was meant to be a temporary split between him and Sian became a divorce, Sian had moved on and met someone else and remarried Dai was happy for her he was a nice guy, Bethan despite all her rebellion had made good grades at school and had gone to University and was now training to be a doctor and is in touch with him at least twice a week,

Dai had moved on he met Steph while on a case before him and Sian had split, she worked for financial company that was being investigated as a link to prostitution in the city and money laundering in the end this turned out that her company was innocent by the time the money had reached them it looked all legit. Dai and Steph had moved in together and after a year she had been offered promotion in the head office at Milton Keynes, Dai applied for a transfer to Thames Valley as a DI but his boss in Cardiff (who was sorry to see him go) knew that a DCI post in the major incident team had come up and put his name forward he was accepted, and the move was on.

Milton Keynes MIT was based in Milton Keynes central Police station but over the last couple of weeks they had been moved to the old Bletchley police station this was a temporary thing while work was being done on the main station in central MK.

Dai swept his id card throw the gate lock and drove the Dolomite in he was surprised to see Dave had got back before him.

"How did you get back so quick" he asked

"Well boss you were so engrossed in your coffee you didn't see me pass you" Dave said with a smile on his face which soon disappeared when Dai proclaimed it was his turn to buy the coffees then.

They made their way inside most of the team had already gathered.

Detective sergeant Lisa Jones was sat at her desk like Dai she had moved up from the valleys and between them they would have fun winding up the rest of the team by talking in Welsh.

"Bore da boss we've had some photos sent over from the tec lads not much to see at the moment"

It fascinated Dai that what years ago would take the photographer nearly all day to do could now take the matter of minutes.

"Right people let's get started I know it early but have we anything to start with a name maybe?"

"Sir a pc doing house to house says a lady thought she heard an argument going on in the underpass as she passed on the top in her car, she had the window down and being an electric car, she could hear shouting from below"

This was DC Paul Stevens the youngest and newest member of the team who had not got round to like the rest of the team calling him boss.

"What time was this" asked Dave

"About eight thirty in the evening sir"

"that's a little early to match with time of death but it maybe something, follow it up see what you can find, the trouble is with these underpasses is they are a little way from the house's so people may not have heard or seen anything" noted Dai to the rest of the team.

Dai took his coffee that Dave had brought in and took a large mouthful it was almost as cold as the one from his thermal cup bloody machine always on the blink.

Dai looked round "right who's not doing anything at the moment"

Dc Steve Carter looked up and then away hoping Dai had not noticed

"Right no good looking away Steve you've be seen, so here's £30 take a car pop down to Tesco get a kettle, tea, coffee, sugar and maybe drinking chocolate and get back here as soon as possible I'm dying for a decent cuppa I think I saw loads of mugs in the old canteen we can use them Oh and get the receipt"

The rest of the day was quite with not much happening the CSI guys had not found anything of significance yet there was still no clue as to who the lad was. Lisa had put the picture up on the white board and Dave had run throw with the team what Ruth had said about time of death and means of death.

Steve had returned with the kettle and everyone seemed grateful to be having a good cuppa.

Dai was in his office there had been a note on the desk for him to contact the chief superintendent when he could so Dai called him and brought him up to date,

He spent the rest of his time going through reports that needed to be done.

Dave was liaising with the CSI, Lisa was chasing up the lad who had made the phone call this was proving a bit of a thing because the name the lad gave was not the name registered to the phone number, Steve was running through missing persons but so far nothing.

At fifteen hundred Dai gave Dave the nod "right mate you up for this post-mortem"

Dave turned green at the thought of it

"Oh, come on I know you can't wait to see the lovely Ruth"

The rest of the team smiled, and Dave went red but grabbed his coat they took Dai's car and headed for the hospital although it only took them about five minutes to get to the hospital, they only just made it to the morgue in time for the post-mortem to start, parking was the one big issue the hospital had and although it had gone through a major refurb and became a university hospital parking was still bad he managed to find in a police car only space near the entrance and put up his board saying "here on police business" When they arrived, Ruth was already set up to go, since covid 19 had hit every were was so sterile Dai and Dave took a clean pair of scrubs each and put them on then facemasks and visors unlike the labs you see on the television this had no screen for you to stand behind and the Doctor gave you there findings over a microphone they washed their hands in bacterial wash and went through to Ruth she looked up and greeted them " morning gentlemen" he glanced at Dave and even under the facemask he could tell he was smiling,

"Shall we start I've had Stella here take the photos already so we can crack straight on" Dai nodded Ruth began

"Right, we have a young male of African, Jamaican origin approx. age 18 to 20, 1,8 meters tall approx. 69 kilos in good shape"

Dai smiled to himself because although he had been brought up in school to use metric, he preferred to use imperial measures his dad had taught him 16oz to the pound 14lds to the stone 12 inch in a foot 3 feet in a yard so while Ruth was telling them this in his mind, he was converting them over.

Ruth continued "time of death is as I thought between ten and eleven last night, cause of death strangulation, you can see here the blood on the back of his head this was caused by the blunt instrument maybe a lump of wood, square in shape you can see the triangle where it hit the skull and cut in" she turned his head so Dai and Dave could see "But this did not kill him, you can see from the marks on his neck that he has been strangled" Ruth lifted one of his eye lids "You can see here that the blood vessels in his eyes have burst this means he was alive after the blow to the head, you can see from the bruising on his neck that whatever was used was quite thick, maybe rope of some kind"

She carried on examining the front of the body checking everything, taking scrapping from under the fingers in case of DNA, between the toes for any needle marks but nothing in her words "this was a fit young man with no signs of drug use"

With the help of Stella, they turned the body over from this view you could see the head wound better but also bruising on the back of the neck one bruise being in a distinctive shape she asked Dai and Dave to look, Dai went in close, but Dave hung back.

"Look here" she said "at this mark there seems to be a bit of fibre in it"

Dai got closer he could see it only small about an inch long, Ruth got a pair of tweezers and picked it off taking a little blood with it she bagged it and gave it to Stella to put with the rest of the evidence they found to go to the forensic

Ruth continued with her commentary

"Buy the looks of this bruise it looks like a knot was in the rope, maybe tied like a noose and pulled from the back" she looked down the body "ah yes look here there's bruising in the middle of the back I'd say whoever did this had the body face down put a noose around the neck then put their knee into his back and pulled tight on it"

"So, the person who did this must have been strong" asked Dave

"No, not necessarily they used their knee to put weight on the body to stop it lifting up as they pulled thus pushing down on the back as they pulled the head back"

"Do, you think they knew what they were doing" asked Dai

"Again, not necessarily they may have tried to do it but realized they could not get enough pull and resorted to the knee that's all I can tell you about the murder side of it I think when open him up I'll find he was a pretty healthy young man so it's up to you, you can stay or go, and I will send you my findings when I get them"

Dave did not wait for Dai to answer he was saying his goodbye's and out the door before he even had the chance to thank Ruth.

Dai thanked Ruth and headed out to find Dave who by this time was out of scrubs and standing by the door,

"Sorry, boss you could have stayed you know me and blood and gut's even the thought of it turns my guts"

"that's, ok but I thought even for the lovely Ruth you would have stayed" Dai said, he knew Dave would go red and he did but quickly changed the subject

"Boss, I had a quick look at the piece of fabric that Ruth found in the neck"

Dai looked at him puzzled he had not noticed Dave looking at it.

"A sorry boss I had a look while you and Ruth were looking at the bruising, I can't be sure, but the forensic guys may confirm it, but I think it's rope"

Dai looked at him gone out "of course it's rope Ruth said that"

"no, boss you don't understand this is old rope, rope today is made up of plastics but the old rope was made up of natural fibres I can't remember what but when I was a kid I use to go out on the lorries my dad, every now and then dad would have to do roping and sheeting to keep the load on and that was the type of rope he used, as I said I can't be sure but maybe forensic will come back with a result"

"Well, if it is there can't be many places that supply it so we may get lucky" Dai answered and headed off to the car. When they got back to the car Dai could not believe it, he had been clamped, and a notice put on his screen about paying a fine to have it released and a handwritten note saying

"Very funny if this is a police car I'll eat may hat, so pay your fine"

Dai took the note and headed round to the parking office Dave stood back "I'll wait here boss if that's ok with you" he had seen Dai in a temper before and did not want to see his bosses wroth that was going to bear down on the parking attendant. By the time Dai reached the parking office his temper had had gone up more. The door was open, so Dai walked straight and slapped the note and ticket on the counter. Sat behind the counter was a big African guy he looked up when he heard the slap of Dai's hand on the counter and gave a false smile

"Good afternoon sir how may I help you" he did not even stand just sat there.

Dai looked him in the eye "it's about this" Dai held up the note "one of your operatives has given me a ticket and clamped my car"

"Ah, yes sir that was me you shouldn't have been so naughty and parked in a police bay with that old car of yours so if you would like to pay that's forty pounds for the fine and sixty release fees so that one hundred pounds total would that be card or cash sir"

Dai just looked at him and reached into his pocket and said "I'm not paying anything"

the guy picked up the card reader and began typing in the amount but stopped when Dai told him he was not paying "well, sir in that case the car will have to stay there, and we will arrange with the police to get in taken away after all it is their space"

Dai held up his warrant card in front of the guy's face "read this go on read it" the guy's face dropped "go on read it" Dai replied "or do you want me to read it for you"

The guy read it out load "Detective Inspector Dafydd Rees, Thames's valley Police oh sorry sir it's just that it's such an old car I thought"

"Yes, well you know what thought did don't you, what's your name" Dai temper was easing a bit.

"Dwayne sir"

"Dwayne what"?

"Dwayne Jonson" Dai gave him a look even he knew who Dwayne Johnson was. "No sir look it's true" he pulled out a piece of paper and showed it to Dai it was his birth certificate "see Dwayne the rock Johnson wasn't around when I was born plus he spells his with the h in Johnson I don't I'm for ever getting teased about it"

Dai looked at him "well, Mr Dwayne Jonson this is what we are going to do, you're going to come back to my car take the clamp off waver the fine and then take a lovely photo of my lovely old car that you can put on the wall of the office and point to it a remind all your fellow workers that it is in fact a police vehicle is that understood"

Dwayne just looked away Dai knew he was embarrassed

"Yes, sir I'll have to get the van and meet you by your car the keys for the clamp are in it"

Dai walked out without saying a word by the time he got back to the car a uniformed constable was stood talking to Dave.

"Ey up boss I was just explaining to Constable Gleeson here your predicament" Dave said with a smile.

At that moment Dwayne pulled up in the van Dave's smile got bigger

"Ey up Dwayne how's the doing? boss been giving you grief has he"

"Oh, hay Dave yes sorry I never realized"

"You know this guy "Dai looked at Dave

"Oh, ey boss we play snooker at the same club everyone there knows Mr Dwayne the rock Jonson"

"See what I mean Mr Rees for ever getting my leg pulled, right give me a minute and I'll have you free to be on your way"

Dai smiled in a way he felt sorry for the guy and as promised within minute they were on their way.

By the time they got back to the station it was almost 5 they checked with the team and nothing much had happened so Dai decided to call it a day.

"Right guy's that's it for today there's not much more we can do see you all back here 08.00 in the morning have a nice evening" Dai said and walked into his office there was another note to ring the chief super with an update but that could wait till the morning.

Chapter Three

Dai woke at 05.30 made himself a coffee and got dressed into jogging bottoms and tee shirt this was his morning ritual he loved to run and he had a set route out of that he took every morning out of the house follow the road down to Simpson village where he would cut through to the Caldicote lake around the edge of the lake to the path that lead to the Fenny lock on the canal then cut through to the Manor fields where the rugby club was then along the river then doubling back along Mill road, Manor Road and home, he got home showered dressed, made coffee, toast and Marmite then sat and caught up on social media Facebook mainly he smiled Bethan had put up some photos of her and some of her mates on a night out it brought back memories of his nights out with the lads from the rugby club back home in Wales.

Dai hit the office just before eight Lisa was already in and had the kettle on the go, he went into his office it was too early to ring the chief super so he checked up on his emails, Ruth had been in touch as she said there was no signs of anything to untoward in her findings there was no news from forensics they should get back later today with any luck.

Lisa popped her head round the door "how be boss kettles boiled do you want a brew or is that a silly question?"

From behind her came the dulse tone of Dave "by heck lass that's good timing tea plenty of milk three sugars, I know don't tell me I'm sweet enough"

Lisa smiled and came back with a quickfire answer "no Dave I was going to say your putting on weight, and you'll rot your teeth with that much sugar"

Dave looked at her as though he was about to explode but broke into a smile when saw that Lisa thought she had overstepped the mark

"ey you cheeky bugger I'll have you know I've actually lost weight just over a stone not that any of you lots noticed"

"How much is that in real money Dave?" asked Lisa

Dai could see Dave working out in his head, like him Dave liked imperial measurements to metric

"Just over 6 kilos not bad ey"

"that's not much" came back Lisa

"that's why I like using pounds and ounce's it sounds better saying 14 pounds"

Lisa walked over the kettle just has Paul Stevens walked in

"If your making tea or coffee mine's white no sugar"

From behind him came the voice of Steve Carter

"And mine's coffee white two sugars"

Lisa's voice rose "listen you lot what's occurring here just because I'm the only woman on the team at the moment doesn't mean I'm a bloody waitress you can all take turns at making the drinks"

"Yes Nessa" Steve said with a smile

"And I'll have less of that I'm nothing like Nessa of Gavin and Stacy" while giving Steve a clip round the ear as she went buy him.

Dai came out of his office and called them all together

"Right thank you for being in so early we just need to get up to speed any news on a name for the victim"

"No sir I've gone through any missing persons over the last week, but none fit the profile of the victim"

"Thanks Steve what about the lad that made the call"

"I've traced him sir a young lad called Darren Yeomans, when I rang the number, we had his father answered when I told him who I was and what it was about he got a little bit angry I could hear him shouting at lad about lying to the police," said Lisa

"Then what"

"I, popped into see him on the way home, when I got there the dad was still going on at him so I had to claim him down before I could speak to him"

"So, what did you get out of him" Dave asked

"well, boss when I asked him why he had supplied a false name and gone off from the scene it all came out, it seems a mate of his had given him some weed to take to another mate and he was afraid if that if he hung around we would question him and search him, at this point the dad exploded even more he went at the lad screaming at him for being involved in drugs and that was it he had told him if ever he got into that stuff he would be out by the scruff of his neck at that point he got physical trying to push the lad out of the door the mother then stepped in but she too got pushed around he was shouting at her that's it you stick u for your precious baby I always told you he'd come to no good"

"Sounds a nasty bit of work" this was Steve

"Carry on," said Dai

" well things calmed down a bit after I threated to nick the dad if he laid one more finger on Darren and his mum, he then went and sulked in the kitchen while myself Darren and his mum stayed in the living room, Darren assured me that the weed was not for him and he had only been the messenger, any way Darren seemed to think he knew the lad not by name but from school he was a few years older than him and had now left but he remembers he lived on Springfield and he thinks he went to one of the churches in the area he remembers him handing out leaflets for it outside the school but that was about all he know before I left the mother pulled me aside it seems the big brave dad isn't Darren's real father and he's pretty handy with his fist's towards him so before I left I gave Darren my card and went into the kitchen and warned the step father I would be back over the next few days and if I saw one hair out of place on Darren's head I would nick him"

"So, no more clues as to who the lad is" Dai asked

"Sorry boss no"

A phone was ringing Paul picked up

Dai caught one side of the conversation

"Sir that was the desk sergeant at central he's got a couple in reporting their son hasn't been home for the couple of nights by the sounds of the description they gave it could be our victim, I've told him to put them in a waiting room give them a drink and one of us would be there asap"

"Right go, take Steve with you and tread carefully we don't know for certain it is him yet"

Another phone was ringing Dave picked up on this again Dai only got half the conversation.

"right boss that was forensics one of the techs worked a late one on the fibre found on the victim it seems it is old rope made out of hemp he reckons it could be really old and been kept in some ones shed or someplace like that, he found traces of what could be brick dust in it and also a small amount of fresh blood and guess what they've done a trace and it's not a match to the victim, they say it's only small so maybe the perp somehow got a small cut before or as he or she was doing the attack"

"Anything on the DNA data base?" Dai asked hoping Dave would come back with a yes and they could go out and maybe make an arrest but no such luck"

"Sorry boss they ran it through the UK and international system but nothing"

"Oh, sod it and there was me hoping for a quick solution to the case"

There was a knock at the office door Dai looked round to see a young woman standing there

"Yes, can I help you?"

"Oh yes sir Detective constable Vicky Campbell sir, remember I'm meant to be joining your team this morning, sorry if I'm a bit late but no one told me you had moved office and I've been over at central for the last half hour trying to find you"

"Oh yes of course sorry come in" Dai had completely forgot about it his mind now taken up with the case

"Right as the lady as just said this is DC Vicky Campbell, she is joining us from headquarters at Kidlington I don't know if you know any of the others, do you?"

"No sir"

"Right so here we have DI Dave Parker, and this here is DS Lisa Jones DC's Steven's and Carter are not here at the moment, but you'll get the chance to meet them soon so grab a desk make yourself at home Vicky, Lisa will bring you up to speed and show you where everything is"

"Thank you, sir,"

"Oh, and it's boss or first name terms here sir to formal"

"Yes, boss thank you"

Dai went through to his office Dave followed

"Dai you never told me about another member of the team I thought you would have told me before she arrived"

Dai felt a little guilty "sorry Dave it wasn't my idea, the chief super he mentioned about a month ago I said I'd think it over and have a chat with you and then totally forgot about it till she walked in I remember him giving me her name and I did look her up she has a good track record. She was brought up in Milton Keynes and still has family here but due to the covid 19 she's not seen them much of them, then her father became ill with it so, she felt she needed to be nearer to them"

"God Dai is old timers setting in or what, but I forgive you it'll make Lisa happy she's not the only female now" Dave said with a smile

Steve and Paul Parked up the car and made their way to the front desk

"Morning Sarg you got someone for us"

"Ah Detectives Stevens and Carter how the devil is you and how are things in sunny Bletchley?" the unforgettable Irish tones of Sergeant Paddy McGinty who by his own confession had now lived longer in the UK than he did Ireland but refused to give up his Irish accent.

"Oh, things are ok it did get a bit over the top yesterday when the coffee machine was only giving out lukewarm drinks the boss sent me out for a kettle tea etc but other than that it's a bit of piece and quite from you lot" Steve said

"Oh, that machine never worked properly when I was there years ago, I thought they would have scrapped it by now, any way you'll be wanting to see your people, I've had PC Grace take them down to one of the interview rooms and get them tea, Oh and be careful she not in a good mood went off mumbling something about all she ever does is make tea and look after people seems your DCI upset her yesterday"

"Thanks, we'll take that in mind do we have a name for the couple" asked Paul

"Be, sure you have it's a Mr and Mrs Okore and their son's name is Diji, oh, and you might like this it's a picture they brought in"

The Sergeant handed it over to Steve who showed it to Paul he took out his phone and tried to phone Dai, but his phone was engaged so he rang Dave instead, Dave picked up almost straight away

"Yes, Steve what you got?"

"Well, boss we haven't seen the couple yet, but the desk Sargent has just handed us a photo of their son and it's definitely him, his name is Diji Okore spelt DIJI OKORE"

Dave could tell the tension in Steve's voice it was never good telling someone that someone had died let alone let a parent know their child had died.

"Ok take it easy on them I'll let Dai know"

"Will do boss do you want me to see if I can arrange a family liaison office while I'm here or will you do that?"

"If you can while your there see if there one around if you no joy let me know"

Steve and Paul made their way to the interview room and arrived in the corridor just as PC Jill Grace arrived with two cups on a tray "hello you two you here for Mr and Mrs Okore? I'm just taking them tea I think they are going to need it they've shown me some photos of their son it is the victim from yesterday isn't it"

"Yes, I'm afraid it is you haven't said anything have you," said Paul

"no. I haven't I'm not that stupid, but I have to admit I did not put two and two together until they showed me a photo then I just felt sorry for them because there was me getting upset because I had to make the tea and these poor people have lost their son, would you like me to stay I've built up quite a rapport with the mother"

Steve looked at her it would help to have a woman in the room "yes that would be great thanks"

All three entered the room Jill handed them their drinks then introduced the two detectives'

"Mr and Mrs Okore this is my colleagues Detectives Steve Carter and Paul Stevens they'd like to talk to you"

Steve did not know where to start he looked at Paul but realized that he would have to be the one to tell them.

"Mr and Mrs Okore as you may be aware there was an incident in the underpass between Fishermead and Springfield two nights ago and I'm sorry to say this incident involved your son Diji"

Mrs Okore began to sob and started to say repeatedly "my son my son what has happened to my son"

"I'm sorry to say your son is dead he was attacked by as of yet a person unknown"

Mr Okore stood shacking his hands "no, no, it can't be my son my son's a good boy who would want to hurt my son you must be mistaken I bet he's somewhere with a friend"

"I'm sorry Mr Okore there will have to be a formal identification but from the photo you have supplied us I'm afraid to say it is your son"

By now Mrs Okore was crying out of control Jill put her arms around her.

Paul for the first time spoke "I'm sorry to ask This but can you think of anyone who might what to hurt Diji Mr Okore?"

"No, no Diji was a good young man he loved everyone, and everyone loved him he was dedicated to the church he did well at school and was at college he wanted to become an accountant I can think of no one who would hurt him"

"Do, you think he had upset someone, some at the church, college, girlfriend maybe?"

"No detective Stevens, no one I would know if it was anyone at the church as I am the minister there so if Diji had upset any one they would have come to me as for college I don't I no he was seeing someone and his mother was always on at him to bring her round but all he would say was "we need to have more time to get to know each other, then when the time is right you can meet"

Diji's mother spoke for the first time between her sobs

"My, Diji was a good man he loved the family me his father his sister Amadi he would not hurt a fly he loved life and everyone, how are we going to tell his sister she looked up to him"

"I'm sorry for you both and I can assure you we will do everything to find out who has done this to your son Mr and Mrs Okore" it was Jill that spoke Paul and Steve looked at her but then could see that her reassuring voice had put both at ease.

"Mr and Mrs Okore as my colleague here has said we will do everything to find out who has done this, and as I said there will have to be formal identification, it doesn't need to be yourself it can be someone who knew Diji well if you don't want to, in the meantime Jill here will run you home we will arrange for a family liaison office to come to your home and be with you we have to be on our way and again we are sorry for your loss" said Steve.

"I, have my car here I can drive us home" Mr Okore said

"I would rather someone took you home Mr Okore you have had a shock, how about PC Grace here drives you home in your car and we'll arrange for her to be picked up?" Steve could see he was still shaking and thought that would be the best way.

They left the room Paul let out a sigh of relief Jill followed them out "thanks for that in there Jill do you know if any of the Flo's are in, we need to arrange one"

"Not sure I'll find out, but I was thinking as I'm running them home could I stay with them"

Steve shook his head "I'm not sure I'll have to clear it with the boss, and you'll have to clear it with your duty Sergeant, but I don't see why not they seem to trust you"

Steve took out his phone and called Dai who picked up straight away

"Steve, what we got"

"Well boss it's confirmed the victim is one Diji Okore 20 years of age, do you want me to contact Ruth to arrange for the Identification"

"No, I'll get Dave to do that you just head back to the office, Oh Dave said something about a FLO did you manage to get one"

"No sir but PC Jill Grace was the one who was with them here when we arrived, Mrs Okore seems to have taken to her and she is taking them home and wondered if she could stay with them?"

"Do you think she will be ok with them? she's not been in the job long"

"Yes, boss she calmed Mrs Okore down and was great in the interview room"

"Ok but clear it with her duty Sergeant I don't want to go treading on anyone's toes, oh and if it's ok asked her to change into civies it's not very nice for people to have a uniformed office in their house and while she at it see if she can find out anything else about the victim"

Dai hung up he was a little bit happier now they had the victim's name but no motive and who he went through to the main office

"Right, folks the victims id is confirmed as Dave said he's one Diji Okore, spelt DIJI OKORE, we need to look into his background, Lisa can you chase up the banks see what we can get, Vicky can you look into social media Facebook, Twitter etc see what we can find there can't be many people with that name, Dave can you give Ruth a ring and see what time we can get an informal id done"

"Yes, boss I still haven't been able to get hold of FLO" said Dave

"that's, ok Dave Pc Jill Grace is taking them home and as volunteered to stay with the family I said she had to clear it with the duty Sergeant but I'm ok with it how about you?"

"Yes, boss that's ok with me but do you think she's up to it she's not been in the job long"

"Steve seems to think so, she was saw to the family when they came into central, and Mrs Okore seems to be able to connect with her"

"Have we got a number for her so I can keep in touch for the id"

"Steve's sending it over now" at that point Dai's phone pinged "there you go talk of the devil"

Dave took the number and wondered over to his desk

Dai went into his office "right if anyone wants me, I'm on the phone to the chief super"

Dave smiled and gave Dai the I do not envy you that call look

Dai saw him "unless you want to do it for me Dave"

"No boss that's all yours thank you"

Dai picked up the phone and dialled the chiefs number it was picked up almost straight away

"Chief superintendent Mackintosh's office how may I help you?" the velvet tunes of Margaret Blackmoor who so it has been said has been secretary to every chief super since the beginning of time and who Dai had to admit sometimes frightened him, she had a sparkle in her eye and a charm that Dai found overbearing,

"Morning Maggie DI Rees here is the chief available"

"no need to announce yourself Dai I know that lovely Welsh voice anywhere," Dai felt himself go red even though she was on the other end of the telephone "I'm afraid his on the other line at the Oh no his just come off I'll put you throw" Dai didn't like going to the Chief straight off he normally delt with superintendent Wilcox but he was in self isolation due to a member of his family testing positive for covid and he wouldn't be back for about four days. "Chief superintendent Mackintosh"

Chief superintendent Leroy Mackintosh had a booming voice to compliment his large build over six feet two of muscle that at the age of 60 could put any younger man to shame and of African origin he had made his way up throw the ranks and had become the first black Chief superintendent in Thames's valley police and was well respected by the those in the force.

"Morning sir DI Rees here just thought I would give you a call to keep you in the loop"

"Ah hello Dai have we made any progress yet"

"Yes, sir a little we now have a name for the victim he's a one Diji Okore 20 years of age his parents came into central this morning to report him missing, they are going to make an informal ID sometime today but we don't really need it they brought in photos of him and DC Carter was able to make an ID from that"

"Okore you say is the father a minister at a church of some kind?"

"I believe so do you know him sir?"

"No not personally I met him briefly his church did some great work helping out in the community during the lock down you know handing out food parcels, collecting prescription for the elderly etc, Dai I have to ask do you think the attack was racially motivated?"

"No sir looking at the note I don't think so it seemed to make out the lad had in some way sinned"

"Have forensics had any joy?"

"No sir they seem to think the note was printed rather than handwritten there getting back to me"

"Do you think we need to do a press conference or put out a media report?"

"It may help to put out media reports on Facebook etc we have a few things that have come up with door to door, but we never know something may come up maybe tomorrow we could do a press conference when we have more info"

"Ok I'll get the media guys on to it, keep me informed please Dai"

"Yes sir"

Chapter Four

Dave had arranged for the id for late afternoon he rang Jill to confirm the time

"PC Jill Grace"

"Oh, hi Jill it's DI Parker here I'm just ringing to confirm the time for the Id, would sixteen thirty be ok with the family?" the phone went quiet for a few seconds

"Yes, sir that will be fine"

"Ok see you at the hospital"

"Oh, sorry sir I don't have transport at the moment, I drove Mr and Mrs Okore home in their car so I wouldn't like to take the mick"

"that's ok just give me the address and I'll pick you up at say 16.10, who is it that will be coming?"

"Mr Okore and his daughter Amandi, Mrs Okore is staying at home a family friend from the church is going to be here for her"

"Have the family came up with anything they think might help?"

"No sir I chatted with them and they are adamant they can think of no one would who would want to harm Diji, oh and sir I've spoken to the sister it seems Diji liked to be call DJ by his friends and she is known as Amanda by her friends she has given me the names of some of his mates but she thinks that he has not seen any of them for the last couple of months he's been a bit quiet as though he had something to hide she thinks he may have a girlfriend but can't be sure this tallies with what the father told DC Stevens"

"Ok do you have a list of names of his mate"

"Yes, sir"

"Can you send it over to DS Lisa Jones at MIT she can then get one of the team to follow up I'll give you her number"

"Ok I'll do that now"

"See you at sixteen ten"

By the time Dave sat down at his desk Jill had sent over the list there was not many people on it.

Steve and Paul had returned to the office

Lisa handed them a copy of the list "right you two we need to chase up this lot friends of the victim, Vicky here has been chasing up his Facebook and twitter so I should think you can get info like phone numbers from there"

Steve and Paul looked puzzled "oh sorry guys this is DC Vicky Campbell she's joined the team this morning, Vicky this is DC's Carter and Stevens Steve and Paul"

"Nice to meet you and welcome to the team, right who's for drink's" said Steve looking at Vicky as though she had to make it.

"Oh no you don't make your own tea and coffees as I said this morning just because we're female doesn't make us waitresses"

"Ok, ok my turn I give in who wants what?"

Dai came into the office from his

"Right guy's any news?"

"I've arranged for the ID at sixteen thirty today I'm picking PC Grace the father and daughter at sixteen ten to take them," said Dave said
"hasn't' she got a pool car?"

"Oh, sorry boss that's my fault I offered for PC Grace to take them home in a pool car, but they had driven there in theirs and didn't want to leave it in the centre parking costing the way it does" Steve replied to Dai's question

"Ok, but see if you can arrange a pool car for her" In the background a phone rang Lisa picked up "MIT DS Jones speaking, ok where"

Lisa was jotting down notes "boss it, looks like we've got another body"

Everyone's ears pricked up

"where" asked Dai

"Underpass between Conniburrow and Downs barn V8 Marlborough Street and H5 Portway meet"

"Ok Lisa, Steve with me Dave you still ok to handle the id with the family" Dave gave a nod Paul, Vicky you two follow up on his mates etc"

"Yes sir" from Paul "yes boss" from Vicky "also boss do you want me to look into the church he has a lot of people that attend there on his Facebook page"

"Yes, good idea see if any of them know anything"

They headed out to the carpark Dai unlocked the Dolomite and leaned over to open the passenger door Lisa jumped in

"Ah boss, do? you think I should take the pool car?" Steve said

"Why what's wrong with mine?"

"Oh, nothing boss I was thinking just in case we have to split up"

"Ok, you may have a point see you there" Dai turned to Lisa

"Can you get on and see if forensics have been informed and make sure the area has been closed down"

"Yes boss"

As the gate opened Dai hit the blue's and two's, turned left on to Sherwood drive and left onto the Buckingham road, Dai had to slow down as he came to the crossing at the bottom and got the V sign from a pedestrian who decided to take his time crossing, out on to the V7 Saxon Street in his mind he was working out which way would be best, he'd turned off the two tones as he went along the road but hit them again as he got to the B&Q roundabouts Dai had never seen the B&Q it was gone before he came to Bletchley and been replaced by a Aldi and Iceland but the locals still called it the B&Q roundabout.

Dai stayed on the on the V7 Saxon Street till he got to the roundabout with the H8 Standing way took the right passed the hospital and picked up the V8 Marlborough Street

"Forensics are on their way boss and so is Ruth"

Dai got to the roundabout that joined the V8 and the H5 Portway above the underpass they needed to be at and found he could not park on the verge he noticed the forensics van turning into Downs barn and followed them in.

They parked up in a street that was nearest the underpass getting out Dai reminded Lisa to pull the handle and lock the door and lean over and push the button to lock the back door.

The forensic guys were getting their gear out of the van and Dai saw team leader Colin Mathews "afternoon Colin"

"Oh, afternoon Dai could I interest you and the lovely Lisa to a couple of nice coveralls there all the rage around here"

They suited up and followed the path that led to the underpass they showed there warrant card to the PC stood by the type and ducked under it; Dai saw Steve at the other end of the underpass he most have parked up in the Conniburrow end.

"Afternoon sir, afternoon Sergeant" PC Joe Clarke was stood by the victim

"Afternoon Joe what we got" enquired Lisa

"Well, we have a young white male approx. 25 to 30 found this afternoon by the gent over there, he does a six till two shift he saw the victim this morning but assumed he was a rough sleeper but when he came back after two and saw he was still there he took a look and called us"

"Dai you had better look at this" Colin was looking over the body he opened the jacket and there pinned to the victim's sweatshirt was a note "he who sins will pay the price"

"Same as the last victim anything in his pockets phone, id etc" asked Dai

"There, no need for that boss I can Id him" Steve had now joined them and was staring at the victim has also gone very pale. Dai gave him a quizzical look.

"His name is Ryan Carter 26 years of age no fixed abode if I remember rightly"

"Carter, you say?"

"Yes, boss he's my dad's cousin's son bit of a black sheep of the family into drugs, petty theft etc I haven't seen him in years I thought he had moved out of the area"

"Steve you alright" Lisa reached out and put her hand on his shoulder

From behind them another voice joined in "hi guys, you all right Steve you look a bit pale"

No one had noticed Ruth had arrived

Dai spoke before Steve could "no Ruth he's had a bit of a shock the victims a relative of his"

"Oh, I'm sorry to hear that Steve"

"Thank you"

"Steve, I think Lisa here should take you home, Lisa take Steve home and get on to the office and get Paul or Vicky here to help me"

"No boss I'm ok really but I would like to be the one who tells his dad I'll ring his daughter Becky see if she can meet me at his house and maybe my dad, Ryan's dad has been on his own for a while now since his wife Ryan's mum passed away"

"Ok but go now I don't want you hanging around here to long"

"Cheers boss" and Steve left

The forensic photographer had finished taking photos of the body in situate and Ruth had begun her job

Dai and Lisa watched over her shoulder and Dai filled her in as to who he was.

"Right as we have an Id for the victim, I'll start with the obvious white male 26 years of age same type of head wound as the last victim and look here around the neck same make's"

She tilted the victim forward

"Ah yes look the same mark on the neck" she pulled up the sweatshirt and jacket to reveal the same bruising in the back "I'd say this was done by the same person"

"Time of death" Lisa enquired

"Well rigor mortis as come and gone I'd say about 11 to 12 hours ago so sometime in the night, I see he has the same note"

"Yes, we'll get the tech boys to take a good look at that the wording and spacing looks identical so they may be right in the fact it's printed"

"Well, I can't do much more here if your finished I'd like to get the body shipped back to the hospital, I can see from his arms he was a user"

Dai seemed to be in a world of his own so Lisa gave Ruth her answer

"Yes, he was according to Steve he was the black sheep of the family been a user for some years now"

Dai came to out of his world

"You alright boss"

"Yes, sorry Lisa I was just thinking why these two people what? do they have in common apart from someone think's they have both sinned, I can understand Ryan theft etc but what about DJ he was a good Christian never been in trouble, but someone believes he has sinned"

"Sir, Mr Kowalska wants to know if he can go"

Dai had forgotten about PC Joe Clarke

"Sorry who"

"The gent who found the body sir"

"Oh yes sorry I'll come over and have a word with him"

Dai and Lisa wandered over to Mr Kowalska

"Mr Kowalska sorry to keep you waiting I'm DCI Rees and this is DS Jones I'd like to ask you some questions if I may"

"Yes, anything to help"

"You noticed the victim this morning I believe about what time would that be?"

"Around five thirty it takes he about fifteen minutes to get to work on my bike I cut down all the redways I like to get there a few minutes before my shift starts and have a cup of tea"

"But you took no notice of him this morning" Lisa asked

"No, I am so used to seeing people sleeping rough under the underpasses I never take much notice at that time in the morning"

"What? Made you take notice this afternoon"

"Well, he had not moved he was exactly the same as I saw him this morning not moved from that spot"

"You speak very good English Mr Kowalska how long have you lived in the UK" Dai asked

"I lived in the UK for ten years now before I moved to Milton Keynes, I lived in Swansea I even learnt a little of the Welsh language like diolch (thanks), prynhawn da (good afternoon) and bore da (good morning) but it is a very hard language to learn I picked up you are both Welsh"

"Yes. I'm from near Bridgend and DS Lewis is from the Rhondda your Welsh is particularly good, Mr Kowalska do you know the victim at all?"

"Yes, I have seen him around, I've seen him a couple of time go into a house opposite me I think it is used by people who do drugs"

"Thank you, Mr Kowalska, if you could give my sergeant your address in case, we need to be in touch then you can be on your way"

Dai wondered back over to Ruth

"You done"

"Yes, thanks I'll be doing the post-mortem, for this in the morning is that ok, I expect my findings will be much the same as the other young man as to cause of death will you be there?"

"No, I've a funny feeling that I will be in a meeting with the Chief in the morning I'll get Dave to come along if you give me a time"

"Shall we say 09,00 Oh and where is your trusted sidekick this afternoon not skiving off, I hope"

"No, he's going with the family of the first victim to do the formal id"

"Oh, I've had to let my number two Stella deal with that as I had to come here well tell him I'll look forward to seeing him"

Lisa wondered over "right boss I've done as much as I can here, I've got a couple of uniform doing house to house, I've had a word with Colin he reckons they'll be here for a while, yet they want to do a complete sweep of the underpass"

"Ok let's head back to the office I need to contact the chief super before he heads off home"

Back at the office there had not been much in the development side a lot of DJ's friends had been traced and they all said he same they had not seen him for weeks some time's months they had kept in touch through Facebook, Twitter etc but most had not seen him.

Dai made his call to the chief

"Hello Dai, I understand we have another body"

"Yes, sir young white male same MO as Diji Okore and we have an identity for this one already"

"Oh, how's that"

"Sir, his name is Ryan Carter 26 years of age small time petty thief and drugs user, he's on our data base but also he is a relative of DC Carter, his father and DC Carters are cousins"

"Oh, I see, how is? DC Carter, has he been asked to take leave?"

"Yes, sir I told him to go home he looked very pale at the scene"

"You mean to say he was at the scene at the of a murder of a relative!"

"Yes, sir when the call came in, we didn't know who it was so DS Jones and DC Carter and me went out to investigate DC Carter got there a few moments after us and it was him that identified the body"

"I see, but has he gone home?"

"No sir he said he was ok he's gone with his father to inform the victim's family, sir I don't think this will affect the way he works he said he hadn't seen Ryan for a long time and thought he had left the area"

"Ok but on your head be it if he screws up and I'd like to see you in the morning 09,00 sharp"

"Yes, sir can I before I go can I request some more manpower, I will need it now we have two bodies to deal with"

"Ok I'll get on to it, see you in the morning"

Chapter Five

Dai was up at 05.30 and made sure he had a clean shirt had one cup of coffee then out for his run, he was back home 07.30

He was not looking forward to his meeting with the chief this morning, he showered, shaved put on the clean shirt and was in the office by 08.00. As always Lisa was first in and the kettle was on

"Morning boss ready for another day at the mad house?"

"Not, really I've a meeting with the chief this morning any news?"

"Oh, I don't envy you that"

"Morning sir" Paul wondered into the office

"Morning Paul good night last night you look a little worse for wear"

"No sir new neighbours they were playing load music at one o'clock this morning I tried the normal thing's banging on the wall etc I didn't fancy going out in the cold at that time of the night but in the end I had too"

"Did they turn it down after that? "Asked Lisa

"Well, it took me 15 minutes to get them to answer the door, it was then answered by a man mountain swearing like hell he was going to rip the arsehole who's knocking the door head off and shove it where the sun didn't shine and if they wanted me to turn down the music call the police"

Lisa laughed "then what"

"He looked a little gone out to see a five-foot eleven skinny bloke standing there in a dressing gown waving a police warrant card in his face, I just warned him I was his neighbour and if I heard any load music from his home after ten thirty in the night, I would nick him right who's for drinks?"

"Me please" Steve was just coming into the room

"And me white no sugar please" Vicky followed him in

"Right 10 minutes for drinks by that time Dave should be here then we'll run through what we've got"

Dave got in just as they had finished their drinks

"Morning all too late for drinks I see" and went and made himself one

Dai came out of his office "right folks now we're all here let's see what we've got Dave how did you get on with the family?"

"Well boss it was very touching the father was very cut up he couldn't bring himself to go in to identify his son in the end it was left to the sister PC Grace went in with her while I stayed with the father, I tried to get things out of him, but he and the family are just as much in the dark as to why anyone would do this to their son"

"Boss there's a message here from the media guys they had a lady been in touch says she saw the argument in the underpass, and she saw the victim was one of the people and although she didn't know the victim, she knows the lad he was arguing with and has given us a name" Paul said

"that's great follow it up will you Paul anything else? Oh, Steve how was things with Ryan's family"

"Ok boss his father took it badly, but his sister told me that they have been waiting for this day for a long time, I left dad with them and by the time I left Ryan's other sister had arrived they were happy that I had been there and done the id, oh and they had no idea he was back in MK the last they had heard from him was about six months ago and he was sofa surfing at mates in London"

"Right Vicky how have we done with social media"

"Nothing more than yesterday, do you want me to follow up on Ryan is if he has any social media?"

"No, no we've got some more bodies coming in this morning so we'll get them on that, Dave I've got to see the super this morning you ok to dish out the work when they arrive, I thought they would be here by now"

"Ok boss do we know who is coming over?"

"No not at the moment the chief said he would get it in hand"

"Ok I'll get onto it"

"Lisa, can you go and give Mr Kowalska a visit, see if he can point out this house Ryan has been seen visiting take Steve with you"

"Ok boss but I think he's a work till after two so it will have to be this afternoon"

"Ok make it then in the meantime Dave I forgot I told Ruth you would be at the post-mortem this morning 09,00 sorry" Dave turned green at the thought of it

"Better get over there now then, I'll give you a call if there's any significant finding's"

"Cheers Dave you can swap with me if you want, I'll go to see Ruth and you can see the chief"

"Ey no boss I know I can't stand post-mortem, but I'd rather be there than see the chief" and before Dai could answer left the room

"Right Lisa being as you are going to be here can you dish out the work when they arrive"

"Yes boss" Dai went back into his office and grabbed his jacket, at that moment that three figures came wondering into the office. The first one spoke looking straight at Lisa and Vicky

"Hello darling's we're looking for someone called DCI Rees we've been told we can find him here"

"And you are?" enquired Lisa

"Oh, I'm DC Bill Smith this here is DC John Price or Taffy to his mates and finally this is DC Alan Bates"

"Ah well I'm not your darling neither is DC Campbell to you I'm Sergeant Jones"

"And I'm DCI Rees" a voice came from behind DC Smith "now DC Smith I have to be with the chief in 15 minutes but when I get back, I'll see you in my office Sergeant Jones will give you your duties for today" he turned "morning Taff how be you and the wife I've not seen you at the rugby yet" although Taffy lived in Oxford he still played rugby for Bletchley as he had lived there before moving to Oxford

"Good thank you, boss I've not had chance to get to the rugby new baby you see"

"Oh yes congratulations boy or girl"

"Girl sir we've called her Bethan"

"Good name same as my daughter's, right I'm off Lisa give me a call if you need me"

Dai could see the look on Smith's face and weighed him up straight away he would have to keep an eye on him he looked like he did not like taking orders from a woman, but he knew Lisa could cope,

Dai made the chiefs office with minutes to spare Maggie showed him straight in

"Morning sir"

"Morning Dai how are you take a seat tea, coffee?"

"Coffee sir white no sugar"

The chief buzzed through to Maggie

"Maggie, could you bring in some coffee please"

"Yes, sir right away"

There was a knock at the door and Maggie came in with a tray with a pot of coffee and two cups, it was so quick Dai wondered if Maggie kept the pot full all day just in case.

"Ok Dai how's it going with the inquiries any news?"

"Ok sir but before we start, I just need to talk to you about one of the DC's you had sent over this morning a DC Bill Smith

"Ah yes sorry Dai I wasn't sure who DCI Rogers was sending over I believe he can be a bit of a handful he seems to not like taking orders to well from a woman"

"I noticed that sir, but I think DS Jones will handle him okay, but I will be having words with him myself when I get back to Bletchley"

"Very well Dai if you have any trouble with him give me a call, now how things going" "yes, sir well we have a few leads to be going on at the moment a witness has come forward to say she saw the first victim arguing with a guy she didn't know the victim but she knew the guy he was arguing with, so DC's Carter and Campbell are following up on that, now the second victim the gent that found him say's he again didn't know the victim to talk to but he has seen him going in and out of a house opposite him he thinks it is used for dealing DS Jones and DC Stevens are going to call on him this afternoon as he is in work this morning and get him to point out the house"

"Have you found any connection to both the victims?"

"No sir not yet I was only thinking to myself yesterday what? joins these two people one good caring Christian the other a petty thief and drugs user the only connection we have so far is the way they were murdered and the same note"

"Well carry on but I think we need to call a press conference social media has got hold of it so now the press is hounding us for fact's"

"Yes, sir and I think the quicker the better"

"Ok, I'll get on to the press office get them to arrange things you ok doing it I've got meetings this afternoon"

"Yes, fine sir just get them to give me a call on my mobile as I'm not sure where I will be"

"Have we any news on the pm for the second victim Ryan Carter is it"

"Not yet sir DI Parker is there now, but apart from there may be drugs in the second victims blood the rest is all the same right down to the markings of the rope which by the way according to the forensic guys could be very old it was made of hemp fibre I've got one of the Dc's checking where it can be brought now"

"Ok keep me informed please Dai"

"Yes Sir" Dai gulped down the last of his coffee

"Oh, Dai how many DC's did DCI Rogers send over?"

"Well three turned up DC's Smith, Price and Bates"

"There should have been four get onto DCI Rogers find out what happened"

Dai took out his mobile and speed dialled headquarters when it answered he asked to be put through to DCI Roger's

"DCI Rogers speaking how can I help"

"Hello Peter Dai Rees, here from MK just to say thank you for the loan of some of your guys but I need to ask how many you sent over"

"Well four as the chief asked for why?"

"Well only three turned up DC's Price, Bates and Smith"

"Well, there should have been DC Billington I don't understand I saw them meet up in the carpark this morning, Dai I'll have to look into this I'm so sorry give me your mobile number and I'll call you"

"Ok thanks one more thing DC Smith he's got off to a bad start this morning with my DS"

"Is your DS a woman by any chance Dai"

"Yes, DS Lisa Jones"

"I thought so that guy has one big chip on his shoulder about women being in charge I've had him over the coals many a time about it, he also thinks he's god's gift to women, and the woman has to be in her place"

"I can see that can I ask a favour after this morning I'm going to be letting rip into him myself and I would also appreciate that after today he does not come back, I can make do with three"

"that's ok with me and if at the same time you want to find out what happened to DC Billington do so in the meantime, I'll find out what really happened"

"Cheers Peter"

Dai headed out to the car park just as Paul and Vicky were heading in

"Hello, you two what are you doing here?"

"Ho hi sir well we went and spoke to the Lady who said she had seen the argument with Diji and she gave us a name one Andris Jansons she thinks he's parents are Polish, Latvian or one of the Eastern bloc countries but he was born here, she then gave us an address for him"

"and"

"Well sir when we went to the house the door was answered by his brother who when went asked to see Andris was quite mad shouting do you guys not speak to each other it seems Andris got into some trouble last night and has spent last night here in the cells we're just going in now to see if we can interview him"

"Ok do you need me to come in"

"No sir I think myself and Vicky can manage ok"

"Ok see you back at Bletchley"

Dai Headed out and Paul and Vicky headed into the custody area

"Morning Sergeant"

"Oh. good morning to you DC Stevens what do I owe the pleasure of your company two days on the run and with new side kick I see"

"Sergeant this is DC Vicky Campbell she joined us from Kidlington and I believe you have one Andris Jansons in custody"

"We do indeed come in last night drunk and affray, we have him in Cell six, nice to meet you Vicky"

"we'd like a word with him if we could, is there an interview room free?"

"I believe room seven is free, is this about last night?"

"No sergeant it's about one of our victims he was seen arguing with him the night he died"

Paul and Vicky went down to the cells and opened six in the corner sat a young man very much the worse for wear.

"Morning Andris Jansons"?

"Ye who wants to know"

Vicky spoke first "well I'm DC Campbell and this is DC Stevens and there no need to be on the offensive we're only here to ask you some questions if you would like to come with us, would you like a drink tea, coffee maybe?"

"Yes, please but just water my gut's not to good think I eat something bad last night"

They lead Andris to interview room Paul stopping by the water fountain to get a cup of water he handed to Andris as they sat down

"Thank you"

"Right Andris" started Paul

"its Andy I like to be called Andy it's more British" proclaimed Andris

"Oh, sorry don't you like your name what is it Polish, Russian?" asked Vicky

"Ya it's Latvian but I live in Britain and it's a lot easier for my mates to call me Andy"

"Ok, now I have to say this is not about the trouble you got into last night"

Andy looked puzzled "we're here to ask you about two nights ago you were seen arguing with one DIji Okore"

"Who said so"

"Andy, we have a witness she saw you and knows you, now was you arguing with Diji Okore on the night he died?" said Paul

"Yes, I was if she say's so"

"What was it about was you trying to get money off him was you threating him"

"No, it was nothing like that it was personal just a silly argument between friends"

Before they had arrived at the station Vicky had looked up his record

"Andy before I arrived here, I looked up your record racial abuse against people of the black and Asian community, and now you are telling us that DiJi and you were friends"

"I can't believe that Andy you were seen arguing, then later that night Diji ended up died, what happened Andy? Did you argue did you try mugging him for his phone, money we know you like to do drugs did he fight back and you got nothing off him the first time but later that night you saw him on his own and decided to get your own back" Paul really let rip

"No, no I could never do that to DJ that's not what happened you don't understand"

Vicky looked at Paul

"Andy, you called Diji DJ"
"ye that's that what his mates call him that's what I call him"

"Right Andy do you want to tell us what happened that night?" Vicky asked

"it's personal"

Paul spoke up "look Andy you need to tell us because at the moment DJ is dead, he's been murdered, and you were the last person to be seen with him a live and arguing at that, how do you think it looks"

"No, you don't understand I could never do that to DJ never"

"Why Andy why would you never do that?"

"it's personal"

"I don't care how personal it is Andy you have to tell us even if it's to clear you we have to know"

"Because I love him there, I've said it I love him, and he loves me"

"What as a couple you mean" asked Paul in shock "but I thought you hated all Black people and Asian's"

"Ye, I did but DJ made me see different" me paused a little trying to think of the words

"Yes, go on," said Vicky

"It started about a year ago just after my mum had passed away, I was angry looking for answers why had this stupid covid taken my mum why did it have to be her, I would be out at night taking it out on people I was very angry I didn't seem to be able to talk to my dad, my brother was away in Latvia and held up by the pandemic I just didn't know what to do"

"Then what"

"One night I was sitting on a wall by the hall I think I was looking for trouble I know there was a church meeting on and that it was attended by lots of black people I needed someone to blame so I choose them but as I sat there, I found myself crying" he paused again "After a while I realised there was someone sitting next to me it was DJ, he asked if I was ok I just told him to piss off before I smashed his black face in he just sat there didn't budge I started to lose my temper with him but still he sat there telling me that was what I needed was to let off steam after a while I just broke down totally and blurted out all of my frustration about mum"

"And then what"

"We ended up talking for what seemed hours I started to realize that I was the one in the wrong he talked sense we became mates"

"But you said you loved him what did you mean by that?" asked Paul

"like I said I loved him we started meeting I felt free talking to him we kept it a secret from our mates, families I had my hard man act to keep up if I saw him in the street when I was with others I would shout racial abuse at him etc, after a few months of seeing each other at what to me I deemed my therapy sessions I blurted out my feelings for him seeing him had made me face my feeling of what I had known for a long time but could never show my dad or my brother they would never understand I think my mum had an idea but never let on god bless her, DJ just looked at me then leant in and kissed me I pulled away for a second but it felt so natural he then said he felt the same about me and thinks went from there"

"What happened the night of the argument?" Vicky asked

"We met up at the underpass I needed to see him I think my dad had begun to suspect something was going on with me I had calmed down a lot I wasn't hanging round with lots of the guys I use to with DJ's help I had weened myself off the weed and drugs I was becoming a better person and one of dads mate had seen me with DJ"

"So why the argument"

"I wanted us to come out to the families I asked about joining DJ's dads church, but DJ would have none of it he kept saying it was too soon he had his family and church to think of I accused him of thinking more of his church than me and if that's the way he felt it was over I then just walked off and left him"

"Did you hear from him after that?"

"He tried phone and texting me, saying he was sorry and that he loved me, but I wouldn't answer"

"What was the last thing you heard from him and about what time?"

"It must have been about half ten he texted to say he was going for a walk to clear his head and if I wanted to meet it, he would be at the normal place"

"But you didn't go"

"No, I was too stubborn I wish I had gone now then maybe he would still be alive"

"Ok that's all for now we may have to speak to you again," said Paul

"Andy, I need to ask was last night the first time you have been on trouble with the police since meeting DJ and how did you know DJ was dead?" asked Vicky

"I heard that there had been someone found dead in the underpass I just knew it was DJ I went and had a look by the time I got there you lot where with him but I could tell it was him the clothes were the same so I just left, and as I said he turned me around I got drunk last night because I was angry at losing him

"Ok thanks for talking to us I'm sorry we'll have to take you back to the cells thought," said Paul

"that's ok and thanks I think I can now face my dad I think that's how DJ would want me to be"

They lead him back to the cells but before they closed the door Paul spoke

"Andy what did you do last night just getting drunk doesn't get you in here"

"I smashed some windows in the hall"

"What hall the one where DJ went to church?"

"Ya I sat on the wall after I had done it hoping DJ would just come out and tell me off but he didn't you lot turned up and nicked me"

"Ok we'll be in touch look after yourself oh just one more thing you said about using drugs do you know a Ryan Carter"

"No, sir why who's he"?

"Oh Nothing"

Chapter Six

Dai was halfway back to Bletchley when his phone went "DCI Rees"

"Hello Dai, Peter here just after I spoke to you DC Billington walked into my office wanting to put in a complaint about DC Smith, seems they set out for Milton Keynes but had only got as far as the end of the road before DC Smith asked her out on a date when she said no thanks he started questioning her about her love life, was she gay is that what it was did she prefer women to men and that if she went with him he would show her what a real man was like"

"didn't DC's Price and Bates step in to help her?"

"Yes, but Smith just told them to shut up it was none of their business this was just to do with him and DC Billington any way by the time they got to Bicester she had enough and got out of the car when they stopped at a set of lights and made her way back here"

"Right, what do you want me to do?"

"Well, he's on his final warning and as he is one of my DC's I will have to be the one who deals with him, are you at MK now?"

"No, I'm on my way back to Bletchley now we're based there for the time being"

"God is Bletchley still in use I thought they pulled that down years ago"

"Well, it almost falling down but it will be base for the time being while the work is done at MK"

"Ok when you get to Bletchley you can have your say with him also get DC's Price and Bates side of things, I suppose you'll want to keep them with you today"

"Yes, if I could"

"Right question him and suspend him from duty then if you can, can you arrange a car to bring him back to me that leaves the pool car with Price and Bates then tomorrow DC Billington can join them as arranged "

"Yes, that fine with me cheers Peter"

Dai arrived back at the office and saw Lisa

"Set mae pethau wedi dod" (how have things been?") looking straight at the back of DC Smiths head

Taffy looked up and smiled

"roedd yn boen iawn yny pen ol" (he's been a right pain in the rear end")

Dc Smith had by this time turned and noticed Dai
"DC Smith my office now and close the door behind you"

Smith entered and went to sit down

"Did I ask you to sit down?"

"No sir"

"Right stay standing, now you got yourself off on the wrong foot this morning walking in the way you did and the way you spoke to my female officers they are not your darling's DS Jones is your superior officer and DC Campbell is a work colleague of equal rank do you understand"

"Yes sir"

"Now tell me in your own words why DC Billington is not here with us"

"Well sir we started out all right we were talking just nicely then I just happened to ask her if she would like to go on a date and she got all shirty on me then when we got to some light for some reason or other, she got out of the car and left"

"Well, that's not the version she's told DCI Rogers she says that when she said no thank you got quit nasty with her asking questions about her sexuality etc in fact you went a bit over the top"

"Well, she would sir it's her word against mine I don't know what upset her she just went off in a huff"

Dai got up from his seat and went to the door

"Price Bates if you wouldn't mind stepping into my office, please"

Taffy and Alan filed in

"Right gentlemen if you both in your own words would like to tell me of the events of this morning that lead up to DC Billington not joining us today you first Taffy"

"well boss I was the driver for today I picked up the pool car and went round to pick up the others when I got to the front of the building DC's Bates and Billington were already there so they got into the car DC Bates in the front DC Billington in the back we waited a while then DC Smith turned up and got in the back next to DC Billington, we hadn't got far when I heard DC Smith asking her out for a date, when she refused he got a bit personal asking her about if she preferred women etc, Alan then stepped in and asked him to pack it up but was told to butt out it was none of our business by the time we got to Bicester DC Billington had enough I think and as I pulled up at some lights she got out and that was the last we saw of her"

"DC Bates"

"Well boss it's just has DC Price said Dc Smith got a bit out of hand I felt so sorry for DC Billington he just would not let it go and as Dc Price said when we tried in intervene, we were told it was none of our business, I told him in the car that he had gone too far this time"

"Oh, come on Taffy, Alan, you know it was only playful banter I never meant anything of it "pleaded Dc Smith

"No sorry Smithy we told you we've had enough you have overstepped the mark we're not putting up with your behaviour anymore" Taffy said

"Ok guys thank you; you can go now and close the door behind you"

"Yes boss"

DC Smith went to follow them

"Not you Smith I've not finished with you, at DCI Rogers request I'm suspending you from duty I have a car coming down from central MK to take you back to Kidlington where you are report to DCI Rogers, I need your warrant card please"

"Sir no, please don't suspend me I'm sorry look I'll ring DC Billington apologies to her but please don't suspend me"

"To late I believe you was down to your last warning so now you've shot yourself in the foot now warrant card please and if you would like to go and wait in the car park for your ride, I don't want to see you in the building ever again"

Dc Smith left without a word just picked up his coat and left, Dai put his head in his hands god that was hard he had never had to suspend an officer before and hope he would not have to again he got up and went into the main office "right who's for drinks?"

"Yes, please boss tea no milk or sugar" Lisa was first off the mark

"Taffy"

"If you don't mind boss tea sugar and milk, please"

"Alan"

"Oh, thanks sir I'd have made it though if you asked coffee milk two sugars"

"No that's ok and as you may have noticed it's boss here or first names"

"Yes boss"

"where's Steve"

"Oh, he's in the loo I think boss" Lisa answered

"what's his poison Lisa"

"Coffee milk two sugars"

While the kettle boiled Dai asked to be brought up to speed on any developments

"Boss Paul and Vicky are on their way back from central they have interviewed the suspect but are pretty sure it's not him they'll tell us more when they get back" Lisa informed him.

"Boss I've tried chasing up any social media on this Ryan Carter guy I haven't found a thing no Facebook, Twitter there's nothing at all" Taffy added

"Sorry Taffy I could have saved you the work on that you may not find a bank account either he never had money always scrouging off other people and if he could the family" Steve had come back into the room

Taffy gave him a quizzical look

"Sorry was you not told Ryan is, was a relative of mine my dad's cousin's son"

"Oh, I'm sorry to hear that" both Taffy and Alan said at the same time

"that's ok we were not that close"

Dave walked into the room and went straight to the kettle that had just finished boiling

"Oh, good it's still hot I'm dying for a cuppa"

"Your just in time I'm about to make everyone drinks what's yours?"

"Tea plenty of milk three sugars and what's wrong boss you not well"

"I'll explain later, how did go at the post-mortem?"

"Ok boss, death was the same as Diji down to the shape of the mark on the back of the head where Ruth thinks he was knocked out" Dave noticed Steve sitting there "oh sorry Steve are you alright with me talking about this?"

"Yes, I'm fine boss fire away"

"Even the knot was roughly in the same spot enough to put pressure on the neck, Ruth seems to think they may be trying to break the neck as happens when the person is hung hence also the knees in the back, as you already know Ryan was a user so lots of track marks, he was also under nourished as though he hadn't eaten for a few days"

"That could be because he was more than likely stoned boss, when his mum was alive, he would turn up and eat them out of house and home, but after his mum died his dad put a stop to it told him not to come back till, he was clean that was four years ago"

"Ok so we know he's been getting his drugs and what food he's had from somewhere we need to find out" Dave carried on

"Boss myself and Steve are heading out later to see Mr Kowalska see if he can point us in the direction of the house he's been seen going in to"

"Cheers Lisa other than that boss we've no more to go on"

Paul and Vicky arrived

"ey up you two how ya get on with finding our lad seen arguing with Diji" asked Dave

"Very well thanks boss thanks to night shift nicking him last night," said Vicky

"interesting"

Dai spoke up "right what did you get out of him if anything"

Vicky let Paul speak

"Well boss we got quite lot, it seems they were a couple the reason they were arguing was because they had kept things secret till now but Andris, who likes to be called Andy wanted to face up to the families"

Lisa piped "sorry Paul did you say Andris"

"Yes Lisa"

"As in Andris Jansons lives on Fishermead"?

"Yes, why do you know him?"

"I've nicked him a few times he doesn't seem the type to be hanging round with a nice church going lad and he said they were a couple come off it he's pulling your leg"

It was Vicky that spoke next "no, truly they were a couple apparently after Andy's mum passed away last year of covid he went out looking for trouble went to the hall where DJ father holds the meeting but when he got there he couldn't do it ended up sitting on the wall crying, that's when he meet DJ since then with DJ help he's turned himself round if you look at his charge sheet you'll see that he's not been in trouble with us at all until last night he said DJ made him stand up to who he really was and it's made him a better person"

"So, what about last night?" Dave asked

"a moment of relapse boss it was the windows of the hall were DJ worshiped, he thought that it was all a mistake and if he broke the windows DJ would come out"

"Did he see DJ after their argument"

"No boss he had texts and phone calls from him, but he was too stubborn to answer or text back the last one he had from him saying he was going out for a walk and he was sorry and if he wanted to meet it would be the normal place"

"The underpass"

"Yes, boss oh and as we were leaving Sergeant McGinty ran out and handed me this say's you need to look at it straight away, some kid walked up the front desk saying a guy in a car had given him a tenner to hand it in"

"Cheers Paul "

Dai opened the envelope inside was two photos and a note

"Paul did Sergeant McGinty say if the young the lad gave them a description of the guy who gave him this?"

"Yes, boss but all the lad could tell him was it was a blue car with very black tinted windows so he couldn't see inside the guy just passed it through a gap at the top"

"Get onto control see if they can get CCTV and get onto forensics get them to get someone down here to collect these"

"Yes boss"

Dai stood there for a moment "right guys we have a development we have someone playing god these have just been handed in at central I won't hand them round as you can understand I don't want anyone else fingerprints on them I inadvertently just added mine"

He put them up on the white board

"As you can see it looks like whoever did these killings followed the victims to get photos of them, the first photo as you can see is of DJ in an embrace with someone, Lisa, Paul, Vicky can you confirm the other person is Andris Jansons"

"Yes boss" all three said

"Right find out if he's still at central we may have to put a guard on him just in case he's the next victim, and this the second victim by the looks of it he's in the middle of a deal does anyone recognise the other person"

All of them shook their heads

"Hold on a second boss it's quite a good photo of the person face on If I take a photo on my phone, I can upload it to the system and see if we get a match" Vicky came over and snapped off a shot

"Good thinking Vicky can you get straight on it I don't want this person turning up dead, now there's this, "he held up the note "as you can see the writing is the same as the notes on the victim's" he put it next to the photos on the white board everyone read it

I AM THE WARRIOR OF GOD, AND GOD SAY'S THOSE THAT SIN SHALL PAY THE PRICE, SO I WILL NOT STOP TILL THOSE THAT SIN ARE PUNISHED"

Taffy was first to speak "how be boss, how can this person say they are the warrior of god and he will kill all sinners when one of god's ten commandments say's thou shalt not kill surely this person is committing the biggest sin of all?"

"Well either they think they have god's permission to do this, or they are just a straight up fruit cake I think I know which one it is, ok people lets crack on see what we can come up with, Dave can I have a word?"

Dave followed Dai into his office he could tell something was wrong "you alright boss"

"No Dave I had to suspend DC Smith this morning I didn't want to, and this morning he overstepped the mark, so I had the job of doing it"

"What Bill Smith I thought I saw him on the way in as I went out"

"Yes, he came in here this morning all mouth calling Lisa and Vicky darling I was going to have him over that when I got back from seeing the chief, but it seems he upset a female officer on the way over here so much she got out of the car and made her way back to Kidlington"

"don't worry about it boss he must have been down to his last warning for sexual harassment I gave him a warning when he was just a PC at Wallingford right chauvinist never ever showed respect for women"

"Cheers Dave that makes me a little bit better oh before I forget can you get someone to put some gloves on and scan in the photos so there in the system before they go to the tech lads" Dai phone was ringing

Dave got up and left

"DCI Rees"

"Good morning sir Liz Mason here from the media office I've been asked by Chief Superintendent Mackintosh to give you a call to arrange a press conference"

"Yes, yes of course"

"Well, I've set one up for 16.00 this afternoon is this ok or do you still need time it will be outside central"

"Yes, that's fine see you then"

Dai hated press conference all the reporters jostling for position and today looked like it could be made even worse because as Dai looked out of the window, he could see big black rain clouds rolling in.

Taffy put his head round the door "boss I've just taken a call from forensic they have some news on the note's"

"Oh, what do they say?"

"Well boss they say they are printed but at first they could not work out the script that was used but then one of the techies noticed that the writing looked like signatures, so they looked closely and sure enough whoever is printing these of is using an Adobe document program but instead of just writing out the sentence in full they are using signature and adding each word as thought it was one"

"that's great what about the type of paper are they able to find out what it is or the printer"

"Not as yet boss but there is another bit of information, both notes had a splash of blood on them, and that blood matches the blood found on the rope fibre"

"that's great Taffy"

Dai spent the rest of the afternoon going through reports and writing up his statement for the press that afternoon.

Lisa and Steve headed out to Fishermead to interview Mr Kowalska they found the house and knocked after a few moments Mr Kowalska answered he was still I his work clothes

"Ah prynhawn da DS Jones lovely to see you"

"And good afternoon to you Mr Kowalska this is my colleague DC Carter may we come in?"

"Yes, yes of course do come in excuse the mess, would you like tea or coffee I've not long boiled the kettle" he led them upstairs to the second floor living room

"No, I'm alright thank you what about you Steve?"

"No, I'm fine as well thank you"

"Mr Kowalska we were wondering if you could point out the house where you saw the victim entering?"

"Yes, of course if you come to the window here you can see it from here, look the third one down from the end there's people going in there day and night all sorts black, white, Asian everyone I have reported it to the police only last week they said they would be in touch, but I haven't heard anything"

"that's great Mr Kowalska we'll take a little walk over there see what we can find out," said Lisa

She was just about to leave when Steve asked Mr Kowalska a question

"Mr Kowalska do you recognise this man" and showed him his phone

"Yes, that is the man that lives at that house"

"Thank you, Mr Kowalska,"

Lisa and Steve left Mr Kowalska to his tea and started to head for the house he had pointed out

"I didn't know you could speak Polish Lisa?"

"it's Welsh you prat Mr Kowalska learned to speak a little when he lived in Wales"

They were almost at the door when Lisa's phone went "DS Jones"

"DS Jones, DS Michaels drug squad can you please keep walking pasted the house you are heading for I'll meet you round the corner and explain"

Lisa put her phone away and kept walking Steve went to go to the house, but Lisa stopped him

"Keep walking we've got to meet someone"

As they turned the corner, they noticed a guy across the road he waved them over.

"DS Jones, sorry to do that to you I saw you go into the house across the road I had to ring central to get a number for you"

"what's going on? Sorry DC Carter this is DS Michaels drug squad"

"I need to ask what interest you have in that house only we've had it under surveillance for the last week it's a main drugs den, we had a tip off from the very house you just went to about it"

"Mr Kowalska was the gentleman who found the body of our second murder victim Ryan Carter he mentioned that he had seen Ryan going in and out of the house so we just wanted to ask some questions of the tenant and we also believe he may be a victim" explained Lisa

"Yes, I am sorry to hear about Ryan, I have nicked him a couple of times and I saw him here about four days ago, funny every time I nicked him, he used to say I could have been a copper just like my cousin I use to ask him who's that then? But he would just clam up he never did tell me his name but every time he said it, he said it with pride"

Steve went red DS Michaels noticed it

"Sorry did you say Carter? Are you Ryan's cousin"?

"Yes, I'm and don't be sorry we were not that close I'm surprised he even remembered me let alone talk about me the states he used to get in"

"I am sorry, now what was this you were saying about Mr Hackett being a victim"?

"Is that his name Hackett"

"Yes, we've been after him for a while, but he dropped of our radar but popped back up again when we got the tipoff"

Steve took out his phone "is this him"?

"yes, that's him Gary Hackett we think he is running a county lines job from here the Met are looking for him as well, we contacted them when we found him here they've asked us to hold fire on nicking him because they have a guy on their patch they believe is about to run a major shipment to him here in MK they want to make a joint bust, but I don't get how you think he'd be a victim and where did you get that photo?"

"It was hand delivered to central this morning then passed on to us with others and a note from our killer basically saying he who sins will pay the price" Lisa informed him

"This photo was taken here on that street, now our team have been in place for over a week now, but no one as mentioned anyone taking photos only the ones, we have who delivered the photos?"

"Young kid walked into the front desk and handed to Sergeant McGinty said a guy in a blue car with very blacked out windows had given him a tenner to deliver it"

"Well, I don't think we've seen a motor like that around, but I'll ask the guys, and as for Mr Hackett coming to grief, we have him under 24-hour surveillance front and back of the house plus he has a few heavies around him"

"Ok thanks for that I'll report back to the boss you ready Steve?"

"Yes sorry, just one question did Ryan drop of the radar at the same time as Hackett only the family didn't see or hear of him for a while"

"Yes, I think he's been working with Hackett for a while not that you would know it from what I gather from a snout is he never asked for money and Hackett never paid him only in drugs he used him to deal them out no one would take notice of a guy from the streets"

"Ok thanks for that Sergeant"

"Your, welcome and again I'm sorry"

"Right better get going Steve can't miss the boss on tv, oh just one thing DS Michaels can you inform us if you see a car matching the one, we said about"

"Yes, sure will"

Lisa and Paul got back to Bletchley long before Dai was due on TV and reported back to him and the rest of the team,

"So, you're telling me the drug squad have this Hackett guy under surveillance and they didn't even notice someone else taking photos of him" Dave said with a laugh

"Yes, boss it seems our Mr Kowalska is a good citizen and reported the goings on a few weeks ago he thought no one had acted on it, as the drugs squad hadn't informed him what they were up to and me and Steve here nearly went bundling in and blow the lot, he says he got my number from phoning central but how did he know who I was"?

"Not sure Lisa"

Vicky spoke up "did you book out a pool car"

"Yes, I did"

"There you go then he took the number of the car and checked in that way"

Dai laughed "bloody marvellous they can spot a cop car in the street but not a car that's connected to a murder, any way I'm off to make my press conference keep me up to date if anything comes in"

Dave shouted after him "mind your make up doesn't run it looks bad on camera"

Lisa joined in "do you want to borrow my lip stick and blusher boss"

"Bugger off you lot" and Dai left

Dai knew he had a good crew in his team even Vicky who just joined had settled in well, Taffy and Alan although they were DCI Rogers men had fallen in well to and he knew he could count on them.

He arrived at central in plenty of time he took out his phone and called PC Jill Grace

"PC Grace how can I help"

"PC Grace it's DCI Rees here" Dai could almost feel her straightening up as he spoke "I'm just ringing to see how Mr and Mrs Okore are and to warn you I'm doing a press release at 16.00 we'll be putting up pictures of Diji I didn't want them to suddenly see him on tv"

"Oh, sir yes thank you they are bearing up well in fact thanks to the members of the church they are getting lots of support every day someone brings food and leaves it at the door, and I'm being spoilt I ask if there's anything they need from the shops I go to go out and there's a car with someone in it they take a list and off they go return later with it all I haven't hardly done a thing"

"Well, I think with the support they have got you may be able to return to normal duties tomorrow and thanks for your help"

"Thank you, sir,"

"Oh, by the way talking of cars you haven't seen a big blue car with blacked out windows hanging around their place have you"

"No sir I have been noting all cars that look suspicious just in case and reporting them back each night for a check"

"Very good PC Grace and thank you again"

Dai hung up and just as he did a voice came from behind him

"DCI Rees"

Dai turned to see a middle-aged woman standing there

"Liz Mason media office sorry we can't shack hands"

"Ho yes Liz nice to meet you in person we've spoken on the phone a few time's"

"Yes, we have but never for something like this, have you got a speech ready?"

"Yes, I have, do you want a read through it I know the chief doesn't want us saying anything too bad about the force"

"No, no I'm sure it will be fine" she looked out the door "I see a lot of the press is here do you want to get started before the rain comes?"

They both left the building to a flurry of flashes from the press and microphones pushed out in front of them Jill spoke first

"Ladies and gentlemen my name, is Liz Mason of the TVP media office if you would just give DCI Rees a moment to give you the facts, he will gladly answer your questions after, thank you I'll now hand you over to DCI Rees" "good afternoon Ladies and gentlemen I'm DCI Rees of the major Incident team Thames Valley Police Milton Keynes division, on the morning of Sunday the 21th March the body of a young male was found in the underpass between Fishermead and Springfield this person has now been identify as one Diji Okore aged 20 he had been beaten and strangled, then on the afternoon of Monday 22nd March a second body was found in the underpass between Conniborrow and Downs barn this person has been identify as one Ryan Carter age 26 he too had been beaten and strangled, We are applying to any member of the public who thinks they may have any information as to why these two men may have been attacked, it does not matter how small the information is we would like to know, you can ring MK police direct or if you wish contact crime stoppers thank you very much for your time"

"DCI Rees, John Brown BBC news are these two people linked in any way?"

"As of yet we have not found a link between them"

"DCI Rees, Alison Kenny Sky news have you any clues yet to who may be doing these murders?"

"We have a few things we are looking at, at the moment but as of yet nothing concrete"

"DCI Rees, Alan Wright the Mirror do you think the person will strike again?"

"Ladies and gentlemen I would like to assure the public that we are doing ever thing we can catch who is ever doing this and that extra patrols are being put on to help with this thank you"

Dai turned and headed back into the building Jill was thanking the press for their time and she too headed in doors.

All this time Dai had not noticed the guy at the back taking photos if he did, he would assume he was press as Dai finished, he wandered of away from all the press guys back to his bike he had to get home he had things to do now he could have a bit of fun with DCI Rees.

Chapter Seven

As he sat in his dark room he had built with his father at the back of the house he was thinking "had DCI Rees got sins would he be one that needed to be punished" he knew he worked within the law of the land but that didn't stop people sinning, look at Diji like him he was a good church goer but then he had seen him cuddling and kissing that other man that was wrong god had created man and woman Adam and Eve so they could be on this earth together it was wrong man and man and the other one Carter, was that it? he had seen him the night the girl across the road had died from an overdose he was at her home he had seen him hand her the package he had killed her and had to be punished, it had taken him a while to find this Carter guy but Diji was easy he had seen him first when he went with his church to deliver food packages they had teamed up with DIji's fathers place of worship and that is where he had met him he was a nice guy but the night he had stumbled upon him and the other guy he realized he was a sinner and god would not like this. He had been brought up in the Christian faith as a young boy he had gone to church with his parents every Sunday, his father was the church warden and his mother use to arrange the flowers and help his father keep the church tidy and now his parents had passed It was his job. He had a passion for photograph the old stuff where you would load a film take your photo then come home and develop it to see the photo appear as it was put in the solution as if by magic his father had been the one to get him into it, he would sit for hours in the dark room watching him seeing photos of himself and his mother in happier times,

He hated technology but he had given in to it he had a computer and a printer nothing fancy like these they advertise on the television just a basic one he needed it now as so much was on line he even had to order his developer and cleaning solution on line, his bank was on line everything was on line it was over taking him, he was thank full for young Jane one of the parishioners daughter who had taken time to show him how things worked and set it all up for him she even tried to get him to start using a digital camera even loaning him one to see how he got on, he had tried it but it wasn't the same so it was sitting on the shelve in the kitchen until she asks for it back.

He looked at the pictures "very good he thought you would think that DCI Rees and that Mason woman were a couple that had just got married him in his suit and her in her matching skirt and jacket" which reminded him he had a wedding this weekend that he was to do the photos for the first in a long time not that there would be much to take photos of the bride, groom, best man and maybe a couple of bridesmaids and family Covid had put a stop to the large weddings.

He locked up the dark room and returned to the house he put the kettle on he had lots to do the photos would be dry by the morning but now he had to write the note, Jill had shown him how to use the program he used to write the note but the first time he did it, didn't seem right the letters were all the same he wanted to be different it was when he came to sign a letter he had to return through email that he noticed that if he used signature on the program and type each word as a new signature the font would be different very clever that would keep them guessing for a while.

He finished up his tea and the note now to get the car ready it wasn't even his car he had learned to drive but never owned a car he loved riding round on his bike along the red ways you could see so much more of Milton Keynes that way, the car belonged to a friend of his he had moved away to America for work and had asked if he could store the car in his garage until he came back that had been two years ago but the friend in all fairness had arrange for him to use the car when ever and once a year would send over money for him to tax, insure and MOT it. He was also looking after his house and would sort any mail and send it on, he never used the car but now it came in handy he was able to visit the police station and not be seen and now it was locked back in the garage if the police went to the address it was registered to and even asked the neighbours they would say that the friend was away for work and they didn't know where the car was all he had to was keep it hidden.

Chapter Eight

Dai and the team had worked late into the night taking calls from the public following up the things they felt could help so at 23.00 Dai had called it a day, he had sent Taffy and Alan off little while earlier as both lived in Oxford a team of extra staff had been drafted in to cover a night shift and sift through anything they may find relevant overnight.

By the time Dai got home had a drink and something to eat it was just coming up for midnight before he climbed into bed, but he still managed to wake up at 05,30 the automatic alarm in his head went off he was going to skip his run this morning he wanted to be in the office early to see if there had been any development, but he knew that if anything had come up he would have got a call.

Dai dressed and headed out to the car there had been a frost and Dai cursed this is the one time he wished he had a modern car on days like this the Dolomite had no heated rear window, but the heater was good he scrapped the car and headed out Bletchley was incredibly quiet at this time in the morning just a few people heading out to work it was a ghost town.

Dai headed into the office and was surprised to find Dave in.

"Morning Dave what's wrong with you shit the bed?"

"Morning Dai no, just couldn't sleep things going round in my head I woke about 04.30 so decide to head in, what about you?"

"Same I couldn't face my normal run this morning like you to many things going on any progress"

"Nothing of significance. CCTV chaps have traced the car from one of the cameras it shows the car approaching the lad the window go down, a little chat then whoever it is hands over the money and the envelope and heads off"

"Number plates?"

"Yes, records show the car is registered to a guy who lives on Stacy bushes, couple of guys went round there but there was no sign of the car or the owner"

"Could he have moved and not registered the car at the new address"

"that's what I thought so I'll get a couple of guys to go to the address this morning and question the neighbours see what they can come up with"

"Anything else?"

"No, just that the kettles just boiled if you want one, but you'll have to wash yourself up a cup this lot are too lazy to do it"

Everyone turned to look at Dave with that "sorry sir" look

Dai went into his office he had paperwork to do no matter how much he had done the day before there seemed to be twice as much the next day. He found his cup from the day before and went out to make himself a brew him and Dave then ran through what the team had to catch up on.

By 08.00 all the team had arrived Taffy and Andy had arrived from Kidlington along with DC Billington Taffy introduced everyone.

"Good morning DC Billington no problems getting here this morning"

"No Sir DC's Price and Bates were perfect gentlemen this morning"

"Right as I explained to the others yesterday its first names or boss for me and Taffy here was not such a gentleman to not give us your first name"

"it's Paula boss"

"Right let us get on shall we" Dai began in the background the phone in Dai's office began to ring Dai ignored it and it went only to start up five seconds later "Dave you ok to take this someone must want me really bad"

"Yes, Dai sure"

Dai wandered into his office and picked up" DCI Rees"

"Morning Dai" Dai was surprised this was a voice he had not expected to hear this morning

"Superintendent Wilcox sorry sir I thought you was on leave due to covid, how are the family by the way?"

"Their good thank you Dai a few more days and we all should be clear to return to normal, and I am but I saw you on tv last night so got in touch with the chief this morning and he's cleared it for me to work from home I'm just sitting here twiddling my thumbs as it is so might as well do something, so what have we got?"

Dai ran through everything they had so far, the superintendent thanked him and gave him his home number to stay in touch with developments.

He wondered back into the main office just as Dave was finishing.

"Right Dave the day planned out"

"ey boss Vicky and Steve are going to see a guy who swears blind he knows who the killer is but from the sound of it he's a bit of a creak pot, Lisa and Paul are going to follow up on the car along with Andy and Paula and poor Taffy here as asked if he could stay as near to the office today as he as a bit of a dodgy stomach this morning"

"Nothing to bad I hope Taffy" asked Dai

"No boss the Mrs had a curry the other night from our local Indian takeaway I found it in the fridge and heated it up when I got home but I think it was a little bit off because since then I've had a touch of Delhi belly"

"It wasn't the couple of pints you had with it then that was to blame"

"No boss ever since the baby came along, I've hardly drank me, and the Mrs take it in turns to do the night shift with her"

"Ah the joys of parenthood, right everyone you know what you have to do so let's get going"

A phone was ringing in the background Vicky picked up "MIT DC Campbell how can I help yes I'll put you through to her, Lisa a DS Michaels for you"

"DS Michaels how can I help you?"

"it's more of what I can do for you DS Jones, we nicked Gary Hackett last night and I wondered if you would like to have a friendly chat with him before the Met take him from us"

"Hold on I'll ask the boss, boss I've got DS Michaels they nicked Gary Hackett last night he wondered if we would like a word with him?"

"Yes, please tell him me and Dave will be over A.S.A.P"

"that's great DS Michaels, DCI Rees and DI Parker will be over to you soon"

"Right folk you all have your jobs for today let's get moving, oh and before we go can someone make sure there is plenty pf bog roll in the gent's we don't want Taffy getting caught short," said Dai

"Thanks boss your all heart" Taffy said with a false smile

Everyone started to leave

"Right boss you ready your car or mine?" Dave asked

"we'll take mine I need to get some fuel while we're out"

"Ok I'll just get my laptop from my car meet you in the car park"

They got too central I good time Dai swiped in and drove into find a parking space two young plain clothes men were stood by the main door

"God Ali I knew Thames Valley were making cutbacks but look at that there having to use old clamped out bangers as pool cars"

Before Dai could say anything, a voice came from behind them "DCI Rees Di Parker, DS Michaels nice to meet you both"

"Nice to meet you to are these two monkeys anything to do with you?"

"No sir these are a couple of our colleagues from the Met"

Dai turned to them "right what's your names"

"DC Jarvis sir"

"DC Sigh sir"

"Now DC Jarvis what was you saying about my car?"

"Sorry sir I never meant anything I was joking"

"Right, I'll give you a tip always be sure of your facts before you go blowing off your mouth when you know the facts you can spout what you like, being a good detective is all about facts without them, we get nowhere understood"

"Yes, sir sorry sir"

"Right DS Michaels lead the way"

"Ok sir I've had him taken to interview room 8 I'm sorry do you mind if I shoot off, I've got to get the paperwork together for him to be shipped to the MET"

"No that's fine"

They made their way to the interview room Gary Hackett was sat behind a table PC Joe Clark was by the door Dai and Dave took a seat opposite Gary Hackett,

Gary Hackett was a large man maybe six foot 250 pounds Dai reckoned he would make a good prop if he played rugby his arms neck and maybe the rest of his body was covered in tattoos.

"Good morning Gary do you mind if I call you Gary? I'm DCI Rees and this here DI Parker we would like to ask you some questions"

"it's Mr Hackett to you and I ain't saying a word without my solicitor being here so you can just sod off"

"Mr Hackett we're not here about your arrest as I said we need to ask you some questions it's about an acquaintance of yours Ryan Carter"

"Never heard of him"

"So, you've don't know him," said Dave

"No, never heard of the guy what makes you think I have?"

"Well, we have this for a start" Dave turned the laptop so he could Hackett could see it "this is you with one said Ryan Carter is it not or have you got a double?"

Hackett stumbled a bit before he spoken Dai could see he was thinking of a good reply

"Oh, him ye I've seen him a round sleeping rough around the city didn't know his name till you just told me"

"So, if you didn't know him what? are you handing him in the photo?" asked Dave

"He asked me for a smoke and a light I was only too happy to oblige got to help these poor souls haven't you"

"look Mr Hackett as I explained we are not here about your arrest for drugs we are here about the murder of Ryan Carter, now as it stands you by the looks of this photo may have been the last person to see him alive we know from our colleagues in the drug squad he worked for you, now do you know where Ryan had been on the night of his death was he making a delivery for you could it have been your drugs that got him killed?"

"Look I had nothing to do with his death he was meant to come to mine about midnight on the night he died but he didn't show I thought he'd gone and got himself stoned or something when he didn't show"

"This was the night of Sunday the 21st" asked Dave

"If you say so but I had nothing to do with is death I was at home all night I have witnesses"

"We know that Mr Hackett, can you think of anyone who would want to kill Ryan?"

"no one at all he was a softy he would wind up anyone but not to the extent they would want to kill him"

"Thank you for your cooperation we've finished with you now" Dai said with a smile "I would normally say your free to go but our friends from the Met would like a word enjoy your trip"

Hackett just curled up his lip in a snarl as they left, and he was escorted back to the cells. DS Michaels met them in the corridor

"All good sir was he any help"

"No not really he couldn't tell us anymore than we knew and as for the night of the murder he said he as witnesses I didn't have the heart to tell him he had the best witnesses going in you lot"

DS Michaels smiled "it's strange to think the evidence we have against him for the drug dealing helped save him from a murder rap, sir I've had one of my lads put all the photos we took on the surveillance of his house onto the system would you like us to send them over to you there maybe something there that we haven't noticed that someone in your team may pick up on"

"Yes, thanks for that DS Michaels and thanks for your help so far, right Dave time to head back to the ranch"

As they got to the car park DC Jarvis caught up with them

"Sir I'd just like to say sorry for earlier I was out of hand" "that's ok DC Jarvis just remember what I said a bout shooting your mouth off "

"Will do sir I hope you don't mind I had a good look round it I see you've had a few improvements done the brakes lights etc"

"Yes, she not a bad old bus, not everyone tastes but I like it and she's fast enough for me"

Dave looked over to DC Jarvis and with a smile said "thank you DC Jarvis and there was me thinking I was getting home in time for tea tonight and you start him on about the love of his life"

"Sorry sir's I'll let you get on your way nice to have met you and if you wouldn't mind me taking a photo of it my uncle is classic car mad, he's got a Triumph Toledo is it?"

"Yes, that's the one down from this, and take as many photos as you like"

Dave gave a big false sigh "bang goes breakfast"

They got back Bletchley just as Taffy was picking up the phone

"Bore dah boss I was just going to ring you young Andris Jansons been released with a warning his dad as taken him home, it seems he's a glazier so as offered to replace the windows in the hall for nothing"

"Anything else come up" Dave asked

"Oh yes boss tech has been on they have taken a look at the photos it seems they were taken and then developed not digital so they can't get a time date or anything from them and no news from the rest of the team I've been keeping an eye on social media just in case anything crops on there but as of yet nothing of interest, someone who knew Ryan has set up a go fund me page for a funeral for him"

"I wonder who that is and if the money will go to where it's meant to" Dave said

Dai was thinking "Dave, Taffy I'm starting to think there's something about this killer"

Dave looked puzzled "what do you mean Dai"

"Well look at it the rope is old rope made from hemp, the photos not digital old fashioned take your time and develop them but the note is printed and cleverly worked out on a computer so we can't trace it whoever is doing this making is our life hard is this someone who is here with future tech and knows how to through us or someone who is stuck in the past and is being made to accept the future?"

"I see what you mean he/she is using both modern and old technology to confuse us"

"Maybe but we'll just have to go with what we've got, right Dave your turn to put the kettle on"

"Ok just this once but if the rest come in, they can make their own Taffy what's yours?"

Dai went into his office a pile of mail had been put on his desk most of it was documents sent over for him to sign but at the bottom was a large brown envelope Dai recognised it as being the same as the one from before he took out a pair of surgical gloves from a box on the side and slipped them on he picked up the envelope it was addressed to him and the writing he could see was the same as the note, he felt it all over to see if there was anything solid in it wires etc no nothing like that so he gentle opened it inside was a photo of him and Liz Mason on the steps of central and a note

"*Dear DCI Rees, that was a good speech you made yesterday but you must understand these people where sinners and sinners have to be punished, you told the people that you will keep them safe but you can't protect all sinners for I am the warrior of god and I have god on my side he will protect me and I have not finished I will track down all sinners and I will punish them*"

Dai was shacking the bastard had been at the press conference yesterday me had taken photos of him he called Dave into the room

"what's up Dai you look like you've seen a ghost?"

Dai handed him some gloves "here put these on and take a look at these"

Dave put them on and picked up the note and photo

"Bloody hell Dai where did these come from"

"Internal mail must have sent it over; he was there yesterday stood right in front of me, and I didn't twig"

"God Dai calm down you wasn't to know how many press was there yesterday 20/ 30 you wouldn't have noticed him if he was hidden in amongst that lot"

Dai was thinking back to last night who he had seen, and Dave was right apart from the press who had asked him questions he had not taken any notice of them

"I'll get on to central for CCTV see if they can come up with anything maybe the car was parked nearby or a face that stands out"

"Cheers Dave I'll ring Liz Mason see if she noticed anyone that was out of place, she must know what agencies where due to be there"

Dave left the room and Dai found Liz Masons number and gave her a call
"Liz Mason"

"Hi Liz DCI Rees, here sorry to trouble you"

"No that's ok how can I help?"

"Liz I need to ask are you are the person that gets the press together you know gives them the times etc?"

"Yes why"

"Did you see anyone there yesterday that you didn't know by any chance someone that you had not invited to the conference"

"No, I saw most of the people I know the BBC, ITV, Sky and the papers but I don't think I noticed anyone untoward there why"

"Well, it seems our killer was there he took a rather fetching photo of us on the steps and has posted it to me along with a note"

"Oh, my goodness the killer was there," she paused for a moment "sorry the thought of it just sent a shiver down my spine"

"It did me too"

"Listen I'm sorry I can't help but I know someone who may be able to his names Brain Patterson he's freelance does a bit of work for the local radio and papers I tried to ring him yesterday to get him there but I couldn't get hold of him so I rang the local radio I knew they would get him"

"Have you got a number for him?"

" Yes, by all means"

Liz gave him the number and he rang it straight away it took a while to answer but when it did it was picked up by a woman

"Good morning this is DCI Rees Thames Valley could I speak to Brian Patterson please"

"I'm sorry Brain's not able to take calls at the moment what it regarding I'm his wife"

"Oh, Mrs Patterson I just wanted to ask him a question about yesterday's press conference"

"I'm sorry DCI Rees but Brain was not at yesterday's conference he's been laid up in bed with covid for the last four days"

"Liz Mason said she tried to contact him yesterday but could not get hold of him why is that?"

"Sorry DCI Rees that's my fault I turned his mobile off I knew if he got one sniff of a story he would try and get out to cover it"

"Thank you, Mrs Patterson, by any chance do you have the local radio stations direct number I need to find out who they sent"

"Yes. I do but I know who they sent it was young Holly Long they always use her if they can't get hold of Brain would you like her number?"

Dai thanked her he was getting that feeling he was going to be going all around the houses on this one he rang her number and got the engaged tone he left it a few moments and went out to find a brew he found one that Dave had been in the middle of making he boiled the kettle and finished making the tea past one to Dave and Taffy and went back and redialled Holly number

"Holly Long"

"Hello, Miss Long, sorry to bother you DCI Rees here I need to ask you some questions if it convenient"

"Hi Mrs Patterson said you would be ringing how can I help you?"

"Miss Long you were at yesterday's press conference, yes?"

"Yes, I was"

"I need you to think Miss Long did you notice anyone who you didn't know?"

"I'm Sorry sir but I'm not up to speed with who is who Brain normally covers the big stories I tend to stick to local; I was too busy being pushed around by the big guys that I didn't even get to ask you a question"

"Sorry about that but I need you to think was there anyone who stood out from the crowd"

"Not that I can think of" there was a slight pause "oh yes sorry there was but I could not make he or she out as we all turned to leave a few of us where chatting and I noticed a person as I said not sure if male or female leaving but whereas most of us went off to our cars or vans, he/she just walked off towards the city"

"Can you describe the person at all"

"Only that they were wearing blue jeans and a parker coat I think that's what they are called"

"Height hair colour?"

"I'd say about one meter eighty thin built, but I can't tell you hair colour the hood was pulled up to cover the face I thought at the time it looked like Kenny from South Park"

"Was he/she carrying anything?"

"Yes, a bag could have been a camera bag but I'm not sure"

"Thank you Miss Long you've been most helpful and what was your question?"

"sorry"

"From yesterday"

"Oh yes thank you I was going to ask was Ryan Carters death drugs related I know of him and have seen him at work outside the clubs dealing out"

"No Miss long it was not drug's related, and thank you again"

"DCI Rees, can I ask do you know anything about the arrest of one Gary Hackett last night?"

"No Miss Long the arrest of Gary Hackett is nothing to do with Ryan Carter it was a totally different matter and I know nothing of why he was arrested"

"But Ryan worked for Hackett surely there's a link"

"Miss Long I can tell you this we know that Ryan worked for Gary Hackett, but I can assure you that Gary Hackett has nothing to do with the death of Ryan Carter so thank you again and goodbye"

"Thank you, DCI Rees but could you keep me up to date on the case I need a good brake"

"Miss Long I am unable to pass on any information about the case, any information will be passed through our press officer Liz Mason"

"Ok thanks bye" and she hung up

Dai went back to the main office "Dave have you got hold of the CCTV guys yet?"

"Not yet I've just arranged for someone from forensics to come and get the note and photo but I don't think they'll find much it looks the same as the last one"

"I got hold of Liz Mason she didn't notice anyone that stood out, but I got hold of a local reporter Holly Long, she saw a person not sure if it were male or female heading away from the conference towards the city carrying a bag that could have been a camera case, about 5ft 9/10 thin build and wearing a parker coat and blue jeans"

"Hair colour eyes?"

"No, she said the hood of the parker was pulled right up said it reminded her of someone called Kenny out of some show"

Taffy piped up "oh I know who that is boss he a little guy in a show, but you never see his face because of his coat and for some reason he always ends up dead then someone says oh my god you've killed Kenny"

"Never seen it, anyway, get on to them see what we can find it cannot be that difficult to spot someone wearing a parker coat"

Vicky and Steve came into the office

"Hi, you two that was quick how did you get on with our guy that says he knows the killer" Dave enquired

They both broke into a smile

"Well come on spit it out what you got"

Steve spoke first Vicky was trying to stifle a laugh

"Well sir it seems our Mr Hendricks thinks himself to be a bit of a psychic he had a vision of our killer he is a real terrible man a worshipper of the devil himself and he is going to strike again, and his vision had become real when he saw him in the papers and the news, he has even given us a photo of him"

"Well come on then show us who this devil is so we can go and make an arrest," said Dave

Vicky now could not contain herself and burst into laughter

Steve to was trying to stop himself laughing "sorry sir but this is him"

He held up a picture taken from a newspaper

Dave and Taffy both broke into laughter

"Bloody hell Dai I never took you as a devil worshipper" Dave was shaking as he spoke

"Very funny I hope you nicked this Mr Hendricks for wasting police time" Dai's face was red but after a few seconds he could see the funny side

"No boss I did give him a stiff warning do you want me to put it on the investigation board?"

Dai himself was seeing the funny side now "god can you see me taking this to the chief here sir we've had a brake through got a picture of the suspect"

Everyone laughed as the rest of the team got back

"Hello what's given you lot the giggles"? Lisa enquired

Steve held up the photo "our witness has given us a photo of the suspect"

The team joined in the banter "well at least you're showing your good side boss"

"Right very funny now let's get on with the serious stuff, how did you get on with tracing the car"?

Lisa spoke first "not too bad but I think Paula got the best lead"

"Yes, boss I have spoken to a lady four doors up from Mr Fosdyke's"

"Sorry who?"

"Mr Fosdyke boss that the name of the owner of the car"

"Yes, sorry I forgot for the moment" apologised Dai "carry on"

"According to Mrs Arnold Mr Fosdyke is away working in America has been for the last two years, and as for the car she has not seen it since the day he left for America she things he may have sold it"

"Boss I've got something else" Andy spoke up before Dai could "another neighbour says she thinks someone is going to the house she saw a light on about a week after Mr Fosdyke left, her husband went over to have a look but by the time, he had got dressed the light was out and the place all locked up he could see no sign of forced entry so left it but about a week later the same thing happened again and has been happening since she thinks someone is going in and sorting the mail for him and making sure the place is ok but the strange thing is it's always at night and never the same night so they have not seen who it is"

"Right let's see if we can find out who this mystery person is and what of the car?"

"boss I've also spoken to a few of the lads around the area it seems the car was well known by them it had all mod cons it had been lowered the windows blackened in fact one of the lads says he saw Mr Fosdyke as we now know him being pulled by a traffic car and told to get the windows redone because they were too dark at the front but that was a few days before Mr Fosdyke left for America, so I was thinking maybe the car had been put into a local garage to have the work done and it's still there"

"Good thinking Steve follow it up will you," he addressed the rest of the team "we know from the lad who delivered the envelope to Sergeant McGinty that the windows where still blacked out as he could not see the driver and the CCTV picked it up so it is still being driven by someone, Paula can you give Steve a handed to chase up the garages in the area but also any self-storage places it may be in a container somewhere"

"Boss I've just had another look at the car details it was taxed, M.O.Ted and insured last year and it's all due for renewal in two months' time but I've just noticed there a second named driver on the insurance a Mr Stephen Clements do you want me to chase it up?"

"well spotted Lisa it could be that Mr Clements works for a garage, but they normally have their own insurance so it may be a friend or relative that has the car check the electoral roll see how many Clements there are in the area and see if anyone knows him, oh and see if anyone knows where Mr Fosdyke works, they may have a number for him, now for those of you that was not here we have had another note and photo delivered this time the photo was of myself and Liz Mason on the steps at central doing the press conference it seems he/she was there the note is basically saying what he said in the first one that he is the warrior of god etc and god will protect him/her and saying he/she will strike again, I have spoken to a witness that saw a person unknown leaving the conference afterwards but the description is not very good brown parker coat with blue jeans about five foot eight or nine of thin build, now DS Michaels of the drug squad has had his team put on to the system photos of the surveillance on Gary Hackett house I need one of you to sift through them to see if we can spot anything they may have missed"

"Sir what's a parker coat?" asked Paul

"it's what Mods use to wear" answered Dave Paul looked at him confused "oh I know what's a Mod Google it your dad may have been one I forget how young some of you are"

"Right folks let's get on Paul look up a parker coat and you can start looking at the photos from the drugs squad"

"Yes sir"

The team worked well into the night and by the time Dai left at midnight they were still on closer to finding the killer.

Chapter Nine

As he sat in his dark room things were running throw his mind tonight he would punish his third sinner he had seen her around the city selling herself to men what was it his mother had called them "ladies of the night" he called them harlots cheap women who should know better, he had met one once he had stayed in London for a conference the church had laid on she was in the hotel he stayed at he had watched her all evening approaching different men some would leave with her, some use to say no, she had approached him asked him if he wanted a good time he ignored her at first but she kept on "oh come on what's the matter are you shy? no are you gay then it doesn't matter to me come on let me show you a good time"

By this time he had had enough he stood up looked her in the eye and at the top of his voice had shouted at her to stop go away called her a harlot and a sinner by which time the manager had arrived and asked her to leave he apologised to him and offered him a complementary drink on the house he had refused this was another thing he didn't like he watched the men with the harlot they had all had too much to drink he was thinking that some of them may be sinners have wives and children at home and here they were going with that harlot the more he thought about it the more sense tonight's kill became he would be justified in the face of god.

The photos had developed by now as he hung them up to dry he was thinking how would he get these to DCI Rees he had used the car the first time and paid the lad to go in, the second time he had just walked up to the door and popped it into the letter box late at night he had taken his bike and had hidden out in the darkness, then there had been the press conference he wouldn't have known about that apart from over hearing one of the ladies helping out with food parcels saying that her friends husband was meant to go but because he had covid he couldn't, it was easy enough to find out the time slip it into a conversation "oh did I hear you say there's going to be a press realise wonder what time that's going to be on?" bingo he had the time, he had taken his bike to it, he had ridden there in his cycling gear he knew just the place to go so no one would take much notice, it was an office block that was no longer in use it had a car park at the rear and a bin area he had locked his bike there slipped the jeans and parker coat he had taken with him over the top of his cycling gear gone to the press conference then done the whole thing in reverse that way if he had been picked up by a camera it would look as if he had just stopped off somewhere and was returning, as for the parker and jeans they were gone he had dropped them along with the ruck sack they were in into a clothes bank he know that way someone would make use of them, now all he had to think of was about tonight.

Chapter Ten

It was gone 12 again before Dai hit his bed, he had taken a voice message from Bethan saying how busy she was with work and that she missed him and warning him that "grancha"(grandad) had a bee in his bonnet and was determined that he the minute the they could travel between Wales and England he was going to see him, the second voice message was from is dad telling him he had prebooked his ticket and that he would be up to see him as soon as he could Dai just smiled that was his dad all over. It did not seem like Dai had had any sleep before his phone was going.

"DCI Rees, Sergeant Cooper here sorry to bother you this early in the morning sir but one of the beat bobby's has found another body"

"No that's ok where?"

"Underpass where Avebury Blvd and Secklow gate meet Xscape side do you wish me to contact forensic etc sir"

"Yes, please if you could, tell them, I'll be there as soon as possible"

"Yes sir"

Dai dressed and was out the door in minutes no need for blues and twos at this time in the morning there was no one around, he voice dialled Dave and Lisa and got them to meet him at the scene.

Dai arrived first parking up he saw the young beat bobby coming out from the underpass he showed his ID

"Right, what we got?"

The PC lead the way back into the underpass "this way sir she's just down here"

The lights in the underpass where out Dai took a small torch from his pocket

"Oh, sorry sir just over here" the PC shone his own torch over to where what looked like a bundle of clothes were

She was sat up Dai could tell from just looking at her this was the same modus operandi as the others.

"Is this how you found her?"

"Yes, sir she looked as though she was sleeping, I asked her name and if she was ok but got no response, so I got in closer that's when I noticed the marks on her neck and the blood on her head"

"The lights are out what made you come down here?"

"I was just doing a patrol of the car parks this area is normally full of rough sleepers when I noticed a light flickering in the underpass, so I got out to investigate that's when I found her"

"What was the flickering light"

"Oh, sorry sir when I came into the underpass, I could just make out someone with a torch whoever it was, was shining the torch on the body and it looked like he or she was searching for her"

"And then what?"

"He she ran off I thought about giving chase, but I thought it was better to deal with the young lady first I radioed through and gave them the details of the person I saw I know there was another petrol just down the road as we had been out to an alarm going off at one of the buildings down there, I hoped they may pick up whoever it was they had gone in their direction"

A voice came from the dark

"Hello anyone there?"

Dai swung his torch round to see Colin Mathews stood there

"Morning Colin sorry to have you out at this time in the morning"

"Oh, that's ok Dai what we got?"

"Young white female about 30 years old looks like the same MO as the other two PC sorry I didn't get your name"

"Pc Jameson sir"

"PC Jameson found her here about half hour ago he hasn't touched anything, you haven't touched anything have you?"

"No sir"

"Good, I'm sorry if we've trampled over part of the crime scene but as you can see, we have no light here"

"that's ok I'll call through and ask for a mobile generator to be sent over but for the moment we have some lights in the van that will do, now can we seal off this area"

"Yes of course"

Dai and PC Jameson walked out from the underpass just as Dave turned up.

"ey up Dai what we got is it the same as the others"

"Looks that way Dave, PC Jameson found a young woman about half hour ago he also saw someone over the body, but he/she ran off towards the Argos building when PC Jameson spoke to whoever"

"Did you not run after whoever it was?"

"No sir I felt my first priority was the young lady it wasn't until I look closely, I realized she was dead"

"PC Jameson radioed in straight away he's made sure the description of the perpetrator has got out; with any luck we'll get whoever it is there can't be that many people around at this time in the morning!

They saw Lisa pull up in her car she got out and walked over.

"Morning boss, Dave what we got same as before?"

Dave spoke first "yes young female this time but boss here says it looks the same"

"bolltau"(bollocks)

"sorry"

"Oh. sorry Dave just swearing under my breath there I thought we would get whoever was doing this before they struck again"

"No such luck but PC Jameson saw someone with the body, and we have people out now looking for whoever it was so with any luck we might get he or she, as Dai said there can't be that many people out this morning"

Dave's phone rang and he picked up and wandered off.

Dai turned to PC Jameson

"PC Jameson did you notice if the person you saw was carrying anything a bag, rope a piece of wood maybe?"

"No sir"

"What! no sir as in you didn't notice anything or no sir the person wasn't carrying anything?"

"No sir the person was not carrying anything"

"Right, we'll have to get a full search team in here if this was our killer somewhere around here must be the tools of his or her trade Lisa can you get on to arrange that?"

"Right boss on it"

"PC Jameson you say the person ran out the other side of the underpass"

"Yes sir"

"Right take your car round there set it so the lights are on that side see if you can see anything that might have been dropped"

The rain was just starting to come down as Dave returned

"Dai that was Ruth she's going to be a bit late getting here her cars gone flat she been on to the RAC and they will be with her A.S.A.P"

Both Dai and Lisa gave Dave a Look

"What?"

"Nothing but since when as the lovely Ruth had your direct line?" enquiries Dai

"I don't know maybe I phoned her at some time, and she saved my number to her phone"

"And since when have you had Ruth's direct number" it was Lisa with the questions now

"I don't remember she gave it to me once while on a case, her works phone had gone flat"

"Oh yes pull the other one" Dai said

"No honest" Dai and Lisa were smiling now "there's nothing in it" but the more he tried to protest the redder he got "oh bugger off you two I'm fighting a losing battle here"

Just at that moment Dai's phone rang "DCI Rees"

"Sir sergeant Cooper here I thought I'd just let you know a patrol as picked a man not far from the scene of your crime near the Sainsburys supermarket their bringing him in now"

"Right, that's good put him straight into an interview room will you we'll be right over"

"Yes sir"

"Dave you with me Lisa are you alright to tie up with Ruth when she arrives? oh sorry Dave would you like to stay here for Ruth and Lisa come with me?"

"No Dai I'll come with you what we got?"

"a patrol has picked up a guy matching our perpetrator just down the road from here their taking him too central now"

"Right, I'll meet you there Lisa keep us up to date"

"Right boss any messages for Ruth?"

"Will you stop it" said Dave going red again.

It only took them a couple of minutes to get to central they probably have walked it as fast

They made their way inside and were met by custody sergeant Cooper

"Morning sir's I've had him put in interview room six, but I don't hold out much hope for you he seems to be away with the fairy's"

"What drunk you mean?" asked Dave

"No sir just not with it, not sure if he's on some sort of drugs or what all he keeps saying is why would the wee lassie not speak to him he was only trying to be friendly"

"Sorry did you say he spoke with a Scottish accent?" Dave said puzzled

"Yes, Sir Glasgow something like that I couldn't understand most of what he said"

"What about a name" Dai asked

"No sir I couldn't get anything more out of him other than why would she not speak to him"

"Boss I've a feeling about this I think I may know who this is, Sergeant can you get on the system and look up one Tommy no sorry Thomas McClintock see if we have anything as to when he was let out of Bayview psychiatric hospital in Oxford, shall we sir?"

Dave leads the way to the interview rooms but stopped before he they went in.

"Dai before we go in, I need to tell you something if I'm right in thinking and this is Tommy McClintock you need to know his background"

"Right go on"

"when I was a DS at Wallingford I had dealing with Tommy, he was in the fire service he was having a bad time of things he had a married a woman from Thailand had a couple of kids with her then he came home one day to find she had left him taken the kids back to Thailand he fought a battle to get them back but the strain of it sent him a little mad obsessed with getting them back he was offered leave but he didn't take it, in all fairness to him and as his boss said he never let it affect the job"

"Until what"

"Until the day they had got a shout to a house fire they got there to find three children trapped inside, Tommy was determined to get into them he got in but was not seen coming out then the whole place blow seems there was a four or five of gas bottle in the house being used for heating, everyone thought Tommy had been caught in the blast, until one of the crew found him in the back garden with one of the children in his arms"

"he'd got out"

"Yes, he was cradling her in his arms saying over and over again I saved her why wont the wee bairn speak to me I saved her, but she must have died in his arms"

"So how come we got involved?"

"well Tommy took the leave he was seeing the services shrink and all was going well until about six weeks later Tommy really flipped, he walked into the fire station one morning and tried putting an axe into the watch commanders head shouting that it had been his fault the children had died if he hadn't dilly dallied about giving the order to go in the kids would have been saved it took about four fire men to stop him but he put one of them in hospital nothing bad just a gash to the arm where he caught it on the axe"

"And you were the one to arrest him?"

"No that was PC Bill Smith and another PC brought him in"

"What the Bill Smith"?

"yes him, after he was brought in I interviewed him I could see that he was not right I felt sorry for him, the watch officer and the fireman that was injured did not what to press charges so he was charged with carrying an offensive weapon he went before the courts and after a review of his state of mind in was decided that for his own safety and the safety of others he would be sent to Bayview, the thing is now adays they would call it PTSD and he would be treated for it"

"Right shall we go and see if it is him?"

They just opened the door when the sergeant Cooper arrived

"Sir Tommy McClintock was not released from Bayview it seems some numpty left a fire door open while work was being carried out and he just wandered off that was about a month ago and he's not been since"

Dai and Dave entered the room Tommy was sat behind the table with his head in his hand looking all the worse for wear his clothes were ripped and he looked as though he had not eaten for weeks and PC Joe Clarke stood in the corner of the room

"Do you wish me to leave sir"

"No that's ok Joe stay if you can"

Dave took a seat "morning Tommy do you remember he my name is Dave Parker I met you at Wallingford"?

"I no, do nothing the wee lassie was asleep I only wanted to talk to her"

"I know Tommy we just need to ask you some questions was the young lady asleep when you first saw her"?

"She was just lying there I tried to wake her I wanted to talk she would not talk I only wanted a friend"

"Tommy did you see anyone else with the young lady"?

"No, no she was asleep all on her own just lying there she must have been cold she looked blue"

"Tommy did you do anything to the young lady why was you leaning over her"?

"I no do nothing she was asleep I wanted to talk I needed to talk"

"Tommy you was seen by an officer you were leaning over the body with a torch shining on her what was you doing"?

"I no do-nothing Mr Parker I swear I no touch the wee lassie I found the torch that's what made me see her it was on the ground shining so I picked it up and that's when I saw her"

"Tommy why did you run when the officer called out to you"?

"He was coming for me Mr Parker he was going to take me back I no want to go back I don't like it there it's a cage they keep me locked up"

"They keep you locked in your room Tommy"?

"I hate it they keep me in, force me to take tablets tell me they are good for me but I no like them they are trying to kill me they hate me; I see them looking at me talking behind my back look at him he's the one that killed that wee lassie"

Dai had kept quite till now

"Tommy you don't know me my name is Daffyd Rees, no one is trying to kill you we all know you saved the little girl you were very brave but we need to know about the young lady from this morning"

Tommy had by now become very agitated and began to sob

"No, no Mr Parker please don't let them send me back Mr Parker please I no like the place"

"don't worry about that Tommy I'll see what I can do" said Dave

"Tommy how did you end up in Milton Keynes and where have you been sleeping"? asked Dai

"I walked"

"You walked what along the roads"?

"No, no I walked the railway in the country I slept in the huts along the line sometimes I got food"

Dai and Dave looked puzzled but PC Joe Clarke spoke up

"Sir do you mind if I say something"

"Go ahead" said Dai

"well about a week ago I got a call out to a break in at one of the contractors huts along where they are doing the works for the new East West rail link, the only things had been taken was some food and a pair of steel toe capped boots, when I arrived the site foreman told me that a few of the huts further down the old line had been broken into sometimes it was the canteen sometimes the locker rooms nothing taken but food until that is the boots went missing"

All three looked down at Tommy's feet to see a pair of steel toe capped boots, Tommy by now was totally sobbing into his hands and crying out

"I sorry Mr Parker please no send me back I no want to go back there I want to stay in the open I on like being locked up"

Dai looked at him he could see that he was not there killer and he felt so sorry

"Tommy when was the last time you ate something"? he asked

Tommy just shook his head

"Tell you what Tommy let's call it a day for now, what say I get Joe here to take you to the canteen and get you a nice hot drink and maybe something to eat"?

Tommy looked up and nodded his head then stood to leave

"Joe here's a couple of quid get Tommy a drink and" he looked at his watch "and as the cook will not be starting till six see if there is food in the vending machine"

"Sorry sir the food vending machines not been working for the last couple of weeks most of us if we're doing night shift bring in packed lunches"

"Bugger ok here's a tenner get someone to run to one of the 24-hour garages see what they can get him some food preferably hot oh and ask them to get a receipt"

"Yes sir" with that Joe and Tommy left

"Well, what do you think"? asked Dave

"Well, I know one thing for sure he's not our killer unless he's got a computer and a printer stashed somewhere. Let us see if we can get him in somewhere round here I'd like to keep him close just in case he remembers something"

"I'll get the sergeant Cooper to give social services a ring see what they can do and he better ring Bayview and let them know we have him"

They headed back to the scene and when they got back Ruth had arrived

"Good morning you two"

"Morning Ruth sorry to get you out so early" said Dai

"Oh, that's ok it wouldn't have been so bad if the bloody car would start, lucky the RAC got out to me in record time and gave me a jump start, seems I need a new battery"

"What we got"? asked Dave

"White female approx. 25/30 years of age same MO as the last two even down to the note the only thing with this one is I think she put up a fight time of death I'd say around ten last night"

Dai and Dave just looked at her

"Well look here the head wound is not so deep I think whoever did this didn't knock her out cold this time just knocked her to the ground, see here there scuff marks on her shoe there are scratches on the front of her legs where she has tried to kick out the other shoe is over there and the toes on her left foot are all blooded where she has tried to use her feet to push herself away from whoever did this"

"Any sign of sexual assault"? asked Dave

"Not that I can see her underwear is still in place, but I'll know more when I do the pm"

Lisa came round the corner "hello your back quick from questioning the suspect"

Dave told Lisa all that had happened

Dai went and looked for Colin Mathews

"Colin you got any thing for us"?

"Oh, hi Dai yes a couple of things, we found a torch just the other side of the underpass it was still lite and there's a make-shift den in the undergrowth that side to looks like someone has been sleeping rough"

"The torch maybe the victims or the suspects but either way if you could get someone over to take prints off one Tommy McClintock he said he picked up the torch and I've a feeling it may be his camp"

"Ok will do what happened with the guy they picked up"?

"that's Tommy McClintock but there no way he could be our killer Ruth said the young lady died around midnight, Tommy was seen with her about 04.00 plus also unless he has a camera and computer somewhere in that den"

Colin cut him off short "ok I get the picture I'll get someone over to do what's what"

"Cheers Colin keep up us to date if you find anything"

Dai wander back to Dave and Lisa and as he passed the victim he took out his phone and snapped off a photo of her "right anything else to report from here"

"No boss I think we're all done here"

"Everything alright with you Ruth" Dai asked

"Yes fine thanks"

"Right, we'll head back to Bletchley if you can let us know when the pm is and I'll send Dave over"

Ruth just smiled but Dave went red and turned and marched off to his car

"Think you hit a nerve there boss" said Lisa with a smile

When they got back to Bletchley Steve and Paul where in

"Morning you two you're in nice and early" enquired Dai

"Yes boss Lisa rang me and I thought I may as well get in now and it seems Paul had the same idea"

"Yes sir I hadn't got much sleep anyway the girlfriend face timed me and we were talking till god knows when"

"What the hell did you talk about for that length of time"? asked Steve

"Well, we haven't seen each other for about two months because of covid she works at the hospital and I'm here it's hard getting the time to talk anyway change of subject the kettle has boiled but you may have to search for cups this lot on night shift don't know how to wash up"

"don't worry leave that to super Lisa" said Lisa disappearing into the paper store and returning with a tray of eight cups "ta dah I washed this lot before we went home last night knowing we can never find clean ones in the morning and has this lot never change or top up the paper in the copier or printers I knew the best place to hide them, right who's for drinks"

"Yes please but I'll make them seen as I'm last in" Lisa turned to see Vicky in the door

"Oh, ok if you don't mind"?

Dai called them together

"Right, everyone we'll get up to speed when the others get here but as you may have heard we have another victim this time a young lady we can't do much at the moment till we get something of forensic, I have got a photo of the victim that I'm going to put on the system, Vicky you alright to get onto that?"

"Yes boss"

"Now some of you may have heard we picked up a suspect, this is not true we have at central one Tommy McClintock he was the one that found the body he's been rough sleeping here in Milton Keynes since walking out of Bayview psychiatric home last month, Dave later on today can you go and see him again see what you can get out of him"

At that moment there was a cough behind Dai he turned to see Alan and Paula

"Morning you two did Lisa ring you too because if she did you must have blue lighted it here in a rocket" enquired Dave

Paula answered "no boss it was so late last night Taffy came up with the idea that we should stay here he found some camp beds and sheets down by the cells so we camped down there we had all brought a change of clothes just in case"

"Oh, and where is Taffy couldn't get out of bed this morning"? asked Dai

"No boss he got a call in the night it seems that dicky stomach he had has now gone to the wife and baby he's had to go home he said he would be in as soon as he can"

"No that's ok I'll ring him tell him to stay at home all we need now is for more of us to go down with Delhi belly, I'm sure someone of night shift would like to stand in for him"

The room went silent

"Right let's get on Vicky I'll download the photo if you can crack on with that I'm sure one of these will help"

"Yes boss and oh here's your coffee"

Dai wandered into his office and plugged his phone into the system to download the photo it was not a genuinely nice photo but it should do to id the young lady if she was on their system. His phone rang

"DCI Rees"

"Morning sir sergeant Cooper here just thought I'd let you know I managed to get hold of social services for Tommy I spoke to a lovely lady Mary they have got a place in a house where he can go for the time being, it seems she knows Tommy she worked at Bayview before coming to social services here in MK and she was more than happy to help"

"that's great have you got the address for it"?

"Yes sir and I hope you don't mind I gave her your number in case she needs to contact you for anything, oh and I got hold of Bayview and let them know we have him they were none too happy about it but as I told them he is helping with an ongoing enquiry now have you a paper and pen and I'll give you the address"

Dai wrote down the address and took it out to Dave

"Dave sergeant Coopers been on he's found somewhere for Tommy with social services this is the address" he handed over the address

"that's great boss at least he's not going into the local psychiatric hospital"

"Yes that's great and it seems the lady from social services knows Tommy she worked at Bayview before coming to MK"

"Boss I know you've only just uploaded the photo but we have a hit she's on the system"

"What already Vicky"

"Yes boss her name is Elena Adamache, 31 years old Romanian by birth been living in the UK for three years now and she has a child"

"How come she on the system"? asked Dave

"She was arrested two months ago for soliciting in the theatre district got let off with a fine and caution as it was her first time"

"Anything said about family apart from the child"? Dai enquired

"No boss but we have an address for her"

"Right take Paula with you see what you can find at the address someone must be there looking after the child"

"Yes boss"

"right folks we now have a name for our third victim one Elena Adamche 31 years old from Romania, Paul can you get onto social media see if there's anything on there, Steve you get onto immigration see if they have any details of her, Lisa get onto the Romanian embassy see if they also have details of family oh and see if we can find an interpreter we may need one, Alan you help Paul out for the moment then when the time is right go with Dave to see Tommy, right you all have your jobs I'm now going to wake superintendent Wilcox"

Dai rang superintendent Wilcox and filled him in with the mornings events by the time he had done that Vicky and Paula were pulling up in the street in Wolverton they had for Elena parking in these old streets was bad they had never been designed for so many cars they found a space and walked back to the house it was a big old house built at the beginning of the 1900's and it had like many of its size had been turned into a house of multiple occupancy. they rang the first bell on the pad it was answered by a man

Vicky hated these things you never knew what was going to come back at you "sorry police here can you let us in please" but this time the door just buzzed and they made their way in, Elana's room was on the second floor they knocked and waited but there was no answer Vicky knocked again

"Hello police is there anyone there"?

From downstairs came a voice

"Hello police lady can I help you who are you looking for"

"Yes sir I'm Detective Constable Campbell and this is Detective Constable Billington and you are"?

"Marius Comea I own the house are you looking for Elena"?

"Mr Comea how well do you know Elena Adamche"?

"I'm her landlord I have been waiting for her to come home my wife Ana-Maria has been looking after the little boy while she was at work but last night she never came home it is so unlike her she loves her little boy she would never leave him for this length of time"

"Mr Comea do you mind if we come in"?

"Yes, yes of course what has happened where is Elena has she been arrested or something as there been an accident"

Mr Comea lead them into the front room "this is my wife Ana-Maria she doesn't speak much English"

Vicky hated this bit "Mr Comea I'm sorry to say the body of a young lady was found this morning in the city centre we have reason to believe it is that of Elena Adamche"

Mr Comea collapsed into a chair his wife sensing something went to his side, it was at that point that Vicky and Paula noticed the small child in the corner of the room the child could sense something was wrong and began to cry Mrs Comea seemed lost as to which way to turn, Paula stepped forward and picked up the child

"There, there little one no need to cry"

Mr Comea looked at Vicky then spoke to his wife Vicky could not understand but could tell from the look on her face that he had just told her about Elena, Mrs Comea eyes filled she turned to Paula and took the child and retreated to the back room.

"Mr Comea did Elana have any other family here in the UK apart from her little boy"?

"No not here her sister came to the UK with her but she as returned to Romania she missed their mother"

"What about the father of her little boy"?

"He is nowhere to be seen he has not seen Daniel since he was born vanished into thin air after promising Elena he would stand by her, after he split from her Elena found he had a wife so she was better off without him"

"Mr Comea where did Elena work"? asked Paula

"She had good job in the city in one of the restaurants she was a waitress made good money, but when the pandemic hit she was what you call furlong"

"Furloughed" explained Paula

"Yes, yes that's it furloughed up until three months ago when they rang and told her she could start her job again they needed clean the place and get it reset for opening"

Vicky and Paula just looked at each other

Vicky spoke first "Mr Comea did Elena always work nights"?

"Yes always it worked well that way she would be with Daniel during the day and my wife would look after him in the evenings and night till she came home"

"What time did she normally get home"?

"It depends sometimes 10.30 but sometimes just after midnight depends on how much work they had to do, when she was not home by midnight last night I tried ringing her mobile but it went straight to answer phone I assumed the battery had died and I thought it strange that she did not contact me she normally rings at some point in the night to see how Daniel is"

"Mr Comea do you think we can see Elena's room and do you by any chance have an address for her family and the address where she worked"?

"Yes of course I will get you the key and while you are up there I will find the address for you but not of her work she never told me which one she worked at"

He went over to a small key chest on the wall and took out the key and handed it to Vicky

"Thank you we'll only be a few minutes"

They went up to the room and let themselves in

Vicky looked at Paula "right now we are out of ear shot it's clear that Mr Comea and his wife didn't know what Elena really did for a living"

"Yes she kept that a secret I wonder what else she was keeping secret"?

"I don't know let's have a look round"

The room was very tidy with just a single bed a cot for the little one a chest of drawers and under the window a small desk most of the clothes where hung on makeshift rails and on the desk sat a lap top Paula opened it and it fired into live

"Vicky there's a laptop here it's not locked but I can't understand it it's in Romanian looks like a calendar with appointments on it"

"Right bag it we'll get the tech boys to have a look with the help of a translator, I've just found this box under the bed there's bank statements here going back a year and looking at them I'd say she was in trouble for money up until three months ago when she started putting in quite a bit of money each week always cash by the looks of it"

"That ties in with when she was arrested she must have stayed on the game to make money"

"She must have been desperate to make ends meet and look after the little one"

"Yes, this pandemic has hit loads of people badly there's also this" she handed Paula a form

"The baby's birth certificate"

"Yes but look name of father"

"There isn't one"

Vicky raised an eyebrow" I think we've seen and got all we need let us get back downstairs"

When they got downstairs Mr Comea was waiting for them he handed Vicky a piece of paper

"This is the address for Elena's family I have tried to write it in my best English for you"

"Thank you, Mr Comea we need someone to do a formal ID of Elena would you be up to that"?

"Yes, yes of course"

"Thank you we'll be in touch with a time and date, we'll also inform social services about little Daniel and they will take care of him"

"No, please myself and my wife will look after Daniel we made a promise to Elena that we would look after him if she was not around I will contact the family someone will come from Romania for him in the meantime we will look after him"

"Mr Comea I still need to inform them you are not the child's legal guardian but I will let them know the situation and it could be that they feel its ok as things are, Daniel knows you, thank you again we'll be in touch"

Vicky and Paula headed back to the car "here Paula can you drive I'll get hold of the boss"?

"Yes sure straight back to Bletchley"?

"Not sure I'll check with the boss he may want us to drop the laptop into the tech guys at central"

Vicky took out her phone and rang Dai

"DCI Rees"

"ho, Hi boss Vicky here"

"Vicky yes sorry I've not put your number in my mobile yet, what have you got for us"?

"well boss we've met Elena's landlord it seems that she had been furloughed up until about three months ago when he said she had a call to return to work to help get the restaurant in order for reopening Mr Comea seemed to think she worked in one in the city but didn't know the name of it, we had a look round her room we found a laptop with a calendar and appointments on it but it's all in Romanian we also found some bank statements which make interesting reading, we asked about relatives here in the UK but he said there is no one there was a sister but she as returned to Romania"

"that's great what about the child is there a father on the scene"?

"The child a little boy two years of age is with Mr Comea and his wife they look after him when she was at work, we found the baby's birth certificate but the father is not named according to Mr Comea he was a married man and fled the scene when the child was born"

"Right get back here we'll start digging into her background"

"Boss do you want us to drop the laptop to the tech guys on the way through"

"No bring it back here Lisa has got hold of an interpreter they should be able to tell us what is on it see you soon"

Chapter Eleven

Last night had not gone to well for him the girl she was a fighter if only he had hit her harder she would not have put up a fight, his parents had told him never hit girls or women it was not right and he never had, he had a respect for them but this girl was selling herself she needed to be punished, he also know that girls could be the most spiteful at school they could be the worse of the lot, the boys could be bad they would fight with him but it was the girls that hurt the most with their name calling they would call him kraut, Nazi, Jew hater all sorts of names that is why when he could he had changed his name to his mother's maiden name of Clements, Muller was the family name and his father had always told him be proud of it but how could he be proud of it when all the time he was reminded of the war and what the Nazi had done to the Jews, people never seemed to understand he was British he was born here his father was born here his grandfather had moved here before the first world war and during the second world war had worked with the allied forces as a translator he hated what Adolf Hitler stood for and vowed he would never go back to Germany, he had often asked his father why he had never changed the family name if the royal family could do it why can't they he would just say "it is our family name and we should be proud of it"

He had waited for his father pass before he changed it out of respect for him but all the time while he was a child he had wished for his father to change it, the house was still under the name of Muller his father had done well for himself he worked at the Wolverton carriage works all his life there had been money that his grandfather left to his father that had been enough to buy the house he now lived in so no need for a mortgage the electoral roll showed him as living at this address as Stephen Muller, his driving licence he had in the name of Stephen Clements and his passport was the same but they had been taken out when he lived for a while in London and he had never got round to changing them why should he, he never used them the last time he used his passport was twenty years ago to go on a holiday with a young lady so it may have even run out now.

He dug out some photos of that holiday ah the happy times with Mary, Mary was a lovely lady he had met he through the church they hit it off straight away she shared his passion for photograph, he had loved her but his mother put a stop to their romance "she no good for you she's been married before she has shamed her faith" it had all got too much in the end Mary could not stand his mother and his mother could not stand her, Mary had given him a ultimatum "me or your mother" he had chosen his mother it was a bad time his father had just passed away and his mother had needed him so the romance had come to an end Mary moved away it was a shame he really loved her. He had tried to find her after his mother had passed away to see if they could get back together but he could not find her, he heard sometime later she had married again and now had children oh if only it could have been him.

For now, he had the new photos to send to DCI Rees. And figure out who the next sinner would be and he had loads to choose from.

Chapter Twelve

Back in Bletchley everything was full steam ahead Dai had spoken to Superintendent Wilcox, Lisa had been onto the embassy and found out Elena's home family details and through them had managed to get a translator that should be here at any time, Steve had got onto immigration they had come back that she was all clear with them and she had all the correct work permits in place, Paul and Alan had trawled through social media she had a Facebook account but it was all in Romanian and the same with twitter there was some English but not much so it looked like the translator was going to be busy when he or she arrives.

As Vicky and Paula arrived back Dave and Alan where just leaving to see Tommy

"Ay up you two howd you get on with the place Elena lived" enquired Dave

"Fine thanks boss it turns out she lived in an HMO we had a look round her flat and found out a few interesting things, it looks as though she was on her uppers until about three months ago then she started make money by being on the game to make things meet"

Alan just shook his head "it's a shame this pandemic as hit so many people so bad"

"It is that Alan anyway we better get moving, we'll catch up on things later"

Dave and Alan left just as Dai came out of his office but before he could speak to Vicky and Paula Lisa spoke up

"Boss sorry with all the that was going on this morning I've only just found this, I had one of the night lads tracing any Stephen Clements in MK he's come up with two"

"that's great now we're getting somewhere"

"Sorry boss not so he contacted them last night one is a twelve-year-old and the other is eighty-seven and in a care home with dementia"

"Sod it we seem to take one step forward two back, right Vicky, Paula what you got for us"?

"right boss as I explained on the phone we have found some bank statements" Vicky spread them out over out "as you can see they go back to January last year, at the beginning of the year all was Rosey regular payments going in from this account and going out to a few payments, this is her mobile provider, this her must be her rent as its made out to Mr Comea and it looks like a regular payment was sent to a bank account abroad maybe home to mum and all the normal things like shopping at Tesco and Aldi"

"Right is there a name for who is paying in like a company"?

"No boss just an account number"

"Paula did you bring back the laptop"?

"Yes boss it need changing but I picked up the charger as we left"

"Great see if there's an online banking app on their"

"Yes boss there one for Central bank"

"Right get on to them see if they can tell us who made the payments in, right Vicky carry on"

"Well as you can see the money started to dwindle about mid-way through last year the payments to the account abroad stopped and it looks also like Mr Comea held back on the rent for her too, but then three months ago money started going back into the account at first only small amounts but these got larger over the weeks"

"From another account"?

"No boss always in cash and always paid in through the automatic teller machine"

"Would the time the money started going in coincide with when she was arrested"

"Yes boss but it looks like being arrested did not stop her"

"She most have been desperate for money for her and the child, talking of which where is the child"?

"he's with Mr and Mrs Comea as I said they would look after him while Elena was at work I said we would have to inform social services but Mr Comea said they would like to look after the little boy, they said they would inform the family in Romania and get someone over to take him"

"And you said the father is nowhere to be seen"?

"No boss he's not been anywhere near since Daniel was born"

Paula spoke "boss I've been onto Central bank they said they could not give me details over the phone I explained that we were investigating a murder but still they said no"

"Right get over there in person threaten them with a warrant if you need to but we need to find out where she worked"

"Yes boss"

At that moment there was a tap on the door Dai turned to see a man standing there

"DCI Rees, I'm Alexandra Borza they said you needed a translator"

"Yes of course welcome meet the team this here is DS Lisa Jones I believe you spoke on the phone, over here is DC Vicky Campbell and DC Paula Billington over the other side there are DC's Steve Carter and Paul Stevens, ladies and gentlemen this here is Alexandra Borza he here to help us with translating Elena's social media etc"

The team welcomed him and Dai brought him up to speed on what they needed from him

"Right Alexandra as she already has the laptop open could you go through it with Paula"?

"Sorry boss I was just about to go to Central bank and find out what I can about who is paying her"

"Ah yes you go and do that Paul can you get onto this"?

"Yes boss it may help also having the laptop to check on her social media as there are somethings we can't see on her profile sight"

"You ok with that Alexandra"?

"Yes that's fine and it's Alex, Alexandra has always been a bit of a mouth full"

Dai went back into his office the internal mail had been delivered no new surprises today thank goodness his phone rang

"DCI Rees"

"Hello sir PC Grace here sorry to bother you"

"No that's ok what can I do for you"?

"Well sir after I finished with Mr and Mrs Okore I had a few days holidays booked but I gave Mrs Okore my mobile number just in case she wanted to talk, well she's just rang me it seems someone has sent an envelope to the house with photos and a note saying there son was a sinner and deserved to die and claiming them self to be the warrior of god Mrs Okore didn't know who else to contact"

"She did right and you did to giving her your number she knew she could confide in you"

"Thank you sir "

"Listen I know you are on holidays but can you do me a favour pop to the Okore's home and pick up the envelope and get it to the forensic guys ASAP and see if anyone noticed who delivered it"

"Oh, I already know that sir it came in the post"

Dai cursed other his breath

"Sorry sir"?

"Oh, sorry just cursing under my breath that throws out the chance of fingerprint's thank you if you could do that for me then enjoy the rest of your break"

"Yes sir thank you"

Dai went through to the main office

"Steve I've just had PC Grace on she's had a call from Mrs Okore someone has posted the photos of DJ and Andy to them can you get on to Ryan's father and see if he's had the same and Lisa see if young Andy has had anything whoever is doing this must know where DJ lived and does he know about the others has he been stalking them"

They both spoke in unison "yes boss"

Dai turned and went to go back into his office

"Boss Alex here has made short work of Elena's calendar"

"Right, what have you got"?

Alex was first to speak "it is a straightforward calendar but nearly every day she's got appointments must of them early evening and all with men, there are no names just Mr J or Mr A but nearly all the meetings are around the theatre district in the city there are a couple that don't mention the theatre district they are marked with things like North, Dun, Lu, etc"

"I was thinking sir these could be short for Northampton, Dunstable and Luton"

Alex spoke up "yes Paul I see went you mean there is one here that just say's Bed I took it that she was talking about bed not Bedford as there is no Mr next to it and it's for two days' time"

"Great work let's see what else we can find"

"DCI Rees I have noticed also there is a diary on here I have just clicked on it but it is password locked if I could get into that maybe I could find out some more"

"That would be great, Paul get onto the tech guys see if they can send someone over to unlock it"

"Yes boss"

"boss"

"Yes Steve"

"I've been onto Ryan's dad and so far nothing has turned up"

"Same here with Andy sir they have not had anything I've asked Andy's dad to inform us if anything does turn up" said Lisa

Dai thought for a moment "I was just wondering does this mean that whoever did this knew DJ and where he lived and the family so he was able to contact them or does it mean that he doesn't know where the other's live"

"Boss it would be hard for whoever is doing this to trace Ryan's dad I mean we as a family have not seen him for over a year"

"Good thinking Steve it could be that whoever this is got the info from the papers, but we only gave the estate where DJ lived and Ryan is down as not fixed abode so they would have no one to send it to"

Vicky spoke up "boss should I contact Mr Comea just in case he has had anything"?

"Yes go with it whoever is doing this may not know that they are not family and sent them, but so far we have not had any photos or a note ourselves but I am expecting them soon, Lisa do we still have patrols going round past Andy's house there's still a chance he could be a victim"

"Yes boss but so far they have not seen anything out of the norm"

"Boss Alex has started on Elena's social media so far nothing"

"Ok Paul crack on see what you can get"

Dai phone rang and before he could speck
"hello Dai, Ruth here I'm just ringing to say that I may be able to do the pm on the latest victim at 2.30 this afternoon if that's okay with you I would have done it later but I have to be at the coroners court at 4.30"

"Yes that's great I'll be there oh and we have a name for her Elena Adamancha"

"You have a name has she been reported missing"

"No, she was on the system she had been arrested for soliciting a while back"

"What about an ID is there family"?

"No family here they are all in Romania but her landlord said he would do it, oh and she had a child a two-year-old little boy"

"Oh, that's such a shame, who's taking care of him at the moment"?

"The landlord and his wife he knows them they looked after him while Elena was at work"

"that's good at least he's with someone he knows and not in foster care"

"that's what I was thinking but you know social service they may see it different"

"Hope not any way I'll see you at 2.30 will Dave be with you"?

"I'm not sure he's out at the moment seeing the guy that found Elena's body to find out if he remembers anything, so I'll see you then"

Dai smiled as he came off the phone as much as Dave denied it Ruth seemed to make it more obvious he went over to the kettle it was still hot he made himself a cupper and sneaked back to his office just as he was about to sit down Lisa called out

"I saw that boss but don't worry I'll make the other's drinks"

"I thought you wasn't a waitress"?

"I'm not but I'm parched so I'll do it"

Dai settled in his chair he just had enough time to catch up on some paperwork and ring the superintendent before he went to the pm and he would have to ring Liz Mason to set up another press conference at some point but just as he took a mouth full of coffee his phone went

"Bloody hell no peace for the wicked DCI Rees"

"Bore da Dai Taffy here"

"Ow, hi Taffy I was going to ring you later see how things are"

"Fine I should be in later whatever it was the family and I had seemed to have eased off"

"No that's ok you take the rest of the day spend it with the family and see how things are in the morning"

"You sure now Dai I don't mind coming in I heard through the grape vine there's been another murder"

Dai brought him up to speed and said his goodbyes he did not have the heart to tell Taffy that he felt safer with him at home the last thing he needed was the rest of the team going down with Delhi belly.

Three miles across the town Dave and Andy were pulling up outside the house they had taken Tommy McClintock too, they parked up and went a knocked, the door was opened by a rather portly lady

"Hello, you must be DI Parker Tommy's been talking about you"

"All good I hope and you must be Mary, Mary this is DC Alan Bates"

"Right do come in Tommy is in the front room he's not said much about the events of this morning I've tried to get him to open up but he just keeps saying that he only wanted to talk with her"

"that's all I could get out of him at the station, he's not with it at all"

"Well, he's not had an of his medication goodness knows when so that could be why"

"I understand you know Tommy from Bayview was he like this there"

"No, he was on medication there it helped calm him down, in fact I think it calmed him down to much it's one of the reasons I left there it was a private run place but they had people from social services in there as well I didn't like the way they worked they ran it more like a prison then a home for the mentally ill I was sorry when I left for the people like Tommy being locked in day after day"

"Well, he's here now let us see if we can help him. Ok if we go in"?

Mary lead the way "Tommy look who's here to see you" Tommy looked up a stared at Dave and Alan

"Right, I'll get the kettle on that will be nice won't it Tommy"? Mary left to make the tea.

"Hi Tommy, how you doing this here is my friend Alan and we'd just like to take you back to this morning to see if there is anything you can help us with"

"you's no come to take me back Mr Parker I no want to go back I want to stay here with Mary I no go back I'll get away again if you take me back"

"No Tommy I've not come to take you back we're going to see if you can stay here in Milton Keynes, but I need you to think Tommy can you remember anything from this morning when you found the young lady"?

"I no nothing I saw her sleeping I only wanted to talk I wanted a friend but she would not wake up she was so cold"

Alan leaned into talk to Tommy "hi Tommy my names Alan we've not met before but Dave here was telling me what a brave thing you did all those years ago if I could, I would shake your hand, and by the sounds of it you wanted to help the young lady this morning"

Tommy held out his hand to Andy

"Sorry Tommy because of covid I can't shake it but I'll tell you what let's do an air high five"

Tommy swung his hand up in an arch as Andy did the same and for the first time they saw Tommy smile.

Andy looked at Dave and the way Dave looked back told him that he was alright to take the lead

"Tommy I need you to think back to last night is there anything that may have upset you we know you have a camp near to where the young lady was found"

"What was her name? I just wanted to be friends"

"Her name was Elena"

"Elena that is a nice name, she looked nice"

"Tommy while you was in your camp did you see anyone or hear anything before you found Elena"?

"I remember the man he came I hide I know he was coming for me so I hide away in my camp stayed in there till he was gone he no find me"

"Did you see Elena Tommy"?

"No, I no see her I heard her screaming and shouting but then nothing"

"Did you not go and see if you could help see why she was shouting"?

"No, the man he would have found me taken me back I no's want to go back I stayed in my camp he no find me"

"Tommy can you remember what the man looked like"?

Tommy was becoming agitated but at that moment Mary walked in with the drinks

"Right Tommy shall I be mother, I hope you are being a good help to Dave and Andy here"

Tommy settled it was as though Mary had a switch that she had flicked

"He was no a big and no a small man and he had a cross"

"a cross"? Dave questioned

"Yes a cross like you have in a church a big one"

"Anything else Tommy"

"a rope he had a rope I thought he would hang me if he found me"

"What about his clothes Tommy was there anything you remember about his clothes"?

"Black, black like he was going to a funeral black all over, black hair too, he vanished into the night"

"Thank you Tommy that's been must helpful shall we have that tea now"?

They sat and drank their drinks then got up to leave

As they got up to leave Tommy looked at them both "Mr Parker, Andy high five" and swung his hand out to them both did the same back

They headed for the door and Dave turned to speak to Mary

"Thank you for your help I can see Tommy really gets on with you but what is going to happen now to him is he going back to Bayview"?

"Over my dead body is he, Bayview don't like it but I'm fighting to get him into the care of us here in the Milton Keynes we have a lovely place here where he can go and not feel he's a prisoner"

"that's great can you keep me informed as to how things go I really feel for him"

"May I ask how you know Tommy DI Parker"?

"I was one of the officers at Wallingford when Tommy was brought in after the attack on his watch commander, I could see then from interviewing him that the death of the child in the fire had affected him I was at the court when he was sentenced I felt then that it was the best for him but now seeing how he's ended up I'm not too sure"

"He would maybe have gone like this anyway who can tell but being at Bayview didn't help, but I can see from talking to Tommy that you helped him he as nothing but praise for you, I'll keep you informed and feel free to visit at any time he'll be here for a while"

As they walked back to the car Andy turned to Dave

"You okay boss"?

"Ye but I can't help thinking if I had done more to help Tommy things could have been better"

"Boss Mary was right we can never tell how things will turn out and you, you did your best at the time and moved on you can't take on every person you have delt with in the past it affect you as it has done Tommy"

"Ye I suppose so but it's still there in the back of my mind I'm going to make a point of keeping in touch now see how he gets on, any way Tommy seems to have got on with you, it was you that got him to open up have you delt with someone like Tommy before"

"Yes boss my eldest brother was in the army did two tours of Iraq and one of Afghanistan saw too much out in both and came home with PTSD he was very much like Tommy but with the right help he came through and that's what Tommy needs and I think Mary is going to make sure he gets it"

"I hope so Andy I hope so, right let's get back and report to Dai now we know for definite it's a man we are looking for thanks to Tommy"

They got back to Bletchley at the same time as Paula, Dai greeted them all

"Alright you three how did you get on"?

Paula and Dave both spoke at the same time then Dave said "ladies first"

"Thank you Dave right boss I went to the bank and at first they were not happy to help until I told them I would get a warrant and make them show me, I was then shown into the manager's office where the manager spent fifteen minutes phoning head office to make sure it was ok to give out the details of the account, but in the end they came through it was an Italian restaurant in the city centre that was paying her wages"

"that's great get onto them see when the last time they saw Elena"

"I've already done that boss the restaurant is just around the corner from the bank and as I headed back to the car I noticed the door was open, I went in and was able to find a manager he said that they had not seen Elena since she was furloughed last year and that they had not rang her to come in to help, it seems today was the first day they have been back in since the lockdown finished"

"How come I thought that some of the restaurants had started to get ready months ago"?

"Well, it seems that during the time the place was locked up some water pipes had burst so the whole place as had to be refurbed"

"Right, Dave any luck with Tommy"?

"Yes boss he was able to give us a description of the attacker white male about five foot nine /ten dressed all in black with black hair, but get this he was carrying a rope and a large cross"

"a large cross"? Dai asked but he could tell everyone else wanted to ask same question

"Yes boss a large cross now I was thinking maybe the cross is the thing he uses to knock them unconscious Ruth did say it may be a lump of wood and a cross can be made up of two bits of square wood"

"Yes could well be, did Tommy say why he didn't help Elena"?

Andy spoke this time "yes boss he was frightened that he had come for him even to the point he thought he was going to hang him so he hide away in his camp"

Vicky gave a little gasp "god it must be terrible to be that frightened that poor man"

"Right, someone get onto our friends at CCTV now that we know what we are looking for see if they can find him"

"I'll do that boss"

"Thanks Paula, Dave what's happening with Tommy now"

"Mary from social service is fighting to get him looked after here she as known Tommy for a while so she's doing everything she can to be honest I hope she manages it I hate the thought of Tommy going back to Bayview"

"That would be good for him let's hope she gets results, Paul, Alex how you getting on with the social media"?

"Fine boss not much on their mainly photos of little Daniel, but we're still waiting on the tech guy to get here and get us into her diary"

"right chase them up we need that A.S,A,P"

"Yes boss"

"Right folks keep up the good work I've a pm to go to, Dave are you coming along Ruth was asking for you"?

"Ok but give me five to go to the loo"

Lisa pipped up "going to spruce yourself up for Ruth Dave"?

"No, I'm not I'm busting to go if you should know nothing to do with Ruth" he looked around the team who all had a smile on their faces "bugger off you lot just pack it up there's nothing going on with me and Ruth and even if there was it's nothing to do with you" he disappeared out of the door.

Dai met Dave in the carpark "you ok Butty"? (mate)

"Yes mate sorry I took so long I think I may have picked up a touch Taffy's Delhi belly"

"I hope not mate I don't need any of the rest of the team going down with it"

"No, it should be okay it doesn't seem as bad as Taffy's"

Dai unlocked the car and leaned over to open the passenger door Dave got in and Dai could not help but notice that Dave smelled of new aftershave

They arrived at the hospital and parked in the police bay.

"Your pushing your luck mate parking here remember what happened last time"

"Not this time Dave myself and Mr Dwayne Jonson have an arrangement now"

They arrived at the morgue a little early Ruth was still in her office

"Hi Dai, Dave" Dai noticed a little smile as she turned to Dave "your early I just got to finish this paperwork and I'll be with you feel free to help yourself to a cuppa"

"don't mind if I do, Dai what about you"?

"Do you think you should what with a touch of Delhi belly"?

Ruth looked up from her paperwork "you've got a Delhi belly I do hope it's not what we eat last night"

Dai raised an eyebrow as Dave went red Ruth saw this

"You mean to say you haven't told the team about us"?

"I haven't gotten round to it yet I wanted to make sure we made ago of it before telling them"

It was Ruth who went red now Dai spoke up

"don't worry Ruth most of us have had an idea for a while but Mr shy here would not let on and Dave you must really change that aftershave it nearly knocked me out when you got into the car"

"I don't know what am I going to do with you Dave Parker? And as for you leave him alone I love his aftershave beats the smell of blood and guts any day, now let us have that tea" said Ruth

Ruth finished here paperwork and they all suited up and went into the morgue Stella was already there camera in hand

"Right gentlemen shall we get started" ruth turned on the large lights above the body

"Right, we have a young white female approx. 65kg one meter sixty tall fair sink, dark brown hair dyed blonde, on the top of the head is a small gash about" she took out a set square with a ruler on it "sixty millimetres long, Stella can you get a shot of that please? There is a small amount of blood but nothing too bad," she moved down to the neck area "on the neck there is bruising consistent with a rope or ligature being pulled tight around it" Stella was there with the camera leaning in as Ruth examined the markings she opened one of the eyes "broken blood vessels in the eye show death was from strangulation, there are scratches and marks on the front of the legs as though she had been dragged along or put up a fight right Stella can we turn her over "?

They turned her over and straight away Dai could see the same marks on her back and the neck as they had seen on Diji and Ryan.

"There are markings on the back that show force has been used to hold down the victim and markings on the neck that coincide with the marks on the front, the backs of her right foot are marked with scratches as with the front of the legs, right can we turn her back please"?

Ruth moved down the body to the pubic area she took out a swob

"There are signs of semen in the virginal area that looks as if she had sexual intercourse last night but no sign of rape" Ruth examined the inside of the virginal area "upon examination I'd say the victim was around two months pregnant"

"You sure"? asked Dai

"Well, I'll know for sure when I open her up and examine the organs but I'd say yes it could be that she hadn't even noticed herself"

Dave raised an eyebrow "so with have a double murder"

"Can you call it murder at that time of the pregnancy"? enquired Dai

"I'd say so he's taken the life of the mother so he's taken the life of the baby"

"If you look at it that way I suppose your right"

Ruth took up a scalpel "right Dave you may want to look away or leave the room at this point"

Dave took the hint and left the room

"I don't know if we're going to be a couple he better get use this this I sometimes have to take photos home with me"

"I think he's ok with photos it's just the live action stuff he can't stomach"

Ruth made an incision from just by the belly button up to just above the breasts

"Right let's have a quick look here just to confirm my thoughts, ah yes as I said about two months"

"Right this poor girl was up to her eyes in it as it was, we think the whole reason for her doing the work she did, was to look after her little boy so god knows how she would have managed with two"

Ruth continued with the pm but other than the fact she had been murdered there was no other concerns.

Dai and Ruth went through and got out of the gowns etc they found Dave in Ruth's office.

"Everything okay"? he enquired

Ruth spoke up first "everything fine she was in good shape fit and healthy, as for everything else I'd say it's the same person that has done all three murders"

"So, we need to step up now and find whoever is doing this, and hope that poor Elena here is the last victim" said Dai

"Well fingers crossed for you; Dave are you still up for dinner again tonight"?

"Sure, what time"?

"Shall we say eight at mine"

"that's great so long as nothing comes up it will give me time to get home shower and change"

"Well, if you come to mine straight away you can shower there you already have a change of clothes there so turn up at whatever time you want"

Dave went a little red Dai just smiled "ok see you when I can"

Ruth leaned in and gave Dave a kiss on the cheek "see you later, oh and don't forget we've got plenty of drinks in"

Dai left the room Dave followed on a few minutes later

"So, how long have you and Ruth been seeing each other"?

"For about two months now we've been staying around each other every now and then"

"So, why all the secrecy"?

"I don't know Ruth was up for telling everyone straight out she's told all her mates and family, but I wanted to hold back telling you lot you know what TVP are like for couples in the force"

"Yes but Ruth not a colleague she a pathologist totally away from TVP, so it wouldn't matter about it"

"I know but we work with her so much that she feels like part of the team"

"Well, I'm glad for you, you need some happiness in your life you miserable sod"

"Thanks Dai but do me a favour let me tell the team"

"My lips are sealed now let's get back see if the team have come up with anything"

They got back to Bletchley

Paul was first to greet them with news but before he could speck Dave spoke up

"Right, you lot listen up there's been a development" everyone turned and looked at Dave "and I should be the one to tell you all and put you all out of your misery, myself and Ruth are a couple we've been seeing each other for about two months now so you lot can stop all the little jokes it's official"

The team all stood and cheered and clapped

"About time you told us we all had a clue the way you would be together" said Lisa

"Well, we wouldn't be very good detectives if we hadn't, we just don't know why you kept it a secret so long"? enquired Steve

"Well, you all know now so let's get on with some work what was you going to say before I interrupted you Paul"?

"Well boss the tech guy managed to get into Elena's dairy and it makes some sad reading I let Alex tell you"

"Well DCI Rees, DI Parker"

Dai stopped him "Dai and Dave please"

"right Dai, Dave I have gone back through the last year or so Elena was a happy go lucky young lady she had a good job loved her little boy Daniel then as we know at the beginning of the pandemic she was furloughed all was going well for her until just before Christmas last year money was becoming tight she could not pay rent etc the restaurant had laid all the staff off so the pay she was getting while furloughed stopped, she was having trouble getting any benefits from the DWP and things just went from bad to worse"

"How could things get worse for the poor girl"? asked Dai

"Well, it seems her landlord came up with a way she could pay the rent"

"What her room for sexual favours"? Dave enquired

"It would seem so"

"Does she mention anything about being pregnant in the diary" Dai asked

"No, why"?

"Well, I'm sorry to say she was two months gone"

"Oh, I'm so sorry to hear that"

"Anything else"?

"Yes in January it mentions her joining a dating agency, Paul as looked it up"

"Yes boss it seems it not so much a dating agency as an escort agency catering for high class men, I've tried to get hold of them but with no joy at the moment, I've left messages for the owner to contact us"

"Do you have an address for them"?

"Yes boss it's an office above some shops here in Bletchley"

"Right get down there see if you can find someone, but it could be that due to covid they have been working at home do we have an address for the owner"?

"No boss"

"Right Paul you and Vicky go see what you can find at the office ask around see if anyone knows where the owner lives, give Paula the name, Paula you okay to chase up the electoral roll on that"

"Yes boss"

"No second thoughts Vicky you and Paula go and take a second visit to our landlord see what he as to say, Alan you go with Paul, I need something to do I'll chase up the electoral roll, Lisa have you got anything for us"?

"Yes boss young Andy's dad has been on he's having trouble with the press he wanted to know who had given out his son's details I assured him it was not us and promised we would look into it; do you think the press have been sent the photo's too"

Dave spoke first "I hope not we've not reviled anything about Andy if it's got out it must be the perp who as leaked it"

"Lisa did he get a name for the reporter"?

"Yes boss"

"Right give it to Dave, you alright to chase up this I know how much you like the press"

"It will be my pleasure Dai"

Dai turned to go into his office just as a uniformed officer walked in,

"DCI Rees"?

"Yes what can I do for you PC"?

"PC Aabir Rahman sir I've been asked to bring this direct to you sir"

He handed Dai an envelope Dai felt a cold chill go up his back

"Where did you get this"?

"I was out on a call in Bradwell Abbey when I got back to the car it was under the windscreen wiper it's addressed to you so I called it in, that's when they told me to bring in straight to you"

"Did you see anyone put it on the car"?

"No sir the call seemed to be a hoax when I got to the site of where the incident was said to be taking place there was no one around I took a stroll round to see if I was in the right place but found nothing till I got back to the car"

"And you saw no one" "

"No Sir the unit that the break in was meant to be in was all locked up with a for sale sign on it the others on each side of it where all locked up too so I saw no one, oh there was a guy on a bike just as I turned into the estate"

"What time did you get the shout"

"At around 16.30 sir I went straight there on blues and twos it took me about 5 to 8 mins to get there"

"And no other units attended"?

"No sir when I got there and saw it was a hoax I called it in so other units where stood down that's before I saw the envelope"

"Right thanks for that, right who's not much to do"

Mike Brown put his hand up, Mike was a civilian working within the team he had been a police officer before retiring but came back when he got the chance

"Right Mike get onto control see if they can get a trace on where the call was made from"

"Yes boss"

Dai stood there thinking it was Lisa that pulled him out

"You alright Boss"?

"No just thinking" he called after PC Rahman

"sir"

"Sorry did you notice if the units had CCTV at all"?

"No, they hadn't sir there was one on a unit opposite but I don't think that was working as that place was up for rent or sale too"

"Right thanks" Dai opened the envelope inside was the photos and the note he showed them to the team "these have just arrived as you can see they are very much the same as the others, now whoever it is doing this is one step ahead of us in delivering these we need to find whoever is behind this"

"boss"

"Yes Mike"

"I've spoken to control the minute they found out it was a hoax call they put a trace on where the call was made from"

"and"?

"it's pinged up on three masts around the city centre the nearest they could get was the Middleton Hall outside John Lewis but then it went dead totally so they think who ever made the call removed the sim card"

"Did they get a number"?

"Yes boss I'm trying to trace it now"

Dai's phone in his office was ringing "DCI Rees"

"Ah Dai Chief Superintendent Mackintosh here I just thought I would give you a ring see if we have any updates"?

"Yes sir well we now have a description of the perpetrator white male approx. five eight to ten slim build and walking around all dressed in black carrying a cross and noose"

"a cross and a noose you say where did this come from do we have a witness"?

"Yes sir one Thomas McClintock saw the suspect from a camp he was in"

"Tommy McClintock the fireman from Wallingford I thought he was in a psychiatric hospital in Oxford"?

"Yes sir he was up until about a month ago when someone left a door open and he just walked out I never realized you knew him sir"

"I don't but I remember the case Dave Parker had something to do with it didn't he and how did he end up here on our patch"

"Yes sir he was with Tommy when it all went to court, so when Tommy saw him it was like getting back an old friend and as for how he got here he walked followed the line that's going to be the new east west link picked up bed and food along the way, social services have got him now a woman called Mary worked at Bayview and knows Tommy so she is fighting to keep him here in Milton Keynes, he doesn't want to go back"

"You say he saw the suspect was he not able to help the young lady when she was being attacked"

"No sir he was to frighten he thought if he intervened the suspect would hang him"

"that's a shame any other news?"

"Well, we have found with the help of a translator that Elena worked for an escort agency so we are chasing that up just in case it is one of her clients bit we are having trouble contacting the owner"

"What about this car that was seen any news on that"?

"we have traced who the car belongs to but the owner a Mr Fosdyke is working away in America for a company that as offices here but no one seems to know the name of it, there is a second name on the insurance a Stephen Clements, I've had one of the team do a search of the electoral roll but there are only two Stephen Clements in the MK area one is only twelve years old the other is eighty odd and living in a care home, I had them ringing round garages and self-storage places within the area but it just seems to have vanished"

"Do you think it could be a cloned car"?

"No sir it's well known on the souped-up car scene here in MK and I think someone would have noticed it running around"

"Do you think we should do another news conference"

"It may help sir we now have three victims and a description to put out there it may help"

"Ok I'm in a meeting this evening so I'll get superintendent Wilcox to contact Liz Mason he's back in tomorrow, just keep me up to date please Dai I want his guy caught"

Dai thought about saying don't we all but finished off with a "yes sir"

Dai came back into the main office

"Dai I've got something but you won't believe it"

"What have you got Mike"?

"I've traced the number the call was made from"

"and"?

"it's Diji Okore's"

"What are you sure"?

"Yes very sure I've checked it twice it's definitely Diji, it was switched on for the few moments that the call was made then turned off again and by the look of it the sim removed we've got no trace at all now"

"That explains why we never found the phones he's keeping them, right we need to find those phones"

Chapter Thirteen

As he sat eating his evening meal he began to think this is good I should have DCI Rees and his fellow officers running round in circles by now, he had made the call from the city centre no one would take any notice of someone on a phone in there, he had

got the idea from one of those American tv cops shows on TV he never really like them his mother would watch them with glee but he would be in the shed with his photography but some nights he would sit with his mother to keep her company, he was not sure of how to remove the sim on a phone but young Jane had come to the rescue he had smashed the screen on his own phone and Jane had shown him how to put his old sim into a phone she had loaned him she said he could keep it till the time came when his contract for a new phone came up again the phone was something he felt he did not need he only got one as a means of checking in on mother, the people from the church would ring him on it but other than that he never really used it he liked the home phone but even that was not used much now he had a cousin in Hereford somewhere and she would occasionally would ring him but he hadn't heard from her since the pandemic hit as far as he knew she could be dead.
His phone was simple it only had that he could make calls and text it had a camera that he never used, a calculator and a calendar but he never used them the phone Jane had loaned him was much the same but when he switched on Diji's he was met by an array of things he never had taken notice of before YouTube, Facebook, Twitter, Netflix and loads more he wouldn't know where to start even trying to make a call had thrown him with his you choose your name or dial your number press the button and make your call but Diji's one had taken him a few tries to make it work in the end he figured it out.
He finished his meal and washed and put away his crockery one of the things his mother had taught him was "a tidy house is a nice house" and he has stood by that all his life, he went out to

his shed the photos of the next sinner had to be developed he had got some good shots of him beating his wife he didn't interfere he supposed he should have that poor woman having to put up with a man like that but he would help her she would not have to put up with him much longer.

Chapter Fourteen

The team had worked late into the night Dave had been and seen the reporter who had been at Andy's home and it turned out to be young Holly Long being young had helped her she had been able to ask around the young friends of the victims and come up with Andy's name and address, Dave had given her a warning about staying away from him and she had agreed,

Vicky and Paula had been to see Mr Comea who had assured them that he had no idea that Elena was pregnant and that it was her that offered him sex to pay the rent and that had come to a stop the minute Elena had got her job back when told that she had not got her job back but was working for an escort agency he broke down and cried.

Alan and Paul had traced the owners of the escort agency and arranged a meeting for this morning.

Dai ran through his normal routine and was heading out the door by 5.45 first stop was the shop around the corner for fresh milk he found his had gone off this morning and he was dying for a cuppa he also knew the night shift would not have bothered to go out and get fresh milk.

By the time he got in Lisa as always was there.

"Bore da Dai kettles on but we need fresh milk" Dai held up the four-pint bottle "duw eich gwaredwr Dai" (God you're a saviour)

"Well, I know this lot would not have bothered so I got some in" he addressed the room "I can see I'm going to have to kicks some butts if some of you lot don't start coughing up for the drinks" the room went quite "if you don't think I haven't noticed that its mainly the day shift putting their hands in their pockets you are mistaken now there's a staff of 35 people in total so I suggest a kitty of a pound each a week that's £35,00 that should be enough to buy tea coffee and milk to last the week for those of you that don't think that's fair look at the price in the machine you'll pay that for one cup everyone agree"

The room spoke all at once "yes boss"

"Right, Lisa grab a tin or something and collect off this lot before they fly off into their beds"

Dave walked into the room "what's the collection for someone leaving"?

"No, I'm just collecting for a kitty for the tea coffee etc boss thinks it's only fair"

"To right too how much do you want"?

"A pound a week will do by the time I've taken money of everyone there should be enough for the rest of the week"

"There you go I see the kettle is boiling so what do you want"?

"Oh, my normal please Dave"

"Dai what about you"?

"If you don't mind cheers Dave"

By the time Lisa had been round the room the rest of the team had arrived "right you lot hands in pockets I'm collecting a kitty for the tea etc"

Everyone put in and Lisa took it into Dai's office

"Right Dai that's everyone can we lock it away in your filing cabinet then each night I'll take a look and see what we need"

"Yes sure but are you ok with being in charge of it we have a lot to do"?

"Yes I'm fine I have to pass Tesco or Sainsbury's on the way home and most nights I pop in for something for dinner I've never just got anything in"

"And I thought I was the only one who lived on padding meals"

"Well, I never seem to get the time to cook real meals and I miss cooking use to be quite good at it, I'll have to cook you a meal when this is all over"

"I'll hold you to that"

Dai wandered back into the main office "right night shift what have we got for today"?

Dc Sparling turned towards Dai "nothing much boss traffic at Slough came through they were on the tail of what they thought could be our mystery car, but after a chase it turned out to be a stolen car on false plates and the driver was known to them a local joy rider and he was believe it or not in the cells at Slough the night of our first victim was murdered"

Dc Mullins spoke next "boss the Romanian embassy has been on they have arranged for the sister to be flown over they also requested if it was possible to make arrangements for the body to be flown home"

"I should think that's ok Vicky can you get on with that when is the sister arriving"?

"They are hoping she will be here next Monday the 28th but it all comes down to covid test if the sister has one and it's positive she may not be able to come but the embassy are trying their best"

"Paul, Alan I believe you are paying a visit to the owner of the escort agency this morning"

"Yes boss I did a quick check on them last night but I couldn't find much so Dc Mullins said he would take a look over night for me any joy"?

" Yes Paul some very interesting news it seems that about a year ago the premises in Bletchley was raided by vice and closed down at that time it was being run and owned by a William Morris but within a few months the place had opened up again under a new name and different owners but on doing a search of companies house I found it is now run by a Mr and Mrs Tailor they are registered as the directors of the company but the person you have arranged to see is the manager none other than Mr William Morris the old owner of the place who happens to be the so in law of Mr and Mrs Tailor"

"Looks like it's a case of keep it in the family, Paul have a word with vice before you go to see them see if they have anything we can use"

"Yes boss"

The rest of the morning seemed to drag on for the team the only ones to leave the office were Paul and Alan

Paul and Alan took the short walk into Bletchley town centre and arrived a few minutes early

Alan tried the door it was locked there was no sign of a bell so Paul rang the number he had it answered almost straight away "William Morris"

"Mr Morris Dc Stevens here we have a meeting with you this morning we are at the front door"

"Yes sorry I'm running a little late this morning my secretary has rang in sick, I'm just round the back of the building now parking up I'll be with you in a few minutes"

"Ok see you soon" Alan gave him a quizzical look

"Says he's running late his secretary has rung in sick"

"Funny, I wonder what his secretary being sick has to do with him being late more like he's been on to the in laws to get their stories straight and she's been given the day off on case she has something to tell us"

"that's what I was thinking" with that the door opened from the inside

"Gentlemen please come in we're just up the stairs on the second floor if you follow me"

"Sorry yes how did you get in"?

"Oh, sorry back door leads out to the parking area"

Paul and Alan followed him up the stairs and into a rather plush office he lead them into another inner office

"Right gentlemen please take a seat I'm sorry I can't offer you coffee or tea the machine takes way too long to get heat up in the morning my secretary normally has it on first thing but as I said she as rang in sick I do hope it's not covid, now how may I help you"?

"Sir we are here to ask you about one of your working girls"

"Sorry you mean one of our escorts"

"If you what to put it that way yes, the escort we need to ask you about is one Elena Adamache"

"Ah yes nice young lady Latvian I believe"

"Romanian sir we need to know who she met up with on Wednesday the 24th of this month"

"I'm sorry I can't give you that information we have very tight rules here and abide by client confidentiality we have some very high up clients who like to keep their private lives just that"

"Mr Morris sir the reason we are asking you this is that Elena Adamache was murdered on the night of the 24th now we need to know who she met up with on that night now you can play ball or we will get a court warrant to get the information we need or would you like me to also have a word with our friends in vice"

William Morris had turned white as a sheet "murdered you say you're not saying it was one of our clients surely not"?

"At this moment we can't say but we do need to contact who ever to eliminate them from our enquirers so if we could have a list of her clients please"

Alan glanced back then asked if he could use the loo "sorry to much tea before I came out"

"Yes by all means back onto the landing second door on the left" Alan got up and left "I'm sorry Dc Stevens I don't have the list of her clients for that night on hand my secretary deals with them they will be in a filing cabinet some where can I get her to give you a ring when she as them and you can collect them"

"But I thought you said she was off sick we need the info straight away"

"Yes she is but we have another girl that comes in around lunch time she'll know where to look"

"Ok but as I said we need the information as soon as possible and if I have to I will come back here with a court warrant for them" Paul got up to leave and handed Morris a card "she can contact me on this number"

Paul walked out onto the landing but Alan was nowhere to be seen he went down the stairs and out onto the street and found Alan standing there with a handful of papers

"Where did you get to and what's that"?

"Well as we were sat there chatting I noticed a reflection in the mirror behind our Mr Morris that's when I asked to use the loo, when I got onto the landing there was a young woman with this lot in her hand"

"What are they and who was she"?

"She's Mr Morris's secretary it seems Mr Morris had her in early this morning to get rid of some of the files, she had heard about

Elena from Mr Comea she is Romanian to she got Elena the job here"

"So, these are the files we need to find out Elena's clients does this mean our Mr Morris knew about Elena's death"?

"No Rosa never told him she thinks he is trying to cover up some of the things the women are asked to do and go to they have two sets of files one for the people like us and the tax man then these to keep a check on what is really happening with the girls"

"Right let's get back to the office and take a look through these then maybe vice would like to take a look to"

As Paul and Alan arrived back Dai and Lisa were heading out the door

"All right you two how did you get on"?

"Not very well with our Mr Morris sir he reckoned his secretary was off sick this morning and he didn't know where the files were but Alan her struck the jackpot"

Dai looked at Alan

"Well boss while we were sat there talking to Mr Morris I noticed a reflection in a mirror behind him I made the excuse I needed the loo and went out on to the landing outside the office to find a young lady clutching these" he held them up to Dai

"Well don't keep me in suspense what are they"?

"Oh, sorry boss it lists of all the people that Elena met on the night she was murdered and of the other girls that work for the agency, it seems Mr Morris was lying when he said his secretary was off sick he called her in early when he knew we were coming and had her sprit away these files she knew of Elena's death she's Romanian to and the news had got round the community from Mr Comea Elena's landlord"

"Won't he notice the files are gone"?

"No boss he asked her to take them home with her, as I said to Paul it seems they have two sets of files one for the likes of us and the tax man the other for themselves with the true activities in it"

"So, she just handed them to you"?
"Yes boss she wants to help catch who ever killed Elena she was her friend"

"Right get to work on them but for the moment don't let on we have them let's see what our Mr Morris gives us instead see how well they match if you find anything report to Dave myself and Lisa have a press conference to get to"

"Yes boss" they said in tandem

A press conference had been arranged for mid-day the family of DJ and Ryan were attending it had been arranged at one of the local hotels in the centre.

Dai and Lisa left his car at the police station and walked over to the hotel Liz Mason was already there as where the families Dai wandered over and introduced himself

"Mr and Mrs Okore, Mr Carter I'm DCI Rees I'm in change of the investigation into your son's murder and assure you we will do everything we can to find the person responsible for it, I have to also tell you that since the murder of your son's there has been another murder a young lady was found the other night and we think that it is the same person who committed your son's murders"

Mrs Okore let out a sigh "no, no this can't be this person has to be caught they have now taken three lives this person is not a Christian god would not allow this"

An arm was put round Mrs Okore it was only then that Dai and Lisa noticed the young white male with the family

"Andy how are you"?

"I'm ok thank you DS Jones Mr and Mrs Okore have been a great help"

Mr Okore spoke "we met Andy when he came to apologise for smashing the windows in the hall he explained about himself and Diji we were shocked at first but when we realised that Diji had been happy for the last year or so we knew that Andy was the reason, he his father and brother have also been a great help to us what has happened has brought us together"

Liz Mason came out and called them all into the large conference room three lots of tables had been set out at social distance Dai saw that he was on the middle table with Mr Carter to his left and Mr and Mrs Okore to his right a microphone was set out on each

Dai took his seat as Liz called the room to order "ladies and gentlemen of the press can I have your attention please" the room came to order "thank you I will now hand you over to DCI Rees"

Dai stood he had thought about staying sat down but he wanted to have a look around the room to see the faces of the press to see if our man in the parker was there again, Lisa had positioned herself by the door and was also on the lookout for him.

"Ladies and gentlemen I am sorry we are here again today to ask for the public's help in finding the murderer of Diji Okore and Ryan Carter, I also have to inform you that on the morning of the 25th the body of a white female was found in an underpass by the Escape building this body has been identified as Elena Adamache a 31 your old Romanian living and working here in Milton Keynes she was also a mother to a two-year-old son and two months with child. We now have some leads to go on and I would like to appeal to the public for any information they have to come forward, firstly we would like to ask if anyone has seen a man matching the description of the photo to my right of me the person we need to contact is described as been about" Dai had to think for a moment "1,75 meters tall of skinny build and wearing a beige Parker coat and blue jeans he was seen around the area of central Milton Keynes on the 23rd of this month we also believe that the same man was seen by a witness on the night of the 24th again in the centre only this time he was dressed all in black and carrying a rope and large cross we would urge the public not to approach this person if they know of him but to contact us immediately, we also would like to ask for help in tracing a dark blue BMW registration number GB 02 ABC it may be parked in a garage near you or a lock up again please contact the police if you have any information thank you I now believe the families would like to say a few words"

The press started to shout out questions to Dai "ladies and gentlemen I will answer all your questions after the family have had their say"

Ryan's father was the first to speak "ladies and gentlemen of the press and public I am here to ask you on behalf of my family for help in finding my son's killer, Ryan was no angel in fact he was awful I know he was into drugs etc but he was still my son, a brother to his sisters a uncle to their children and we loved him he did not deserve to die like this at the hands of a mad man so please if you have any information at all pass it on, I have every confidence in DCI Rees and his team in catching this man but any help they can get will be helpful thank you"

Mr Okore spoke next "people of Milton Keynes I can only echo the words of Mr Carter, DCI Rees and his team need all the help they can get in finding the killer of our son's and that poor young lady, Diji our son loved everyone the church was his life we have just found out that he had a new love in his life a partner who had made him happy he did not deserve to die at such a young age so please, please if you have any information at all come forward with it also if you do not feel you can go the police come to me at my church you can talk to me in confidence and I will pass the information to the police thank you"

Dai stood "thank you if you could all wait a moment while the families leave I will gladly answer any of your questions"

Dai stood and said his goodbyes to the families then turned to the press he saw a young face in the crowd being jostled by the big guys of the national press Holly Long

"Right any questions Miss Long do you have one"?

Holly a little surprised "Ho yes sorry, DCI Rees you say you are looking for a blue BMW is the owner of the car a suspect and why have you not been able to find him or the car"?

"The car was spotted just the once the registered owner we know is working away in America and we have not been able to contact him as of this moment we believe that he may have sold the car before he went to America and whoever he sold it to has not registered it in their name or it has been put in a lock up somewhere till he comes back and that someone from said place maybe using it"

The questions went on for a few minutes more, then Dai called time and headed back to central to pick up the car.

He had sat in the hotel foyer listening to DCI Rees and the families giving their statements to the press no one had taken any notice of him he was just a man sitting having a cup of tea but from where he sat he could hear every word and see them all, he was shocked when he heard about the woman having a child and being with child, but she was a slut a woman who sold herself to men she had one child that now would be a bane on society and she was going to have another child possible by two different fathers, as for Ryan his father admitted he was bad, how could a father love a child who had done the things he had done dealing drugs to young people if his father condoned that he was just as bad, and Mr Okore sitting there like god oh mighty if you cannot speak to the police come to my church I will see that your information is passed on to them and all the while that lad who was with his son is stood behind him he was not a man of god if he let his son be with another man, there was no mention of the other sinner the man he had taken last night, had they not found him or where they just not saying ?, he had sent out the photos taken of the man beating his wife days before so unlike the others he had sent them before he had taken the sinners life, he had taken a bus to Aylesbury and dropped them in the post there so they should get the photos soon. Now to work out who next and work out how they had got a witness he had not seen anyone that night but someone must have seen him.

Dai and Lisa got back to Bletchley not much had happened to put their inquiries ahead of what they already knew, Paul had a call from Mr Morris that the list he needed was ready to collect whenever he was ready so he had gone and collected it he was ready with it when they got back.

Dai called the team together "right what have we got anything useful"?

Paul spoke first "Sir Mr Morris has given a list of Elena's clients for that night"

"And"

"Well, it's a little different to the one his secretary gave us the names of the people she met are the same but the services given and prices are totally different"

"Can we trace who these people are"?

"Not from the list Mr Morris gave us they are just names but the list his secretary gave us has bank details on it so Alan and I have taken to checking with the banks as to who accounts they are and names and addresses"

"How many people for that night"?

"Just four sir we have so far traced three but the last one we are having a bit of trouble with it's an overseas bank and they are closed at the moment"

"that's great anyone of interest"

"Just a local councillor we've spoken to him and he assures us that when he left Elena at eight pm that night she was ok, he was back home at eight fifteen"

"Can anyone vouch for that"?

"Yes sir, his wife" Dai and Lisa smiled "he has asked that we don't mention any of this to his wife as far has she knows he had gone to see an elderly relative who as luck as it she's doesn't speak to"

Lisa seemed to see red "So he's using an elderly relative as an excuse to go and have his leg over dirty old sod"

"His wife may well find out if we find he is lying to us" explained Dai

Lisa was still seeing red "I hate people like him what is wrong with them his poor wife being lied to, I know of his wife seen her around they live on the same estate as me she's a lovely woman"

"Now, now Lisa come down off your high horse I'll tell you what if we find out he is our suspect I'll let you tell the wife how's that"?

"It would give me great pleasure"

"For now, though you can take a look at the video the tech guys did of the press conference see if our guy in the parker was there this time, Vicky can give you a hand she's got a keen eye for faces"

"Yes boss I also did a video of my own I took a walk around the areas the I thought the tech guys may have not got a camera shot so I'll download that too"

"That's great, Paul Alan you continue chasing Elena's clients for the night, where's Taffy and Paula"?

Paul spoke first "Oh sir they have gone to the Blue lagoon fire brigade reported they have got out a burnt-out BMW wondered if it was ours so they have gone over to see"

Dai knew the Blue lagoon it was a local nature reserve man made when one of the brick yard pits was filled with water, It was a lovely place but had also become a haven for young people to meet on hot summer nights to swim, drink and take drugs in fact his first job in Milton Keynes had been there when the body of a young man was found in the water he'd gone swimming after a few drinks and smoking some weed got into difficulties and drown, his mate that were with him thought he was messing about and when he didn't surface that thought he had swam under water to the other bank and gone home they were so stoned themselves it wasn't till the next day that the body was found that they realised what had happened.

"And Dave"

"He's gone to see Tommy he had a call from Mary the social worker saying Tommy was going on about something she wondered if it was to do with the case"

"Ok I'll be in my office if you need me"

Dai's phone was ringing as he walked in he went to pick it up but stopped a cold shiver went down his spine there on top of his in tray was an envelope he knew what it was even before opening it he put on a pair of gloves and looked the print was the same but this one had been sent by Royal mail it had a HP 21 post code he went to his laptop and put in post code checker the result came back as being Aylesbury area, he gingerly opened the envelope inside was more photos showing a man beating a woman and the same note.

He walked back into the main office "right everyone I've just got this in the post I need to know have we had any more reports about a body mainly that of a male"?

"No boss nothing at all why"?

"because of these" he held up the photos "same MO right down to the note, I take it our killer is against men hitting women and therefore this man could be or already has been the next victim we need to find him"

Vicky took the photo from Dai and scanned it in "I'll get onto the tech guys to collect it boss then I'll see if we can get a face match from the system"

"I'll start looking through domestic violence files see if we have had any reports in the last few days that may match I'll also see if anyone has been reported missing"

Dai's phone was ringing again "cheers Lisa I'll have to get that"

"DCI Rees"

"Hello Dai Superintendent Wilcox here, I saw your press conference I think it went very well any progress"?

"No sir but we have had a new development we've had more photos sent and a note but this time we don't have a body to go with it"

"No, body you say could this mean the killer has not struck yet I do hope so"

"I can't be sure sir the killer went out of his way to post these photos via Royal mail they were sent from Aylesbury so either he had the person in mind and is looking to kill him or we haven't found the body yet and the photos were meant to arrive after the body was found"

"Right, I'll get onto central and have them have patrols checking out places to see if they find anything"

"Thank you sir may I suggest they check out estates with underpasses that link them it seems to me the killer is using them to keep out of sight"

"Anything else useful from our enquiries so far"?

"Not really sir we have got the names of Elena's clients for the night she was murdered but so far we have only been able to trace three of them the team have spoken to one of them he's a local councillor but he has an alibi for the time she died the other two they are about to talk too and one we will have to wait till his bank open's to get his home details"

"You are getting their details from their banks how come"

"Well sir Elena worked for what they like to call them self an escort agency we got an address for it and DC's Steven's and Bates paid them a visit this morning the manager told them that his secretary had called in sick so he could not get the list for them at that moment but DC Bates notice a young woman in a mirror and made his excuses and went out to see her while Dc Stevens stayed talking to the manager one William Morris"

"William Morris you say didn't vice have something to do with him"?

"Yes sir they closed him down a while back but it seems he has reopened with his in laws as the new owners he's now a manager"

"And who was the young lady DC Bates saw"

"It turns out she was the secretary she was also a friend of Elena's Morris had called her in early to make some of the files disappear he asked to take them home but when she saw us there she gave us the files in the hope it would help"

"And these files had names and bank details on"?

"Yes sir bank details how much they were charged what service they got the lot, it's a bit different from the list Mr Morris gave us, as not only does it have Elena's contact for that night but also the other girls that work for him I was thinking maybe vice would like a look after we have finished with them"

"Good thinking, I want to see that man go down and so far we've not been able to get him but we'll have to be careful as to how we got the files I don't want him accusing us of taking them without a warrant"

"Well sir he gave them the young lady to take home with her so we could say that she was arrested with them on her or that she volunteered to give us them because she felt they may help the case"

"We'll have to think long and hard about this one but yes by all means pass them on to vice, anything else"?

"No, sir that's about it"

"Ok keep me informed"

"Yes sir"

Dai put down his phone his throat was dry he was not sure if it was the thought of there being another body or that he just needed a drink he went out to the kettle to find Dave standing there

"Ey up Dai great minds think alike ay do you want one"?

"Yes please I'm parched, how did you get on with Tommy"

"Ok he seems to have settled in very well at the home where he is for now Mary told me they have managed to get him moved over into the Milton Keynes care system"

"That's great what could he tell you"?

"Well now he's back on his meds he's calmed down a bit Mary said it will be a good while before he is totally right because he was off them for so long, but he seems to think he had seen the killer before at one of the soup kitchens in the centre"

"That's great do you think it would help if we took Tommy around them to see if he could point him out or what"?

"Not at the moment Dai he's still very fragile Mary said he has been having nightmares about it"

"Poor sod if he hasn't got enough on his mind now he has this, right have you seen this"? Dai handed Dave a copy of the photo

"Bloody hell Dai when did this come"?

"As far as I can tell this morning's post the envelope is post marked Aylesbury so either our killer has been on a road trip or like the other times he's had someone else do the donkey work"

"We haven't got a body yet have we"?

"Not yet but you bet your life there will be one this guy doesn't show any signs of stopping"

"Do we know who this is so we can warn him I know he's shown beating a woman here but surely that wouldn't make him a target"

Before Dai could answer Lisa spoke up "Dai, Dave I think you better see this control have just had a Mrs Hanson on her husband Derek has not come home from his work and she's just come home to find an envelope with photos of her husband and her in it"

"Right Lisa you with me, did she say where her husband worked"?

"Yes boss one of the factories on Redmore it's within walking distance of their home"

"Did she not worry this when he was not home"?

"No boss she leaves for her work before he comes in, they cross over so it wasn't till she got home she realised something was wrong"

"Right Dave you get onto control get them to send units to the underpasses between Redmore and Beanhill if he's anywhere that's where he'll be"

"Sure thing"

"Oh, and get a forensic guy to meet us at the home address to pick up the photo and note, although I think we are bashing our heads against a brick wall with that so far they've all been the same"

Dai and Lisa headed out by the time they got to the address a forensic van was already parked outside as they pulled up Colin got out

"Afternoon Dai, Lisa what have we got"?

"Afternoon Colin I thought you would have sent one of your team out for this little job"

"I would but I'm sort on staff, two have had to self-isolate"

"Oh, who's that"? enquired Lisa

"The Livingstone twins, one of their siblings as tested positive so they are off for the next nine days"

"That's the trouble when you have families working together one down all down"

"Don't I know it, right back to work as I asked what do we have"?

"Missing male not been seen since yesterday" Dai told him

"So why am I here"?

"Because the wife as received a note and photos and buy the sound of it they are the same as ones we received at the office this morning"

"But we have no body yet"?

"No, Colin at this very moment is calling in teams to search the underpasses between here and Redmore"

"That's within spitting distance of here and no one has seen this guy"?

"Not a dicky bird right shall we get on"

Dai let Lisa lead the way he found that letting a woman approach another woman who was in distress was better it put them more at ease.

Lisa rang the doorbell it was answered almost straight away by a very pale looking thin lady with a big bruise on her face

"Mrs Hanson I'm Detective constable Lisa Jones this is my boss Detective chief inspector Dai Rees and this is Colin Mathews from our forensic team may we come in"?

"Yes of course I'm sorry to be troubling you knowing that silly old sod he's got drunk and kipped over someone else's house, it's the photos that I'm worried about its freaked me out to think someone has been watching us and taken photos"

She lead them into the main living room "please take a seat can I get you teas or anything"?

They all shook their heads "no thank you"

Lisa took the lead again "Mrs Hanson do you mind if we take a look at the photos"

"Yes sure and there's the note too" she went over to the table and picked up the envelope and went to hand it to Lisa

"Sorry can you give it to Colin it will have to be taken and checked,"

She handed it over and Colin gently opened it and took out the photos and note Dai and Lisa looked at each other the photos were the same as the ones sent to the office but the note was totally different in its wording

It read "I have seen your man sin against you but you need not worry anymore as god is on your side and he has tasked me to cleanse all sinners you shall be free of this man"

"Mrs Hanson I have to ask have you any idea when these photos were taken they must have been taken here from outside this house and why you didn't ring us earlier about them"

"No, I can't say they could have been taken anytime, Derek's not a bad man we have our ups and down like any couple, and I thought he was at work I was going to ask him about them when he came home, but his work rang to say he wasn't there I had a feeling something was wrong"

"Mrs Hanson looking at these photos this is more than a up and down is that how you got the bruise on your face"?

"No, I walked into the door"

Just then a voice came from the hallway "mum tell them the truth" a young girl of about fifteen came into the room

"Emma go back to your room this doesn't concern you"

"Yes it does mum we're fed up listening to you covering for dad he's too handy with his fist against you what that note said is true he's a sinner and good riddance to him"

"You don't mean that go back to your room" my voice rose an octave has she shouted at her daughter

Dai spoke up "Sorry Emma have you seen the note"?

"Ye and the photos mum left them on the side when she went to phone you, mum you know when they were taken it was last week when you had that big fight with dad that's when he gave you that black eye, go on mum tell them the truth for once stick up for yourself"

She turned and went back to her room.

"Mrs Hanson is that correct the photos must have been taken last week"?

"Yes it must have been Monday of last week he was on holiday I was late home from work I work at the hospital as a cleaner night shift Derek went mental accused me of seeing another man. He drinks you see oh when he's with his mates he all charm and wonderful to me but behind closed doors it's a different matter"

"Did you not report any of this to the police"?

"No, I took my wedding vows for better or worse and I have stuck with them, do you think something has happened to him as I said this all could be a mistake and he's sleeping off a drink somewhere"

"Mrs Hanson we can't say at this moment but we have people out at this moment looking for him in the meantime we will have a family liaison officer come round and stay with you if that's ok"

"You do think something has happened to him don't you that's why you are here, it's that killer isn't it the one who has killed those others" she looked straight at Dai "I knew I'd seen you before you was on the telly this morning, you think its him the killer that's had for my Derek" with that she broke down and began to sob Emma appeared back at the door and then put her arms around her mother

"I'm sorry mum I didn't mean the things I said" she looked at Dai and Lisa "do you think it could be him the killer as taken my dad"

Dai looked at her he seemed lost for words "Emma as of this moment we cannot be sure of anything we are covering ever angle that is why we are here now we have people out looking for your dad, but let's hope it's as your mum said he's sleeping at a mates house, Mrs Hanson do you have a resent photo of Derek"

Dai Lisa and Colin flinched back as Emma retorted back "what more resent than them ones"?

"No Emma sorry that came out wrong do you have a photo that shows more of your dad's face we can't really see it on these"

Dai could see Emma thinking she seemed to have taken control after her mums sudden outburst

"Yes sorry I've got one on my phone I took it last month at my little sisters birthday it's a nice one he's sobber in it, it's the only birthday that I ever seen dad sobber at thanks to covid he seemed to like celebrating birthdays more than us kids it would go on all day we'd be at home while he was out with his mates"

Lisa spoke "Emma are you on What's app"

"Ya I think everyone is now a days why"?

"If I give you my number can you send me the photo"?

"Ya sure"

As Lisa and Emma exchanged numbers and the photo was sent there was a knock at the door Colin being closest answered it to find Pc Jill Grace standing there

"Oh, hi Colin I didn't expect to see you is DCI Rees here"?

"Yes come in"

"No, I think it's better he comes out here could you get him for me"?

"Yes Sure" Colin went inside "Dai PC Grace is outside she wonders if she can have a word"?

Dai apologised to Mrs Hanson and went out

"PC Grace what can I do for you, I thought you was on holidays"

"Sorry sir I was but we're short of a few PC so was asked in. i rang the office and they said you was here and I thought it would be best to tell you in person rather than phone you, the body of a white male has been found in the underpass between here and Redmore where it goes under the Redmore roundabout"

"Do you think its Derek Hanson"?

"Well sir theres no phone or wallet but we have found a wage slip in his name beside the body it could have fallen out when the killer went through his pockets"

In the background Colins phone was ringing "Ok I'll be right there I'm just round the corner, Dai I have to shoot as I said I'm down on manpower, can I ask a favour"?

"Yes sure go ahead"

"I was hoping to get prints of Mrs Hanson and the daughter but I will not be able to I know it's not right but if I leave a print scanner with you can one of you do it"?

"Yes sure but I'll have to time it right I now have to tell them we have a body"

Colin went to get a scanner from his van and PC Grace was saying here her goodbyes when Dai stopped her

"PC Grace can I be cheeky too I was wondering you did such a good job with Mr and Mrs Okore would you mind staying here with Mrs Hanson and her family just till the FLO arrives me and DS Jones will have to shoot off at some point and I don't want to leave them alone"

"Yes sure sir in fact I'll let you into a little secret I've asked for a transfer to become a FLO"

"That's great I think you'll do well at it, but for now shall we get this over and done with"

"Sir"

Dai and Jill were brought back to their senses when they heard a voice behind them it was Lisa

"Mrs Hanson please come back inside DCI Rees will be back in a moment"

Mrs Hanson was shaking and firing questions at Dai ten to the dozen "what is it? why is she here? Where has the other guy gone? Tell me it's Derek they've found him haven't they"?

Dai put his hand on to Mrs Hanson's Arm but she pulled away "Mrs Hanson I need to talk to you but I think it's better we do it inside please"

"Where is he take me to him I need to see him"

Jill put her hand out "Mrs Hanson my names Jill I'm going to be with you for a while, now what do you say we all go indoors and let DCI Rees talk to you in there we don't want the neighbours knowing all your business do you"

With that she turned and went back into the house and took a seat

Dai followed "Mrs Hanson I'm sorry to say that the body of a white male has been found in an underpass not far from here, we have reason to believe it is Derek"

Emma was beside her mothers, by now as she broke down into tears "how do you know it's him you could be mistaken"

"We have found a wage slip with his name on it"

Emma was next to speak "what about his phone wallet where are they"

"We thick like the other killings that the killer may have taken them with him"

"Why has he done this to these people why kill my Derek I just can't understand it"

"I'm sorry Mrs Hanson but until we catch whoever is doing this I can't answer your question as I don't understand it myself"

Mrs Hanson calmed down a little at this "Yes I understand but whoever is doing this must be a nut case taking lives like this what gives him the rights to do that"

"Who knows what goes on in the minds of some people Mrs Hanson, Mrs Hanson me and DCI Rees have to leave now but Jill here is staying with you can she get you anything"?

"No thank you and my name is Jane I've only just taken it in you've been calling me Mrs Hanson"

"Right Jane Jill here has our number so if there's anything you need to know she can contact me, oh and I'm sorry to say she will need to take yours and Emma's fingerprints"

Emma looked up shocked "What for"? "

"Don't worry it because you both handled the photo and note we need to eliminate your prints that all"

"Oh, will it hurt"?

"Oh Emma of course it won't, will it Jill? and you've seen it done on the telly loads of time's"

"No, your mum is right it won't hurt at all in fact you don't feel a thing it's just like scanning your fingerprint on a mobile phone if you have it locked that way no more ink and paper that went out with the start of the tech boom"

"Ok then but mum you go first"

Dai and Lisa said their goodbyes and headed out to where the body had been found

"Dai, Jill seems to be doing a lot of FLO work now she's good at it we need a good FLO do you think you could talk her into being one"

"No need to she already put in for a transfer to it, I'll put in a good word for her but I wouldn't mind her being with us she'd make a good detective"

By the time they arrived at the scene Ruth and Dave were there

"Afternoon Ruth is it the same as the others"?

"Yes I'm afraid so Dai right down to the note he's been dead about 18 hours I should think"

"Ey boss that would tie in with the time he finished work at six last night" said Dave

"Someone must have seen him before now surely" asked Lisa

"You would think so more people must use this underpass on the way to and from work how many factories are on this estate"?

"There's two car showrooms, one clothes distribution warehouse but that as now closed a food factory but I think that's closed too, three or four small units and the Royal mail vehicle workshop" Dave said of the top of his head.

"That's quite a few places to have staff so I can't understand why he's not been found"

"I've driven down onto the estate a few times boss and the road is lined with cars down one side plus the car showrooms I should think that their guys have their own cars, and I'm not sure if it still does but the food factory if it's still open use to bus people in so it maybe that not many people use this underpass, plus the bus stops are up on the Standing way so the other end of the estate"

"So far we have four murders all in underpasses that means or killer must be following them to know their routes, Right let's get back to the office must of these places will be closing now we'll come back in the morning and ask around I want to know if anyone has seen anyone hanging around"

Dai didn't relish the thought of another late night but that's what it was going to be.

Chapter Fifteen

The team had again worked late into the night it was one in the morning before Dai got into bed, Taffy and Alan had managed to book into a local hotel Steve had offered one of them a bed for the night but they had both refused he was quite surprised when Paula had ask if she could take him up on the offer Dai felt a little pang of guilt there was he rattling round a three bed-room house all on his own but he had gotten use to his own company he could walk around as he liked too.

Dai woke at five and tried to get back to sleep but no matter how hard he tried he could not too much was going on in his mind again he got dressed, it had been a few days since he had gone for a run maybe that will help him think he was about to leave when he saw the house phone flashing to say there was a message he pressed play and his dads voice came back "Dai bach I'm fed up with this covid I've decided to come up and see I've got my ticket as I said I'll be on the seven thirty train to Paddington in the morning that gets me into Paddington at around ten thirty by the time I get to you it should be around two thirty in the afternoon"(Dai bach small or little Dai) he sighed that all he needed now was his dad turning up in the middle of a major case it was too early to ring him now but he would the minute he got into the office this morning a second voice made Dai jump "Hi dad sorry it's late I hope you're not in bed I see on the news you have a major case on but I've had a little run in with Grancha he determined to come and see you I've tried to talk him out of it but you know what he's like stubborn old sod, sorry I shouldn't talk about him that way but he is, any way I'll give him a call in the morning see if I can talk him out of it love you" good thought Dai if anyone can stop him it would be Bethan.

Dai hit the office at seven thirty and as normal Lisa was in

"Bore da Dai trust you slept well"?

"Bore da Lisa no I've had about four hours to many things on my mind, and to top in all I had a message on my phone to say my dad's on his way up this morning"

"Oh, is he allowed to travel with the restrictions from Wales to England"?

"I don't think so but I have the feeling he's going to do it any way, Bethan has tried to talk him out of it and in her words the stubborn old sod will not listen"

"As he had his jab"?

"Yes he had the first one a few weeks back I tried to explain then that he needs the two but he was determined to come he feels safe after one, I'd better get into my office before he leaves and try and put him off"

"Good luck you forget I know your dad and Bethan's right, but he's a loveable old sod as well can't wait to see him"

"Cheers the thing is I just don't know what I'm going to do with him while this case is going on any way best give him a ring"

He went into his office and speed dialled his dad's home but got no answer he tried his mobile just in case for once he would pick up but to no avail, he scrolled through his numbers till he came to his cousins Gareth's number, Gareth ran the local taxi in the valley it picked up straight away "Rees's taxi where would you like to be picked up from"? it was not a voice Dai knew "can I speak to Gareth please"

"Who calling"?

"It's his cousin Dai"

The voice went up an octave "Dai how lovely to hear from you, it's Megan"

Dai was taken a back a little Megan was Gareth's youngest daughter was she at the age to be working it had been so long since he had seen them "hi Megan sorry I was not with it how long have you been taking calls at the office"?

"I left collage last September but due to covid have not been able to take up my university position so dad had a job going here so I took it, it will fill in till I can get to go to university"

"That's great what are you hoping to do"?

"I would like to follow your Bethan in to medicine she's helped me with my exams" Dai cast his mind back and remembered Bethan telling him that she was helping one of Gareth's girls but he assumed it had been his eldest Bronwen "anyway would you like to speak to dad"?

"Yes please and good luck"

Megan shouted out to her dad Dai felt his ear drum rattle "Dad pick up Dai's on the phone, I'll put you through bye"

Gareth picked up straight away "Dai how be you butty (mate) long time no hear from, it's nice to hear from you but I've a feeling I know why you are calling,"

"Yes sorry to ring you but have you by any chance heard from my dad"?

"Sorry Dai I have I spent twenty minutes on the phone to him last night trying to talk him out of getting the train to come and see you but you know what he's like out of all my uncles he's the most stubborn, I even sent Uncle Stan round to try and talk him out of it he booked a cab for Half six this morning"

Uncle Stan was Dai's fathers youngest brother who after Gareth's father Harold had passed away had taken Gareth under his wing in fact it was he that had started the taxi company all the family loved him he had no children of his own so had spoilt all his nephews and nieces to death.

"I take it even he had no luck"

"I'm afraid not I got a call from him calling your dad all the names under the sun"

"So, he's already left I know now he will not answer his mobile so I better get used to the fact he is on his way it's all I need right now"

"Sorry about that butty but we tried, I saw on the main news last night you have a big case on you looked good on the telly put a bit if weight on mind you"

"Cheeky bugger I'm still the same weight as when I was at home"

"Well, they say the telly adds ten pounds to you so we'll put it down to that, you still playing the rugby"?

"Yes had our first game last week proud to say I scored the winning try, what about you"?

"That's great, no Butty I tore my calf a while back and it's not healed to well so I've had to give up but I still go and watch and do some coaching from time to time"

"That's a shame any way I'll have to go good to talk, by the way what time did dad leave"?

"My driver picked him up at six thirty as he asked so he's well on the way now"

"So, no chance of turning him round"?

"Sorry Butty no he's well on his way back, oh and by the way when you speck to Bethan thank her for all her help with Megan she's been a great help"

"Will do catch up with you soon I hope"

"And you bye"

Dai hung up and went into the main office Dave had arrived and so had Steve and Paula "Morning boss" said them both in unison

"Oh, morning you two I trust you got a good night's sleep and are ready for today"?

"Yes thank you, boss Steve's bed was a lot more comfortable than hotel beds"

Everyone looked round and Paula went red when she realized what she had said

"Oh no I didn't mean Steve's bed I meant the bed in his spare room" everyone just looked "it's true tell them Steve"

By now Steve had gone red too "yes it true I've got a partner so nothing happened between me and Paula, I'm going to make tea who wants one"?

"That's it Steve change the subject" said Lisa with a giggle in her voice "oh and we have another one keeping little secrets do we like Dave, who's the lucky girl" "it's lucky boy actually His name is Brian and he works in a bank so there my little secret is out as of am I"

Everyone turned and clapped Dai spoke first "congratulations hope you both are happy together"

"Thank you, boss I've been waiting for a long time to tell everyone but just hadn't got the guts to do it I was freighted that some may not like it"

Dave spoke "ey bugger everyone else lad the world is a far better place now adays more open to others good on ya, right you said you was making tea so get on with it lad I'm parched" he turned to Dai "morning Dai you don't look to happy this morning dropped a pound and found a penny"

"Oh, nothing Dave just a problem with my dad"

"What I hope he's ok mate he's not been taken ill has he"?

"No, no such luck I found a call from him on my answer phone this morning saying he was on his way here. I tried ringing him to put him off but he's already left one of my cousin's taxi's dropped him at Bridgend Station this morning and now he's turned his phone off he won't ring me on my mobile because he knew I would talk him out of it so that's why he left a message"

"Bloody hell Dai that's all you need at the moment can't you get British transport police to intercept him and take him home they could say he's breaking covid rules"

"No mate I'll just let it ride I don't want to cause any trouble for our friends at B,T,P he a grumpy old sod as it is I won't live it down"

"Ok but it was worth a try"

Steve looked up from his desk "Boss there's a message here for you from one of the forensic guys something about rope"

"Ey that would be me cheers Steve" said Dave

"What, we got Dave"?

"It seems one of the forensic guys was fascinated by the rope bit he sent it down to Chatham docks museum seems they still have a rope making place that makes it the old way for ship's and boats they have confirmed it was made of hemp maybe in the early seventies and that loads of it was sold to London brick here in Bletchley for as I said roping and sheeting so it could be that our man as a tie in with the old brick works"

"That interesting but why have rope that is so old he must have stored it somewhere and when did the works close"

"Not sure I'll have a quick look" Dave Googled up the works "It closed in nineteen ninety so the rope has been laying in someone's shed since before then"

"Well, we've worked out who ever this is seems to be living in the past so we'll just have to keep working on that "

"Ha but here's another thing rope like this was also supplied to Wolverton works so he could have a connection with that"

"Right, that's another thing we'll have to look at that too"

"And sorry there's more it was used on the canals to tow the barges with"

A voice came from behind Dai and Dave they both turned to see Paul had arrived

"Sorry boss it's a narrow boat on the canal not a barge"

"What's the difference there both boats Mr smarty pants"

"Well boss a barge is a boat that is normally about nine to ten feet wide and is used to carry large bulky goods a narrow boat is as it says is narrow around six feet ten inches wide it still carries goods but has to be the size it is to fit into the locks"

"Well, you learn something every day in this place I stand corrected to tow the narrow boats"

"I see but I think with the brick dust it may be more of a chance it's from the brick works but we'll not rule out the other two but for now where are we with yesterday's victim"?

"Well boss some of the night shift lads went around Redmore it seems the old clothing warehouse still has security and CCTV covering the road, they were able to pick up our victim going past one of the gates at eighteen o five but there was no one after that went past on foot, while they were there a mechanic from one of the garages stopped them and he also confirmed seeing Derek it seems they pass each other each morning and evening and just say hello" said Lisa

"What about his work"? asked Dave

"we've got an appointment this morning at ten"

"Right, I'll take that if that's ok with you Dai"? enquired Dave

"Yes that's fine I think Superintendent Wilcox is back today so I may be summoned to a meeting with him this morning" with that Dai office phone began to ring "see talk of the devil I bet that's him now"

"Fiver says it not" chipped in Dave

"Ok you're on" Dai went into his office and picked up Dave followed "DCI Rees ah hello superintendent Wilcox how are you"? Dai looked at Dave and rubbed his finger and thumb together

Dave just slumped took out his wallet and handed Dai the fiver

"Hello Dai, I was hoping to get back in today but now my youngest has now tested positive so it looks like we are going to be in isolation for a little longer so you'll have to bring me up to speed over the phone" Dai did a little fist pull back and in his mind said yes "Dai you still there"?

"Oh, sorry yes sir just thinking there so sorry to hear that and hope he gets better soon" he was about to say more when he was interrupted

"My youngest is she"

"Oh, sorry sir I've only ever met your sons" Dai felt as if the ground had swallowed him

"So, you have you met them at the rugby are you still playing"

"Yes sir had our first game last weekend we won"

"That's great I'll have to bring the boys down to watch when all of this is over now what have we got"?

Dai was on the phone for over half an hour bringing the super up to speed and by the time he got off his coffee had gone cold he walked into the main office "right anything existing happened in the last half hour"

"No boss except this has been sent over" Lisa handed Dai an envelope his blood ran cold "Don't worry Dai it's not from the killer it's from the forensic guys and girls take a look"

Dai opened it up and inside was two photos both of shoe imprints they both looked the same photo

"So, we have a shoe print"

"Yes but one was taken from the scene near yesterday's victim and the other was from near our second victim, both were found by a bush at the entrance to the underpass they think our killer stood behind the bushes till the victims came along, Colin left a note to say can you give him a call and he'll tell you more"

"Thanks Lisa I'll do that now" He went into his office and dialled Colin

"Colin Mathews"

"Hi Colin Dai, here you wanted to speak to me"?

"Yes I trust it you've seen the photos of the shoes"?

"Yes thanks what can you tell me about them"?

"Well as you can see they are large size thirteen to be exact, but whoever wears them is small about five foot eight or nine" Dai's mind slipped back to primary school and his teacher there, he was five foot six and wore size fourteen shoes he had to have them made for him, all the kids called him Coco after the clown but he was a lovely teacher he came back while Colin was still talking " so that means or man must have his shoe's made for him and they are shoes not trainer the print is very similar to Doc Martens but not as there is no makers mark in the sole like with Doc Martens"

"How can you tell he's not very big"?

"The pressure of the imprint is not very deep as of that for say a large man with that size feet and also we noticed that the back of the heel is worn down quite well this could be that the person puts their heel to the ground first or they may even have something wrong with their leg"

"So, our man as you said must have them made I'll get one of the team on to it they may come up with our mysterious Stephen Clements cheers for that Colin"

"Oh, Dai there's one more thing since we sent over the photos one of the team as found a piece of black thread on one of the bushes were they found the shoe print we've analysed it it's pure wool it's been woven I think it may have come off suit jacket or trousers could be tailor made like the shoes this could tie in with your guy all dressed in black, I'll get back to you as soon as I find anything else"

"Right, cheers Colin catch you later"

Dai put the phone down and sat there thinking his mind went back to the first press conference to see if he could visualize someone like that, there was the BBC guy no me was over six foot, the guy from the Mirror he was small but he didn't have a parker coat. No matter how he tried Dai could not come up with anyone that fitted that bill the only one was the man Holly had seen but she only saw him from the back and they had no joy finding him on CCTV. He went back into the main office.

"Right, everyone I've just had Colin from forensics on we now have some new leads who's into fashion"? Vicky put her hand up "oh good you'll love this one I need you to get onto specialist shoe companies find out if any of them have a gentleman from Milton Keynes who has size thirteen shoes made for them mainly a Mr Stephen Clements and it's also a long shot someone find any tailors in MK that make suits again if you have any joy for our Mr Clements"

"Yes boss, I'll get on to that straight away, you do realize I'm a shoe fanatic"

"Ye lass keep your mind on the job no getting carried away and ordering new shoes while you are at it" pipped up Dave

"Yes boss but there's nothing wrong in window shopping"

Steve spoke up "Boss if you don't mind I'll give Brian a ring he has his suits and shirts tailor made I'm not sure who buy but he can give me the name I can follow up from there save a bit of time searching the net"

"That will be great but don't give out any details of the case's" answered Dai

"I never discuss anything of the case with Brian he goes green at the site of blood on the telly even though we know it's fake"

"We know someone else like that don't we Dave"?

"Oh, come on I'm not quite that bad I can watch a good horror movie in fact me and Ruth sat down and watched an old Saw movie last night I quite enjoyed it"

"I can't watch horror movies I find myself laughing at them halfway through the Mrs gets well upset" added Taffy

"That's just the Welsh sense of humour" butted in Alan

Lisa retaliated "Ha watch it butty you've got three against one here"

Everyone one laughed and Dai gave a discrete cough

"Right people let's get back to things that matter, how are we getting on with the other three victims"?

"Sir, over the last few days I've been taking a look at the photos the drug squad sent over I've found nothing of interest on any of them we've got Ryan coming and going but no one that looks like our killer" Paul said

Lisa spoke next "Oh talking of the drug squad they have passed the go fund me page for Ryan over to fraud when looking into the accounts of Mr Hackett it was found he set it up and all moneys was going straight into his bank account so far it is nearly three thousand pound they've asked the service provider to close it down and see if they can get the money back to those that have donated"

Everyone one gave a little gasp at hearing this

"Cheeky bugger even tried to make money off the dead, no disrespect Steve" Dave looked at him

"No that's ok boss, as it is his father had already made plans for a day like this he had taken out life insurance on Ryan hoping he would never have to use it, but it will be enough to bury him and pay for a stone"

"The Romanian embassy have been on and confirmed that Elena's sister will be here Monday to collect her body and the child and return them to her home and wondered if someone from the T.V. police could meet them they would like some details of the case so they can keep the family informed" Vicky said

"Yes sure when will they be in MK"?

"They are looking at Tuesday that give's the sister time to get to the UK and settle down"

"That's fine I'll deal with that myself anything else"?

"Yes, Ruth told me to tell you, the PM on Mr Hanson will be at three this afternoon" added Dave

"Great I'll go for that and seeing as I don't have to see superintendent Wilcox now I'll come along with you to Mr Hanson's place of work" Dai's mobile and office phone began ring at the same time he looked at the mobile it was Bethan he hit the hang up button he know Bethan would understand it was a bad time to call, he went into his office and picked up "DCI Rees"

"Good morning Dai" Dai felt himself go red the velvet voice of Maggie Blackmoor

"Oh, morning Maggie what can I do for you"?

"Oh, you could do lots for me Dai but I'm ringing to say the Chief would like to see you this morning at ten" Dai heart sank and he felt himself go redder that's all he needed he'd already spent time going throw everything with Wilcox now he'd have to do the same with the chief

"Yes that will be fine see you then" Dai hung up and picked up his mobile and rang Bethan back she picked up straight away.

"Morning Dad how are you"?

"I'm ok I take it you had no joy with your Grancha"

"No sorry dad I'm off today first time in weeks so I've shot over to his house but he's not here"

"That's because the stubborn old sod left at six thirty this morning one of Gareth's cab's took him he's caught the seven thirty train"

"If I realized he was leaving that early I would have got here sooner, did Gareth not try and stop him"?

"He spent time on the phone with him last night trying to talk him out of it but with no joy he even sent your great uncle Stan round to see if he could talk him out of it"

"And still no joy, I know it's a bit of a long shot but can't you get someone from one of the other police forces to pick him up and bring him home he is breaking covid rules"?

"Dave Parker already suggested that but it would just cause to much paperwork for whatever force it is so I'll just have to wait for him to get here"

"Oh, dad I am sorry I should have got here earlier and stopped him"

"You are not to blame for this Bethan he has a mind of his own and no one was going to change it so stop worrying"

"Ok but I do worry ever since he had that mild heart attack last year I've done nothing but worry"

"I know but as I said he's got a mind of his own now you go a enjoy your day off I'll ring you when I pick him up from the station and let you know he's arrived ok"

"Ok love you loads and speck to you later"

"Love you too bye"

Dai hung up he felt a pang of guilt Bethan was a good daughter and since he had moved she had taken it on herself to look after his dad he just didn't know what to do he had suggested to his dad that maybe he could move to Milton Keynes to be near him but no he wanted to stay in the valley to be near his mother's grave maybe he could talk him around this time. He went back into the main office

"Right Dave change of plan I knew I would not get off that easy I've got to see the chief super at ten so you'll have to take Mr Hanson's work on your own"

"That's fine with me. Jill Grace has just rung she will meet us with the family at the id with Ruth"

"I didn't realize an id had been arranged when is it"?

"Oh, sorry I thought you had been told it's three thirty tomorrow"

"Oh, thank god for that I thought I would be splitting myself in half then"

Taffy spoke up "Oh boss vice have passed on a message they have found a flat in Campbell park that Elena and the other girls use, they thought it was funny that Elena was working so paid Mr Morris a visit they realized the girls could not be using hotels because of the covid, when they got Mr Morris and his in laws in it all came out, seems the mother-in-law wanted nothing to do with it spilled the beans on the flat the lot"

"Anything of interest for us"?

"Loads of hidden cameras they are going through the footage now to see if there is anything can help us"

"Right keep me up to date with whatever we get"

A phone rang in the background Mike Brown picked "Boss that was the Hr of the company our Mr Fosdyke works for, one of the security guards recognised the number plate when you gave it out and reported to HR, it seems he's in the middle of a Brazilian rain forest at the moment and they have no way of communicating with him, I asked if they knew where his car is but they have no idea"

"Are they following it up"?

"Yes boss they are going to try twice a day to contact him and as soon as they do they will have him contact us"

"Well, that puts Mr Fosdyke out of the picture so who the hell used his car"?

"More to the point boss is where is it, it can't just have vanished"?

"That's true Dave someone somewhere must know where it is"

Paul spoke next "Sir the overseas bank as finally come up with the details of Elena's client the guy lives in Buckingham"

"Great you and Taffy go pay him a visit see if he can tell us anything, he must realize by now that he may have to be contacted"

"Will do I'll ring ahead and arrange to see him"

"No just go you ring ahead and it gives him time to make up a story surprise him"

"Yes sir"

"Right, I'll be in my office if anyone needs me"

Dai sat in his office going throw the paperwork he looked at the clock the time had flown it was nearly nine twenty he would have to make a move to see the chief super, he was brought back to his senses by a knock on the door frame he looked up and there stood Vicky "yes Vicky what can I do for you"?

"Boss I've had a bit of luck with the shoe companies the third one I tried has a Mr Stephen Clements on their book's"

"Do they have an address for him"?

"Yes, boss but it's in London and Steve asked me to say he's had no joy with tailors here in MK do you want him to widen the search"

"Yes that would be great you get on to the Met see if they can find this Mr Clements and tell Steve to look at tailors in Savill Row London I remember one of my uncles buying a suit from there he said they were the best tailors in the UK"

"Will do boss"

Dai picked up his mobile and jacket and headed out to the car park just as Dave was doing the same thing "You off to see Mr Hanson's work"?

"Yes mate"

"don't suppose you want to swop you see the chief I'll go and see his work"?

"By eck Dai no way when I reach DCI then I'll take on seeing the chief but till then you're on your own"

"Worth the try keep me up to date get me on the mobile if you feel it something the chief needs to know"

"Will do"

By the time Dai was sitting down to tea with the chief Dave was at Derek Hanson's work there was no one at reception so he wondered straight through to the warehouse he could not see any one but a voice came from one of the corners

"Whatever it is mate we're not buying"

"Mr Bridesdale D I Dave Parker Thames Valley Police"

"Oh yes sorry I didn't realise what the time was I'm up to my neck in it this morning what with this happening to Derek and the other lad who works here being off, you don't mind if I work and talk I've got an important order to go out"

"No not at all I just need to ask a few questions that's all sorry I have to ask where was you the evening Derek was murdered"?

"I was here till about 18.30 Aiden the lad and I were finishing an order off"

"Did Derek not stop and help"?

"No Derek a creature of habit 18.00 on the dot out of the door, it wasn't so bad while everything was in lockdown he couldn't get to the pub he'd sometimes stay, but the minute they said the pubs could open that was it back to his old ways"

"So, you managed to stay open during the lockdown"?

"Yes we're only a small company but we supply parts for making PPE to some of the major manufacturers so it's kept us going"

"And Derek's drinking that didn't affect his work"?

"No, he was very good at it the only way it affected his work was I had to make an excuse to stop him driving the van but the pandemic helped with that"

"How come"?

"Well, some mornings he would come in he looked sober but I knew he had a hangover I could smell the drink on his breath I was afraid that if I let him drive the company van he would be pulled for drink driving so when the pandemic happened I made out we had to much work I needed him here and started using a courier company for now to do the deliveries"

"So, he did drive the van"?

"Oh yes that was his job driver warehouse man I didn't realise he had a drink problem till he'd been here about six months, he came in one morning so drunk I had to send him home, next morning he came in apologised said it would never happen again and it never has but I've always got that niggle in the back of my mind but as I said it never affected his work from that day on but I know it affected his home life"

"Oh how"? Dave played it a little coy he wanted to see what he know

"Yes I know his wife Jane and daughter Emma I feel so sorry for them I saw what he could be like first-hand one time Derek had left his wallet at work so I ran it round from what I can gather

Derek and Jane don't normally see each other till later in the night him working days and her at the hospital in the nights but this particular evening Jane was at home she had some holiday booked, when I got there it was like World War three going on"

"Did it not stop when they saw you"?

"No, I'm afraid I was a bit of a coward, I saw Emma coming up the street so I gave her the wallet I never knocked at the house, he came in the next morning rating that he had lost his wallet and all along the bitch of a daughter of his had it he was still mad about it"

"Did you not say you had given it to Emma"?

"Yes I did he apologised to me but I don't think he ever apologised to Emma"

"How do you know that"?

"About a week later Jane rang to see if Derek was working late he was not home, we got taking and I told her what I had seen and asked if she was ok I explained about giving the wallet to Emma and asked if she was ok, Jane explained that he had not mentioned a word to them he was still blaming Emma"

"Then what happened"?

"I tried keeping an eye on Jane and Emma I would phone just to make sure they were ok, but then Derek found out and went mental at them and me threatened to smash up this place kill me and Jane accused us of having an affair the lot"

"Surely you couldn't keep him on after that I'd have fired him on the spot"?

"I know I should have said this is his last week he was finishing tomorrow his last day I didn't fire him on the spot because I didn't want to hold back his money for the sake of Jane and Emma they didn't deserve what that got from that man so I gave him a weeks' notice"

"I see have you got anyone to replace him"?

"Aiden's back tomorrow and as of Monday my son is going to help out till I find someone, I have to ask would it be right for me to go and see Jane and Emma see if they need any help"?

"I shouldn't see why not the covid rules have changed now you can meet people, and I also think that because you were in contact nearly every day with him and he with is home that may class as a bubble"

"Thank you I'll pop round tonight"

"I have to ask do you know of anyone who may have been after Derek you know someone he may have upset"

"Apart from myself I don't think so, and I can assure you I never killed Derek Hanson and I never met his drinking mates so I can't tell you anything about them"

"Ok Mr Bridesdale that's all for now if I need to contact you any more I've got your number and here's my card if you need to contact me"

"Right thank you, do you think it's the same guy that murdered the others"?

"We seem to think so, oh by the way you haven't by any chance seen a dark BMW hanging around"?

"No, I'm afraid not we don't see much going on we normally have the doors closed and we're so used to seeing cars coming in to here and having to turn round because they never realised it is a cul de sac mind you we did see some poor sole on a bike come a cropper last week myself and Derek were loading the van for the courier this guy on the bike came down saw the gap in the trees over there and must have thought he could get to the red way went in head first"

"Was here hurt"

"Not bad a few cuts to his hand and knee and he ripped his lycra shorts me and Derek went and helped him gave him some plasters and off he went"

"Ok thanks again"

Chapter Seventeen

He sat eating his evening meal the news was on they still had not said anything about his latest victim, apart from Diji his last victim was the only one he had contact with to talk to, why? had he gone to his work that day he already knew his routine but he just wanted to check it over one more time it was stupid of him and to come off his bike like that he had seen the gap and just gone for it without thinking, his hand was hurting from the cut on it, his leg had healed well but his hand was not so good it had got an infection in it and was weeping he may have to see the doctor at this rate, the other guy had been nice provided him with plasters and dug his bike out of the bushes a good Samaritan but his victim all he seemed to do was smirk at him never actually laughing at him but he could see it in his eyes he deserved to die people like him. He finished his meal and washed up the dishes just as the news ended but it ended with an update into the murders in Milton Keynes to say that another body had been found. He thought about his next victims he had them lined up this was going to be harder a couple man and woman but this man and woman were sinners they were having an affair he didn't know them personally but thanks to the gossip of the ladies at the church he had found them he had followed the man he found where he met the woman he know what nights they met so he was prepared but it wouldn't be tonight, tonight he had to get his gear ready for the wedding on Saturday tomorrow night Friday the day they met for their night together he would be ready.

Chapter Eighteen

Dai had spent a good part of the day bring the chief super up to date as he was leaving Jill Grace was coming in

"Afternoon sir"

"Afternoon Jill how's things with you"?

"Good sir, I've just left Jane Hanson there's a FLO with her and Emma, Jane as taking it really bad although Derek was such a bastard to them she loved him"

"They say love is blind and as she said she took her vows and felt it would be wrong to leave him till death do us part is what it says and she took it to mean just that"

"I know it sounds awful to say sir but I think Derek getting killed like this may give her a new start in life"

"It's not awful you could be right she may make a good new start but it may also make her depressed turn her the other way into sadness let's hope it's the first"

"Oh, Mrs Okore rang me while I was with Jane news travels fast due to the internet now, she wanted to know if it was the same killer"

"What did you tell her"?

"Nothing sir I told her out straight I could not discuss the case, but I think she had put two and two together "

"That's good" Dai's personal phone was ringing in his pocket he took it out and looked at the number "sorry I have to take this"

"That's fine sir bye"

"Bye Jill, Dad where are you"?

"I'm at the station I thought you would be here to meet me, and who's Jill"?

Dai had not realised he had pressed answer before he said goodbye to Jill his dad would pick up on the slightest thing

"Dad I've been in a meeting with the Chief super and Jill is a work colleague now stay at the station I'll be there in five"

"Ok see you soon"

Dai drove out through the gates and turned left onto Witen Gate through the first set of lights and right at the next onto

Midsummer Blvd this took him straight to the Central MK train station Dai hoped his dad was in an area that was easy to park and just go he would drop him at home before he went back to Bletchley. He was lucky a car was just pulling away from the kerb as Dai turned in he whipped into the space and got out to see if he could see dad but there was no sign of him Dai made his way the main entrance but there was still no sign of him his phone began to ring he picked up

"Dai bach where are you, you said you would be five minutes"?

"Dad, where are you more like it I'm at the entrance to the station and you are nowhere to be seen"?

"I'm outside the station by the taxi rank but there's no sign of you have you got the same car"?

Dai made his way outside "Right I'm by the taxi rank where are you"

"By the taxi rank looking at some big grey boards around what looks like a building sight"

Dai's mind was thinking "Dad what station did you get off at"?

"Well, I was meant to get off at Milton Keynes but the train stopped at Bletchley so I got off their I thought it would be easier what with you living in Bletchley"

"Dad I'm a Milton Keynes, look it will take me a while to get to you now I need you to take a walk, cross over the road where you are walk around the grey boards just past them is the

Bletchley police station go to the main door use the buzzer and tell the duty sergeant who you are and get Lisa Jones to come and meet you I'll be there as soon as possible"

"Ok Dai bach, I'll see you then sorry about that, wasn't the fire station where the grey boards are now"?

"Yes it was they pulled it down after they built another one, look dad I'll see you there"

Dai headed back to Bletchley and by the time he got back his dad was in full stream sitting with a cup of tea in hand telling the whole of the room stories his dad caught him coming in.

"Dai bach I was just telling them of the time when you was little how you fell in the river fully clothed and came out blacker than you went in, and how you was caught by your uncle Teddy riding the arial"

Dai's mind went back to his childhood the happy times he had, the river Garw ran though the village it started up in the mountains above Blaengarw and ran right down to Aberkenfig where it joined other rivers to form the river Ogmore, the river itself was fed by streams that came down off the mountains but some of these ran through the pills of coal slack so they ran black turning the river black too, the slack was taken up the mountain by the arial that you could say was a ski lift but instead of seats it had buckets to carry the slack when they got to the top a trigger would operate and turn them over to empty all the kids of the village use to rid it even if they got caught like he had they would still go back for more.

"Hi dad I see you've made yourself comfortable"

"Yes Lisa was kind enough to make me a cuppa I needed after that journey, pandemic my arse there seemed to be more people on the trains than ever"

"Yes and you was one of them, you know you shouldn't have travelled from Wales to England, I tried ringing you this morning to stop you but you turned your phone off, you knew if you did that I couldn't get hold of you"

Dai suddenly realised the whole room was staring at him he went red now was not the time to have a go at his dad Lisa broke the silence

"Listen Dai we haven't got much to report why don't you take your da home get him settled in and come back later we can get you on your mobile if we need you"

"Yes, yes good idea, come on dad say goodbye to everyone I'll take your case"

Dai picked up his dads case and headed for the door it seemed to take a while as everyone seemed to want to say goodbye personally this was typical of his dad he could go anywhere walk into a room not knowing anyone and by the time he left the whole place was his best friend, In the car his dad was silent

"Look sorry dad I didn't mean to shout at you like that it's just that now is a bad time at work but you must admit that you turning up like this is not on"

"I know Dai Bach but it seems that it's been a lifetime since I've had contact with anyone this covid as driven me mad "

"What do you mean? you ring me at least twice a week Bethan try's see you as much as she can then there's your brothers you keep in contact with them"

"I know but it's not the same as face-to-face contact being able to talk to someone have a drink with them, Bethan set me up on this Facebook thing so I could keep in contact with friends it helps a little but it's just not the same"

"Well, you got Bill and Vera next door you must be able to see them make up a little bubble with them you are in and out of each other's house's all the time and you and Bill use to love going to the working men's club for a game of snooker"

"Dai don't you remember Bill passed away last year"?

"Dad you never told me how and when"?

"I'm sure I told you, he was one of the first to die from covid he got it and was gone within the week they recon him having COPD didn't help"

Dai cast his mind back has long as he could remember Bill had been bad with his chest he remember one time as a teenager seeing him coughing up blood into a hanky.

"Dad I didn't know what about Vera she's still next door in the house surely"?

"Oh, I'm sure I told you about Bill, and as for Vera, up until he passed away Bill was looking after her she had a stroke back in 2019 couldn't do much for herself so Bill stepped up to the mark became a good house husband I helped out as much as I could I'd go shopping for them etc but after Bill passed I couldn't help out Vera was so bad the family felt it was better she went into a home she passed away a few weeks ago nearly a year to the day Bill did"

"Oh, dad I am so sorry you where such good friends and I'm sorry It must have slipped my mind about Bill" by this time they had pulled up outside Dai's house "right come on then let's get you settled in I'll put your cases in the middle bedroom you had before, the beds all made up"

"Duw da (good god) son It's been two years since I last saw you I hope you've changed the sheets"

"Yes I have you cheeky old sod I know I work all the hours god sends but I do try and keep the house clean I never know who might drop in at the last minute, mind you I have to admit no one's been here in the last year"

"Dai don't get yourself so uptight I'm only messing I remember when you and your sister was little it was so strange Bronwen was the girl we expected her to be the tidy one and you the messy one being the boy but no she was messy as hell clothes left all over the house books and records never put away, but you everything had its place and if it was not there, there would be hell to play, now after all these years I'll let you into a secret remember that leather jacket you had you brought it with the money you earned in the butchers you never took it off you kept it so clean if you saw a crack in it out would come the dubbing"

"Yes I remember it I wore it till I grew out of it, what of it"?

"Well, the one you so carefully looked after was not the one you brought"

Dai looked puzzled "of course it was, I brought the thing don't forget down in Bridgend"

"Sorry do you remember about a week after you brought it you went away with the school on some trip to some sort of camp"

"I remember that it was summer camp I wanted to take my jacket but you and the school would not let me in case I lost it"

"Well while you was a way Bronwen decided to borrow it, we didn't realise what she had done till after a few days your mother noticed the jacket was not behind the door where you had left it"

"So, what happened to it"?

"Well, it seems she borrowed it and her and some of her friends went out for a sneaky drink and smoke during a disco at the hall they got seen down by the square and chased by a group of lads, they ran but it was not till later that she noticed she had not picked up the jacket from where she had taken it off she went back for it but it was gone"

"So how come my jacket was there when I came home"?

"Well, your mother took Bronwen to the post office drew out some of her savings and made her buy you a new one before you came home and we have never let on till now, mind you one good thing did come out of it Bronwen stopped with the sneaky drinking and smoking"

Dai's mind went back to that time "well I must say dad it has solved a mystery for me after all these years"

"What's that boy"?

"I all ways wondered how Dicky Morgan ended up with a jacket like mine when his poor family hardly had two pennies to rub together, he must have found it that night"

"That may well be it son"

"Anyway, dad I have to get back, now you remember where everything is there is fresh milk in the fridge and there's pie in there too if you want one you just need to heat it up in the oven oh and oven chips in the freezer oh and talking of Bronwen does she know you have come up here"? Dai's sister has married young and left the valley and was now working as a legal secretary for a firm in Gloucester and like him kept in touch with their dad as best they could

"No, I never told her, I'll be fine son do you want me to cook something for you"?

"Well don't you think you better and while you are at it ring Bethan and let her know you have arrived and I'm not sure what time I'll be home it could be late but thank you"

"Ok but I'll cook any way you can warm it up when you get home"

"Cheers da, see you later and don't wait up as I said I don't know what time I'll be home"

Dai made his way out to the car he had to admit to himself as much as he cursed his dad coming it was good to see him and he looked so well apart from being down in the dumps he just hoped he would have time to spend with him when this case was over he was just about pulling into the station carpark when his phone rang he pressed the answer button that had been mounted on the Triumphs steering wheel "DCI Rees"

"Hi dad that's so formal I was just ringing to see if Grancha had arrived ok"?

"Sorry Bethan I'm driving and didn't look at who was caller ID, yes he's arrived and I've just settled him in at mine, I told him to ring you and let you know"

"That's good I was so worried about him, I tried ringing him but his phone is engaged"

"Ha that means he's on probably on the phone to your auntie Bronwen he never let her know he was coming"

"He never told her because he knew auntie Bronwen would be in the car and down in the valley to stop him he knew what he was doing, anyway dad I'll let you get on I know you are very busy with the case speak to you soon"

"Yes ok I just hope this thing is over soon and we can get back to normal it would be nice to see you"

"That would be nice bye dad" and with that she was gone, Dai made his mind up that when this was all over the case, the pandemic he would go back to the valley he needed a holiday and that would be a good place to unwind he made his way back into the office he saw that Dave was back,

"Ok Dave how did you get on with Mr Hanson's work"?

"Not too bad there wasn't much they could tell me apart from tomorrow being his last day"

Dai gave him a quizzical look "how come"?

"Well, his boss knew about his drinking, he was employed as a warehouse man driver but because of his drinking and some mornings him coming in smelling of drink he had to take him off the road, he found out about his home life when Hanson had left his wallet at work one evening he took it round to the house just in time to see him beating up the Mrs"

"So how come this is his last week and why did he not stand in"

"Well Mr Bridesdale is not a big guy and he admitted he felt he had better not, he saw the daughter in the street and gave her the wallet, then he got a call one evening from Hanson's Mrs seeing if he was still in work he'd not come home, they got talking on the phone and after that Bridesdale would give her a ring every now and then to see how she was, Hanson found out threatened to kill them both and smash up the workplace said they were having an affair etc so he told him that was it he couldn't take anymore from him"

"I thought he would have sacked him on the spot for that"

"So did I but I think he felt sorry for his Mrs and the daughter so he paid him up till the end of the week"

"Well, they won't get any money now with him ending up died like he as"

"I wouldn't be so sure Mr Bridesdale seems to me to be the type of man who will pass on the money to Mrs Hanson, he knows what she has been through"

"That would be good if he did, right guys who's got some good news for me"? everyone looked at Dai but not a word was said "oh come on someone must have something"?

Vicky spoke first "the Met have been on they have visited the address we got for our Mr Clements but with no joy it seems he moved out over ten years ago and no one has seen or heard from him since"

Steve was up next "boss I did as you said and rang round tailors I could find in Savile row London there are just over fifty of them"

"And"?

"Well, I struck lucky on the forty-eighth they have a Mr Stephen Clements on their books but that's where the luck runs out the address they have is the same one Vicky got from the shoe manufacturer"

"So, who is this guy he can't have just disappeared someone must know who he is?, right we need to change tactics on this if someone could start looking up census forms etc see if they can throw something up, and someone try spelling his name different ways maybe somewhere along the way it's been miss spelt Steven not Stephen and Clemants not Clements no disrespect to anyone but sometimes people write things how they say it or they mishear and it ends up being spelt wrong"

Mike Brown put his hand up "I'll follow up the census boss and electoral rolls, but I'll add in a little bit extra I've been tracing my family tree on Ancestry I know I shouldn't but sometimes you get better results from that"

"I've come to a stop on the shoe side of thinks at the moment so I'll give it ago with the spelling" said Vicky

"I'll give you a hand I'm sitting here twiddling my thumbs at the moment and two heads are better than one"

"Cheers Lisa"

"Right folks you all have your jobs to do lets crack on, but first who's turn is it to make the drinks"?

Everyone turned to Alan "Oh come on I made it this morning for everyone"

"No didn't you cheeky sod I did I had to top up the tea caddy and sugar because no one else did it"

"Ok Lisa you win what's everyone poison and I mean that I'm terrible at making tea"

Dai wandered into his office Dave followed "alright Dai seems I missed out seeing your dad, he arrived with no trouble"?

"Apart from the silly old sod getting off at Bletchley instead of Central yes all was good"

"What was wrong with him getting off at Bletchley you live in Bletchley seems logic to me"?

"It was but I was wandering round central looking for him, I got him to walk round here by the time I got back here he had made himself comfortable and was regaling the team with stories from my past"

"Oh, nothing to embarrassing I hope"?

"No thank god, I've settled him at mine now he knows little bit of Bletchley so knowing him he's out for a walk somewhere"

"I'll have to catch up with him after this is all over have a drink"

"We will do"

"How did you get on with the chief super and the man eater Maggie is she still after your body"

"Oh, don't it make me shiver even thinking about it"

"What Maggie or the chief super"

"Maggie you stupid sod, any way the super suggested another press conference but as I said to him we've not got much out of the last two so I don't think we'll get much more with another one, we'll just rely on the news channels and press giving their daily coverage"

"That seems ok to me" Dave looked at his watch "Bloody hell Dai weren't we meant to be at Mr Hanson's PM at three it's three ten now" with that his phone went "Ruth sorry we're running a bit later we'll be there it ten ok Right love you bye"

Dai and Dave made the hospital in record time when the got to the lab Ruth had already started the PM "afternoon you two hope you don't mind me starting without you I've lots on today"?

"No not at all, anything different about this one"? asked Dai

"No nothing apart from the blow to the head he managed to fracture the skull this time I think after the girl he wanted to make sure he was out cold, I'm not sure until I look at the skull but it may well be that the blow to the head was cause of death in this one there was lots of bleed out from the wound more than the others"

"But he still strangled him"? enquired Dave

"Yes just the same right down to the marks but these are not so prominent as the others as I said I think the blow to the head killed him so the heart stopped before he strangled him"

"You think he didn't realise that the blow killed him or do you think he did and just carried on the way he has been"

"Not sure Dai"

"Anything on the body that might help us"?

"No not I've found a thing I checked under his nails for a man they are very clean not a thing under them"!

"That could be because he worked for a company that makes components for PPE companies I was at his work earlier and his boss washed and scrubbed his hands each time he put a new component into a box "

"That explains that then, I gather he was a drinker"? all the time they were talking Ruth had been working on the body directing Stella to point the camera here then there and talking into a microphone giving details of what she found

"Yes he was"

"I can see from the liver it has cirrhosis if he hadn't been killed now he'd have died in the near future of it".

"It was that bad hay, what makes a woman stay with a man like that".

"You never met her Dave when I saw her she broke down in tears she still loved him but also to felt tied as she said to me I took my wedding vows from death do we apart and for better or worse"

"God I thought that type of vows had gone out years ago, we're not having that at our wedding are we Ruth"

"I didn't know we were having a wedding! Dave Parker have you just proposed to me here in the middle of a PM"?

Dave went red "Well yes it looks like I have so I better ask probably Ruth Pickford will you marry me? and sorry I don't have an engagement ring at the moment this all came on rather fast but I will get one"

It was Ruth's turn to go red now but she remained silent then for the first time that Dai could ever remember Stella spoke up "oh god Ruth say yes before the poor man changes his mind"

"Yes, yes of course I will and don't worry about a ring I don't need one to show you love me"

"Well, you are both well covered in PPE are you going to kiss or just stand there"? asked Stella

"No, I think we'll save the kissing for later when we are alone don't you think Dave"? she turned and smiled at Stella and Dai it was their turn to turn red now "right now that's over shall we carry on with work"

The PM went on for about another half hour then Dai and Dave said their goodbyes to Ruth and Stella then they made their way back to the car, Dai opened his door got in then leaned over and opened Dave's but he stopped him getting in
"hold on mate I've just got to get something out of the glove box" he reached in and took out a small box then Dave got in
"here you are mate you don't have to take it but I think it may come in handy now"

Dave took the box and opened it "bloody hell fire mate what's this I can't take this"

"Yes you can it's the ring I gave to Steph when we got engaged, she gave me it back when we split up"

"But it's yours" Dave said speaking over Dai

"No, it's not it's been in that glove box ever since the day she gave it me back I'll tell you the truth I forgot about it till now"

"I can't mate you would be better off giving to Bethan"

"God mate do you think I would give Bethan anything of Steph's she hates her, anyway she's got my mother's ring's engagement and wedding so she has no need for them so take it"

"Mate what can I say thank you, I must say it's a beautiful ring thank you again"

"You are welcome mate"

"Look mate let me pay you for it how much was it"?

"Listen butty you have just offended me I don't want anything for it take it as a wedding gift from me"

"Sorry mate but I will let Ruth know where it came from"

"That's up to you mate now shall we get back to Bletchley"

When Dai and Dave arrived back at Bletchley Paul and Taffy had got back from Buckingham

"Alright guys how did you get on"?

Taffy spoke first "Ok boss he couldn't tell us much yes he had seen Elena that night he had arrived at 21.00 hours and left at 22,00 hours he was back in Buckingham at 22.20"

"Duw da (good god) Taffy those times are spot on how the hell did he come up with them"?

It was Paul that spoke this time "it's all down to technology boss his car is very smart it has a built in sat nav computer that logs every trip he's new to the area so he's using it a lot it shows him arriving at Campbell Park at 20.55 and leaving spot on 22.00 then pulling up at his house at 22.20"

"Well, that rules him out did he have anything useful for us"? Dave asked.

"There was one thing he can't be sure but he thinks he saw someone follow Elena away from the flat"

"What do you mean he thinks he saw someone he either did or he didn't"?

"Well sir as he was pulling away Elena came out of the front door of the flats he saw her waved she waved back, when he had gone passed her he looked in his mirror and he thought he saw someone come out of the shadows behind her but he could not be sure he thought it could be just the light casting shadows"

They could see Dai was thinking

"Dai you alright"?

"Sorry yes Dave I was thinking if it was our killer why did he wait so long to kill her he could have struck anywhere along that road"

Steve spoke "Boss while I was on the beat here in MK I use to patrol that patch there is no underpass from Campbell Park to the theatre district the road crosses over the Marlborough Street so the first underpass is the one where Elena was killed"

"Right let's get on to the CCTV boys again see if they have anything for us, oh and see if we can get anything from shops in the area that may have CCTV"

"Sorry boss that may be hard with the shops"

"Whys that Steve"?

"Well boss if Elena stayed to the main footpath from Campbell Park to where she was killed the road is a duel carriage way so the shops are set a good way back from the main road plus on the Xscape buildings side the car park is another two road widths, there may be something on bus stops or a passing bus may have got something but other than that it could be a problem"

"I see but give it a try anyway"

"Yes boss"

"Right any more news for me"?

Mike Brown was the first to speck "Well boss I've followed up mainly on the London census and electoral rolls at first to see if Stephen Clements moved to anywhere in the London area there are a few but none of them moved from the address that our Stephen Clements was at so I started to cast my nets further starting in Kent and moving up from there county by county but as of yet I've only had one glimmer of hope"

"What's that then Mike"? Dave enquired

"A woman in Kent boarding house remembers a guest called Stephen Clements staying with them at the time of the two thousand and one census, she remembers him because he was the only person staying with them at the time that's how he showed up as a boarder at that address"

"Was you able to get any more details of him from her"? asked Dai

"No, I asked if she still had the details of him from that time like address etc but she was unable to help, in two thousand and six they started shifting all there written files on to computer and discs but then they had a large fire lost nearly everything so all records etc went up in smoke"

"Bugger so there was nothing she could tell us"?

"She couldn't but her husband remembered he was religious it was for at religious meeting he was in Kent but other than that nothing"

"This could be our guy Paul, Taffy start ringing around churches see if any of them had a religious convention in Kent in two thousand and one we might strike lucky if you can't get any luck with local churches get on to the bishops or whoever it is in charge of the church see what they know, Mike keep up with the census and electoral rolls but now see if there are any vicars, priests etc by that name right folks let's keep up the good work we'll get this nut case sooner or later sooner I hope"

The rest of the night dragged on nothing much was happening in any way to catch this man every time they felt they had something, something came up to be put in its way. Dai was tired he decided to call it a day at ten that evening that way he could get home to his dad he sent the rest of the team off too, Taffy and Alan headed out for their hotel Paula had arranged to stay at Steve's again so he bid them all good night and left making sure the night team would inform him the minute anything came up.

Dai got home about ten past ten and as he opened the door the smell of cooking hit him it was a smell he had forgotten he missed the fact of having the smell of fresh food and not a microwave dinner he walked into the dining area his dad had left a note on the table "Dai bach I did as you said and didn't wait up there's a dinner under a plate for you in the kitchen good night son see you in the morning". He walked into the kitchen and lifted the plate steak pie, mash, peas and gravy stared back at him he was surprised it was still warm he popped it in the microwave and went to the fridge and got himself a pint can of mild he poured it as his meal heated up he then took a sip, that first mouthful always tasted the best he took both through to the dining room and sat at the table this was the first time in a long time that he had sat at the table he normally sat in a chair in front of the telly but tonight he felt because he his dad had gone to the trouble of cooking he would sit there. It didn't take him long to finish the meal and his first pint he took his plate into the kitchen and was just washing up when he noticed his dads reflection in the window

"Oh, hi Da I thought you was asleep"?

"No boy I was sat reading my book I heard you come in but I wanted to get to the end of the chapter I'm on, I'm at the part where they have nearly caught the killer"

"You and your crime thrillers it's nothing like that in real life Da" Dai was pouring himself another pint "Do you want one"?

"Don't mind if I do and I know it's nothing like that in real life you forget I have a son who's a detective"

"Who's that then"? Dai went to the cupboard and got his dad a glass and then to the fridge for the can he handed both to his dad"

"You, you silly sod anyway I don't mean to pry but how's the case doing I see on the telly there's been another body found"

"Not too bad we seem to have hit a brick wall just can't find out who this guy is"

"Oh, you know it's a man then"?

"Yes we have had a witness who saw him just before he killed the young woman, I may have seen him to but I can't remember"

"How come"?

"Well, it seems he was at the first press conference we had he took a photo of me and Liz Mason the press officer on the steps of central Milton Keynes police station then sent it to me saying I will never catch him he has the lord on his side"

"What is he some sort of religious nut case going round saying the lord is on his side"

"Looks like it from what he can gather he uses I large wooden cross to knock his victims out then strangles them with a rope"

"Bloody hell boy this man needs catching and I have every faith in you that you will do it"

Dai had begun to wonder if they ever would catch him every lead they had turned up a blank, the car was nowhere to be found the mystery man at the press conference seemed to be a phantom just disappeared, and as for the name Stephen Clements every one of those they had traced had drawn up a blank. "I don't know Da he so far as eluded us no one can give us any information on him or the car he used both seems not to exist"

"Now you listen here boy you've buggered up on a few things in your life but this is one thing you will not bugger up you and your team are working hard to find this guy so if it takes a few more days or even a year I know you will get him"

Dai had this feeling an even bigger lecture was coming from his dad he went to get himself another drink "Thanks da, do you want another or do you want something stronger"? Dai poured himself a measure of whiskey "and sorry what do you mean I've buggered up somethings in my life"?

"Well, your marriage for one thing, then meeting that little tart that you was with and moving here"

"Da we've had this out before I thought you had come up for a nice visit and here you are bringing up the past, a past we cannot change what is done is done"

"So, you say son but did you ever try and get back with Sian think of what Bethan thought of all of this, and me and your mum what we went through"

"Look da I've told you before I know I was in the wrong I put the job before family and yes I would have loved to have had a second chance to get back with Sian and Bethan and be the family that you and mum wanted from me but by the time that came about Sian had moved on I wasn't the one that made the split, and as for Steph I admit that was one big mistake they say love is blind and at that time it was, and as for moving here I like it, the move has helped me with my career I have as you said a good team and I'm sticking with them now can we change the subject"

"Sorry boy I just hate the fact of you up here all on your own and the rest of the family are in the valley"

"I know Da I do miss the valley and the closeness of the family but it would have been the same if I was back home I'd be stationed in Cardiff or Swansea I'd have a flat or house in either and I would still not be at home in the valley, talking to Gareth this morning made me realise I must take a holiday and get back home"

"You spoke to Gareth this morning what for"?

"To see if I could stop you,"

"Oh right"

"Anyway, another thing that made me realise that I had missed so much in the valley was the fact Gareth's youngest Megan was now working for him and when the time comes is going to university"

"Oh, I thought I told you about that too, Bethan has been helping her they've become more like sisters than her real one's they spent a lot of time at mine as Ava and Shelly use to come to Gareth's and Mary's with the kids it was like a play school there so she could not study"

"Look Da it's getting late I have to be up early in the morning so let's get some shut eye nos da" (good night)

"Nos da boy see you in the morning"

Dai's eyes seemed to shut the minute his head hit the pillow but it seemed no time at all before the alarm went off, he woke to the smell of bacon cooking he got washed, dressed and went downstairs to find his dad in the kitchen

"Bora da boy, sit yourself down I've done you a bacon and egg sandwich got to start the day right, now tea or coffee"?

"Oh, coffee please Da how long have you been up"?

"About half hour say half six"

Dai looked at the kitchen clock it said seven he was sure his alarm was set for five thirty

"Is that the right time I'm normally up at five thirty"

"Yes boy, your alarm went off at that time this morning but you was out to the world so I reset it for seven"

"What did you do that for I have to be in the office, now I'm late"

"Look boy you looked like you needed a good night's sleep and you said it yourself last night you have a good team they can manage without you for an hour now get that sandwich inside you before it goes cold"

Dai could not argue with that and the sandwich did taste good even if he wolfed it down

"Diolch (thanks) for that Da but you shouldn't"

"Look boy, while I'm here I might as well do something useful even if it means getting a good meal inside you, you look as though you need it, now get going I can see you are dying to get to work"

"No that's ok Da I'll finish my coffee if the team needs me they can get me on the mobile, look Da sorry if I was a bit off last night it's just this case"

"Look Boy forget the case for ten minutes, now it was nice seeing Lisa yesterday she's looking well, but I didn't see Dave"

"Lisa is doing well she mentioned taking her inspectors exam maybe next year, and Dave was out getting a statement from the last victims boss, oh and he's getting married"

"Good on Lisa, and when did this happen with Dave I didn't even know he had a young lady"?

"Neither did we the team knew there was something going on with him and Ruth but he would not admit it then the other day it came out, then yesterday at a post-mortem he proposed to her and she said yes"

"Who's Ruth and how come he proposed at a post-mortem"?

"Oh, sorry Da you haven't met Ruth yet she's the pathologist who is dealing with the case and while we were at the PM yesterday something was said about wedding vows and Dave mentioned marriage and with that he proposed"

"Well, I heard of some places to propose but never a mortuary but good luck to him hope he's happy, no one on the scene for you yet then boy"?

"Da don't start I'll take my time and find the right one this time I won't make the same mistake, as mum use to say I won't let my balls rule my brains"

"Right, that's good, what about Lisa is she still single"?

"Yes Da she is still single now don't you go getting in your head to play match maker I like Lisa but as a work college and nothing else"

"It hadn't crossed my mind boy I was just asking but she is a lovely woman"

"Da stop! I'm going now before this goes any further, I may see you later but you never know what will come up today"

"Ok boy good luck hope today's the day, see you later"

"Cheers da"

Dai hit the office about eight everyone was in Dave greeted him first

"Ey up Dai had a sleep in this morning"?

"Yes sorry about that, dad decided when my alarm went off and I never heard it he reset it to seven so I'm running late"

"By ek of course you're not, nothing much has happened over night in fact we have no new leads at all"

"What nothing"?

"Zilch nothing this guy seems to have vanished off the face of the earth according to the night lads and lasses they've had no joy with any of the follow ups, no new CCTV, no witnesses nothing on name checks or anything else"

"God will we ever get this guy" at that point the whole team seemed to talk at once

"of course, we will boss" with Lisa adding "you've got the A team here Dai you know we will, he'll slip up at some point then we'll have him"

Chapter Nineteen

As he sat in the kitchen with his tea and toast he couldn't help thinking about tonight it was going to be hard to punish the two of them but it had to be done they had sinned against the lord what? was it the seventh commandments said "thou shalt not commit adultery" and the tenth "thou shall not covet another man's wife" this man was doing both these sins not only was he cheating on his wife but he was lusting after another man's, he had heard this from his favourite source of local news the ladies from the church he could learn a lot from them and also going round the homeless people they loved to talk he would talk to them about all sorts how the government was handling the pandemic, to classical music some of these poor soles on the streets were quite intelligent who through no fault of their own had ended up on the streets, one young man he spoken to had even gone to Oxford and got a degree but thanks to a few mishaps in life had ended up on the streets of Milton Keynes these people he felt sorry for but the people who sinned he had no time at all for. He finished his breakfast and washed up the dishes, he then went out to the garage he had to check his bike he had gotten a puncture on his way home the other night and he'd had to repair it he checked the tyre all over it was still up he slipped the wheel back onto the front forks and tightened the nuts hand tight the great thing about racing bikes was everything was so easy to take off and put back no spanners etc except for the tyres they could be a pain he thought for a moment some of the guys at the cycle club had gotten none puncture tyres maybe he would invest in some of them maybe he could ask one of them to help him purchase them, he checked his new rucksack it was plenty big enough to hold the cross and the rope also his clothes he wore when he did gods works, he could easily have kept his racing gear on but it didn't feel right he needed to feel he was gods warrior but in his racing gear he never felt that way his love of god and his cycling was two sperate things and they should not cross at times like these each had their use but both gave the same effect he could go places and no one would take any notice of a man in racing gear on a bike passing through and no one noticed the way he dressed for his church work he was just him. He went back into the house and changed into his cycling gear but he still had time to set up his bag for tomorrows wedding it sent him back to what he had to do and the young couple that was getting married would they turn out to be sinners he would hope not but these days you never know. He spent an hour getting things together then set out on his run he loved Milton Keynes no matter where you are in the town you could hit countryside within minutes today would be a good run he tried once a week to do one long run say over thirty to forty miles some said he was mad but he loved the open road this would be what he would do today but he would take his time he didn't need to be back in MK till after six he would go straight to the underpass where the couple meet, he always carried his camera with him when out on his bike if he found somewhere to take photos of the wildlife and country side he would. He got back to MK at about five thirty he headed for an area he know he could leave his bike and slip his clothes over his riding gear he got to the underpass at just before five fifty he hid himself in the bush he had found to keep an eye on the underpass he stood back and waited but by six fifteen he began to worry there was no sign of the couple he could see the carpark where they always left their cars but there was no sign of either. He headed back to home this had thrown him this was not meant to happen he would have to find out tomorrow when he was the church. Then tomorrow night he would get his next victim he already had him lined up he had seen this man stealing from a food bank he had followed him he felt sorry for him at first to be that desperate to steal from a food bank but when he followed him he found him selling the food, the more he kept watch him the more he learned about him, he found him begging in central MK then followed him to his big BMW and to his plush home this man was stealing from the good citizens who gave him money, money he could see he did not need, he had taken photos of this man out in his begging clothes and on nights out in his best, flash gold watch smart top of the range clothes and always a wallet full of money Saturday would be the night for him the time when he was out showing off to his friends despite the pandemic this man had always met with his friends he imagined he was one of these people who did not believe in the pandemic and the vaccine.

Chapter twenty-one

Friday and Saturday was not a good day for the team they had gotten nowhere, churches had been rung round but no one could help, as the vicar or priest at most of them had not been in the parishes in two thousand and one, finally someone found someone at an office of a bishop that could confirm that there had been a church convention in Canterbury in two thousand and one but they did not have details of everyone that went as it was arranged by the churches themselves who was sent so back to square one.

But Sunday morning the team hit the floor running Dai had only just got into the office and a call came in that a body had been found Lisa had taken the call

"Dai that was the duty sergeant we've got another body"

"Where now"?

"Another underpass this time between Bancroft and Bradwell where the V6 Grafton Street meets the H3 Monks way"

"Right folks lets saddle up Lisa you with me, Alan, Taffy get a car and meet us there" Dave had just walked in "sorry Dave no drinks this morning we've got another body"

"Bloody hell where now and who"

"Between Bradwell and Bancroft, not sure yet Lisa just getting the rest of the details"

"Right, what do you want me to do"?

"I know you don't like doing this but can you ring Superintendent Wilcox and bring him up to date you'll find his home number on a pad in my office, then stay here and liaise with us and the others, as it's a Sunday Paul and Paula are going to church this morning to see if they can find anyone that may know our Mr Clements"

"Right Dai I'll get onto that; do you want me to give Ruth a call"?

"I've a feeling that the duty sergeant will have already been in touch"

"That's ok I'll do it anyway, and by the way she said to thank you for the ring"

"You're welcome you told her it was from me"?

"Me and Ruth are open with each other and when I told her how I came about the ring and how Bethan didn't need it she was happy"

Dai left the room Lisa went to follow but paused to ask Dave a question but before she could Dai shouted to her

"Lisa are you coming we've got a body to see"

"Ok I'm on my way" Dave turned and went to Dai's office Lisa took that as I don't what to talk about it so left it at that she knew with enough badgering she could get it out of Dai. When they got to the car Lisa started the questions

"So, what's this with Dave and Ruth and a ring then Dai"?

"Oh, nothing Dave will tell you in his own time"

"Oh, come on now you can't leave a woman in suspense especially when jewellery is involved "

"Look no Lisa I'm not saying it's up to Dave and Ruth to give you the news" Dai decided to take the A5 or as the locals called it the A5D as the old A5 Watling Street still ran through Milton Keynes and the D stood for diversion to Stacy bushes then go into the area along the Monks Way

"So, there is news I knew it, are they getting married"?

"Sorry It's not up to me to say now let's just concentrate on the job in hand"

"Their getting married aren't they"

"Look Lisa I'm not saying a word I told you it's up to them to tell you the news themselves now stop you're as bad as my Da"

"Ok but at least tell me a little bit"

"No, No, no I will not be badgered on this I know you to well Lisa Jones you have a way of getting info out of me I don't want to give out now let Ruth and Dave give you the news and don't let on you heard anything from me"

Lisa put her hand up in a mock salute "Yes boss"

They hit Bancroft in under ten minutes Dai saw a patrol car parked on the grass verge and pulled in behind it Taffy and Alan followed. Dai went to the boot of his car and took out some coveralls and handed one to Lisa he looked back at taffy and Alan "Guys see if there is any coveralls for you in that car I just realised these are my last two"

They made their way down the embankment as a PC was making his up

"Morning Sir"

"Ah PC Rahman isn't it"

"Yes sir"

"Right lead the way PC Rahman and fill us in with what you know "

"Well sir we have the body of a white male 42 years of age that goes by the name of Christopher Barker"

"Do you know him"

"No sir unfortunately his body was found by his two sons, apparently he goes out once a week to a friend's house drinking and playing cards on Bancroft they realised he hadn't come home last night so this morning went looking for him they found him in the underpass"

"Oh, nasty what did they do when they found him"

"While one of them rang 999 the other tried CPR but of course it was no good, when I saw the body I could tell he had been dead for a while"

"Who's with the body now"

"Sir the ambulance team have just left and PC Jackson is with it now"

"Where are the son's"

"You've just passed them sir they are in the back of my car"

"Right Lisa, Taffy you go talk to them see what you can find out, Alan you're with me Thank you PC Rahman"

"Sir there is one other think"

"What's that"?

"They haven't told their mother yet that they have found him"

"What"?

"They are frightened to say anything to her, she nine months pregnant due any time now"

"Duw da" Dai called after Lisa "Lisa you better come here"

"What's up Dai"?

"I've just found out from PC Rahman here the boys have not told their mother yet she's nine months pregnant, so I think you better take them home now and inform Mrs Barker I'll come along as soon as I can"

"Will do"

Lisa made her way back up the embankment and Dai turned and headed for the underpass he could see Colin was already there.

"Morning Colin"

"Morning Dai, Alan looks like our killer has struck again from what I can see"

"Same note I see"

"Yes and these this time" Colin handed Dai an envelope even before he opened it Dai knew what it was

"Same as the other's photos and a note" Dai looked at the photos at first he could not make them out they seemed to be two lots of photos of two different men one lot was definitely Mr Barker but the other's where of some of what looked like a scruffy homeless man he handed them to Alan "Here Alan what do you make of these" Alan looked at them

"Not sure boss but I think they are the same man, look here" Alan pointed to a point on one of the photos "both are wearing the same ring"

By now Dai was reading the note this one was longer than the rest and addressed to him

"Dear DCI Rees, I hope this note comes to you, I bet you are wondering why I have killed this man and what his sin is, well I'll tell you he steals from the poor and plays on the good nature of ordinary people begging for cash from them then going home to his fine home to change into his fancy clothes and drive his fancy car so that is why I killed him he is a sinner. I trust you are well The Warrior of God" He handed the note to Alan

"Bloody hell boss he's getting personal now"

"Looks like it we need to catch this guy as soon as possible" from behind them came a voice

"Morning Dai, Alan, Colin" they turned to see Ruth

"Morning Ruth I think we could have saved you a journey this morning same MO the lot he's even left the photos and the note with the body this time"

"Well, I'll have a quick look see if there is anything else that may help then will get him back to the morgue don't suppose we know who he is and how he came to be here"

"His name is Christopher Barker he was found by his son's this morning he'd been out drinking and playing cards at a mates house and when he hadn't returned this morning they went out looking for him"

"Is there a Mrs Barker"

"Yes Lisa has gone with them now to inform her, the boys hadn't told her what they had found"

"Right let's take a look, I see he's on he's flat on his back"

"Yes one of his son's tried CPR and ambulance crew also attended"

At the time Ruth was starting he examination Lisa was pulling outside the house of Christopher Barker, she hadn't been able to get much out of the lads only their names and some details of why they had gone to find their dad, the boys lead the way into the house calling out for their mum as they went, Lisa and Taffy looked at each other as a woman that looked no more in age than the boys appeared from the living room they saw the look of shock on her face as she saw them and one of the boys just took her in his arm and hugged her.

"Mrs Barker I'm DS Lisa Jones and this is DC John Price I'm afraid we have some news for you about your husband Christopher"

"What, what has happened to Chris Liam, Dean what has happened to your dad"?

Before Lisa could speak Dean spilled it out in between tears "Dad's dead mum we found him dead"

"No, he can't be dead you are wrong he's had an accident they've taken him to hospital you've made a mistake" she said pulling away from Liam

"Mrs Barker can please come and sit down this is a shock for you but what Dean said to true your husband has been found dead in the underpass between here and Bancroft, unfortunately it was Liam and Dean that found him"

Mrs Barker pulled both boys to her "Oh you poor things you poor, poor things" she lead them into the living room and took a seat the tears where running down her face she looked at Lisa and Taffy

"Was he in an accident or is it the same as the others that have been killed"?

"We believe it could be the same person that as killed before but at this moment I can't confirm it"

Liam began to speak "Mum I'm sorry we tried everything we tried mum but we could not save him"

"Listen Liam, it is Liam isn't it"?

"Yes"

"I'm sorry to say that your dad may have been dead long before you found him so you did your best but there was nothing that you did could have saved him, now what you say that you and Dean here show me where the kitchen is so I can make everyone a drink and leave your mum here to talk to Lisa and you can tell me all about your dad" Taffy lead the boys out of the room.

"Mrs Barker I'm so sorry for your loss but I have to ask you some questions are you up to it"?

"It's not Mrs Barker myself and Chris are not married it was something we were going to do after the baby is born" tears flooded her eyes again Lisa leaned in close and put her arm round her "I'm the twins step mum their mum had some sort of a breakdown after they were born Chris come home one day to find her gone left the boys with his mum never to be seen again, Chris as done a great job bringing them up on his own"

"They seem very nice lads and by the looks of it they think the world of you"

"Oh, we get on like a house of fire the age thing doesn't seem to bother them I'm only seven years older than them but they just see me as mum I'm the only one they have known"

"If you don't mind me asking how did you and Chris meet"?

"Chris was running a pub and advertised for a live-in barmaid come housekeeper I went for an interview got the job after a few months we realized that things between us where happening I got on well with the boys we realized that we liked each other and just things went from there"

"Does Chris still run a pub"?

"No Covid and the lockdown put paid to that he had to sell up that's how come we're living here in rented accommodation"

"Oh, I see, sorry I haven't even asked your name"

"It's Chloe McLaughlin"

"Right Chloe you don't mind if I call you Chloe"? Lisa looked at Chloe who had a look of pain on her face "are you all right"?

"I'm fine just a twinge I've been feeling them all night, that's why I set the boys to look for Chris"

"Ok Chloe I need to ask where was Chris last night"

"Oh, he'd gone to his mate Graham's house for drinks and cards, I'm sorry to say Chris was one of the people that believed the pandemic was a scam even though it took away our living all the way through it he has made Saturday night his drinks and card night with his mate" Chloe let out a sharp scream

"Look Chloe are you sure you are all right"

"Yes I'll be fine as I said it's just twinges"

"Do you have an address for his friend and did he always go to the friend's house or did the friend come here"?

"Yes sure" she called through to the boys "Liam, Dean can one of you write down Graham's address for the Detectives please no he always went to Graham's I wouldn't have anyone in the house just in case they brought the covid bug in what with being pregnant" she let out a little gasp and Lisa notice a wet patch appear on the chair beneath her "Oh my god I think my waters have just gone"!

"Chloe how long have you been having the pains and how far apart are they"

"As I said since last night they started off light but now I'm getting a pain every few minutes"

"I thought so I can see it on your face, Chloe I think you are in labour I'm calling for any ambulance" Lisa dialled 999 "ambulance please" she waited as she was put through and explained the situation "Right Chloe an ambulance is on its way they should be here in a while"

"Oh, this is not right it happening to quick"

Lisa was still on to the ambulance operator "Listen I think this baby is coming quicker than we think would it be better for me to put her in my police car and get her to the hospital that way"?

"No keep her there if needs be you may have to deliver it have you help there"

"I have my colleague here and the lady who's in labour two stepson's"

"Right pass the phone to one of them" by now taffy and the boys where back in the living room one boys each side of Chloe holding her hands Lisa handed the phone to taffy and put in on speaker "right now what"? asked Lisa

"Right, I need you to get mum into a position for her to deliver this baby, on the floor with her back slightly raised and her leg's apart"

"Right Chloe you heard the lady let's get you into position and I'm sorry but we'll have to remove your knicker's"

Chloe lowered herself off the seat onto the floor resting her back against the seat and with Lisa's help they removed her knickers at that point both boys looked away Lisa looked up "Liam, Dean can one of you go and get a towel so we can cover your mum" Dean left the room and came back with a large bath sheet towel and handed it to Lisa "thank you right Chloe let's get your modesty covered" she used the towel to cover Chloe so all the boys could see was the top of her knees "right operator what next"?

"Right how far are the contractions"

"They are coming think and fast now"

Chloe let out a scream "oh my god I feel I need to push"

"Did you hear that" asked Lisa to the operator

"Yes I did I need you to see if you can see anything see if baby's head is crowning and Chloe on the next contraction I need you to push"

"Right Chloe let's have a look" Lisa bet down to see "I can see something it's only small but I think it's the head"

"Lisa I need you to help Chloe now as she pushes I need you to guide the head and as it comes out make sure that the umbilical cord is not round the neck"

"Ok got that come on Chloe you're doing great, right that's it the head is clear and there's no sign of the cord"

"That's great now Chloe with the next contraction I need you to give one big push and see if we can get your baby delivered"

Chloe let out a deep breath and pushed and everyone looked at Liam has he gave a little scream "Ah mum you're squashing my hand"

"Right Chloe I can see the shoulders and arms, that's it good keep going, that's it's born"

Taffy got up from next to Lisa in all that was going on no one had noticed that the paramedic had arrived and was at the door Taffy let him in.

Taffy spoke to the operator "The Paramedic is here now, thank you"

"Ok I'll leave you in his hands and well done to your colleague"

The paramedic was with Chloe by the time Taffy got back into the room

"Right Chloe I just need to cut the umbilical and then make sure you are alright" with that he bent down and cut the cord and handed the baby to Lisa "It's a little girl"

"Liam, Dean say hello to your sister who wants to hold her first while the ambulance man helps clean up your mum" Liam stood forward

"Me, first as I'm the eldest"

"Only by minutes any way it was agreed with dad it would be him first then you then me" the boys seemed for a moment to forget what had happened to their dad

Chloe called Lisa to her and took her hand "Her name is Christine after Chris it was going to be Lily but after today I think Christine is better something for us to remember Chris by and she needs a second name do you mind if I call her Lisa after you as you was the one that helped her into the world"

Lisa went red "No not at all, now do you need us to contact anyone"

"There's Chris's parents and mine but I think the boys can deal with that there's just one thing I need you to do"

"What's that"

"Find the bastard that has done this the father of my children and lock him up for good"

"We will do I promise we'll get him; we're going to make a move now but a Family liaison officer will be here soon she'll help you as much as she can if you need to speak to me here's my number"

Lisa and Taffy did their goodbyes and went to the door the paramedic followed he looked at Lisa "are you all right love you look a bit pale"?

"Yes I'm fine all got a little bit too much in there but I'm ok"

"Ok I couldn't help but overhear what Chloe said to you I have to ask what happened to her husband"?

Lisa still didn't seem right so taffy spoke "I'm sorry to say he was murdered last night that's why we are here to give her the news then she went into labour"

"I heard the shout this morning are they the two sons that found him"?

"Yes they are"

"Oh, poor souls I'll get back into them and stay as long as they need you never know in circumstances like these someone may go into shock" he looked again at Lisa "Are you sure you're all right"

"Yes I'm fine and thank you for that as I told Chloe a Family liaison officer should be here soon so don't tie yourself up to much"

"No, it's okay my duty is to the patient so I'll stay as long as needs but I will echo the words of Chloe catch this bastard" with that he turned and went back into the house Lisa and Taffy headed for the car just as another ambulance pulled up they took no notice of them and headed into the house Lisa stood beside the driver's door with the keys in her hand Taffy took them from her "Here I'll drive"

They sat in silence for a little while before Taffy broke it

"You all right cariod"? (Cariod love) with that Lisa burst into tears Taffy pulled the car into a layby and leaned over to Lisa "yno, yno (there there) cariod you let it all out you did brilliant in there"

"Thank you but I can't help thinking that, that little girl is going to grow up not knowing her father and there's Elena's son left without his mother and the baby she was expecting and all because we can't catch this nutter"

"listen here you, you said it to Dai yesterday we'll get him he'll slip up somewhere along the way then we've got him now dry those tears and let's head back to the office and have a good strong cuppa"

"I could do with something stronger"

"So could I but we're on duty so let's get back"

They got back just after Dai and Alan Dai saw them come in

"All right you two how did it go"? he looked at Lisa "bloody hell Lisa you all right you look like you've been crying"

"Yes I'm Ok"

"No, she's not listen here you lot this young lady here has just delivered a baby girl I think she's still in a little bit of shock because I know I am"

Dai and Dave spoke at the same time "what how come"

Taffy was by the kettle now "go on Lisa tell them I'll make you a strong cuppa"

"Well, you know you told me she was nine months pregnant it seems last night she started having contractions they tried phoning Chris during the night but couldn't get hold of him that's why Liam and Dean went looking for him this morning for some reason they couldn't get hold of his mate he was playing cards with. Anyway, we got there told her the news she took it rather badly sat down I got Taffy to take the boys to make tea for us then as I sat talking her waters went then it all happened so quick I phoned for an ambulance but by the time it arrived I had delivered the baby with the help of the ambulance operator"

Paul spoke up "and where was you when all this was going on Taffy hiding"

"Bloody cheek I was holding the phone any way it's nothing to me I was there when my Bethan was born"

Lisa was sat her desk she still looked a bit pale Dai went to the drew in his office came back out and handed Taffy a bottle "Here put a drop of that in it I think she needs it" Taffy handed her the drink she took a sip looked at them both and smiled

"By that hits the spot"

Members of the team where coming over and shacking Lisa's hand or giving her tap a on the shoulder to say well done, Dai called the team together

"Right, everyone let's get down to business, as you now know we have another body this morning one Christopher Barker aged 42 married with children, as normal a note was left with the body but this time the killer also left the photos, now I need to find out all we can about Mr Barker as the note implies that he was a wrong un, Lisa are you up to telling us what you got out of Mrs Barker before all the action took place"

"Yes I'm ok right to start off with Mr Barker is not married Chloe is his girlfriend they were going to get married after the baby was born, up until the covid pandemic he ran a pub but due to the lockdown he had to sell up, the boys are his from his first marriage seems the wife had a breakdown after they were born and walked out on them after a few months Mr Barker then looked after them for a good few years before taking Chloe on as a Barmaid house keeper then it all went from there with them Mr Barker was a none believer in the pandemic he made every Saturday night during it a cards and drinks night with his mate at his house the mate never went to theirs as Chloe unlike her husband believed in the pandemic"

"Did she say what he was doing for a job now"

"No sorry I never got that far"

"Boss before it all kicked off with the baby I was talking to the lads in the kitchen It seems he had a part time job at one of the supermarkets driving one of the online shopping vans"

"Do they know which one"?

"No, they're not too sure he never really talked about it they use to ask him how his day was and all he would do is say ok nothing more than that"

"Right Taffy you follow that up ring round the supermarkets see if he worked for one of them"

"ok boss" Steve put his hand up

"Yes Steve"

"Boss my local supermarket does a thing where if you order online a small amount it is delivered by taxi it could be he worked for one of them"

"Right Taffy follow up too, now our killer has changed tacked on this one he has left a note saying why he has killed this victim, he also left two photos that at first I thought was of two different people but as Alan pointed out they are wearing the same ring in the photos now in the note he points out that our victim is stealing food and conning people into thinking he is homeless to obtain cash from them" Paul put up his hand "yes Paul"?

"Sir do you mind if I take a look a closer look at the photo"

"Sure, what are you thinking"? he handed the photo to Paul

"Sir a while back I nicked a guy who was doing the same thing I just wondered if it was Mr Barker" he looked at the photo

"Well,"?

"No sir it's not him"

"Ok team we need to step up the mark on this I don't want any more bodies on our hands, someone follow up on his social media Facebook. Twitter, etc now this photo looks as it's been taken outside the McDonalds in the city I need for someone to get some copies made and get up there and show them around see if anyone knows Mr Barker and what he was up to Dave you and me will go and see his mate he was playing cards with see if he can throw some light on things"

Vicky put up her hand "Boss do you mind if I go to the city I know it's a bit of a cheek but I missed breakfast this morning I could do with something to fill me up"

"Ok and take Paula with you and don't take too long on the food"

"Cheers boss" Taffy piped up

"You don't mean to tell me you eat that rubbish do you I can't stand them"

"It's better than the curries you eat look what the last one did your stomach"

"That wasn't the curry did that it was a bug anyway you can't beat a good chicken korma, rice, poppadom's after a good few pints and what's more you can have what's left for breakfast the next morning" the sound of the men in the team agreeing with Taffy got a little louder

"Oh, you're disgusting you lot warmed up curry for breakfast"

"Don't knock it till you've tried it" came out from a few of the team

"right folks let's get on you all have your tasks to do so let's get moving" Dai and Dave went to leave when a voice came from behind the team

"Dai sorry but I think I have found something"

Dai looked round to see Alex the translator standing there he felt himself go a little red he had forgotten he was there helping with Elena's stuff "Sorry Alex what have you got"?

"Well, I've been reading throw Elena's diary it been pretty hard because she has used a sort of code for some of the things she has been doing but I came across this one thing" he turned the laptop to Dai,

"Sorry, what I'm I looking at"?

"Yes sorry my fault I forgot you don't speck Romanian, this page here it's from about the time she started working for the agency. She describes a time when one night she was approached by a man who called her all the names under the sun a hoar, sinner everything and that she needed to stop what she was doing and turn to god"

"Does she describe this man"

"Yes about 1,76 meters tall wearing and black jacket and trousers and how do you say the thing round his neck that a priests wear"

Dave spoke "A dog collar"

"Yes that's it, and what's more he was carrying a large cross, she said he freaked her out"

"Bloody hell it looks like our killer was in touch with Elena, does she say anymore weather she saw him again"?

"No, she mentions him only the once"

"Right Lisa ring round the other families see if a priest has been in touch at any time it maybe that he has been just to recon the victim's, I'll be on my mobile if anything comes up"

"Dai and Dave headed out for Bancroft and Mr Barker's friend they found the house and knocked the sound of a large dog greeted them from behind it and a voice shouting at it

"Tyson back get here now" they could hear the sound of the dog scratching at the door "Tyson come here it's no one for you, sorry whoever it is give me a moment to put the dog out" they waited a few moments longer before the door was opened "sorry about that his bark is worse than his bite but he can be very playful when you are trying to talk to people, now gents what can I do for you

"Mr Collins I'm DCI Rees and this is DI Parker we would like to talk to you about Christopher Barker"

"Yes please come in can we get you a drink tea, coffee the wife's just put the kettle on" Dai said yes to a coffee and Dave a tea he called out to his wife "Patsy two more cups love one coffee one tea, sorry how do you take them" Dai asked for it white with sugar Dave asked for white with three sugars "the coffee white with sugar tea white three sugars and make it strong we have a fellow Yorkshire man" he turned to Dave "where are you from"?

"Just outside Rotherham you"

"Oh, I'm a Leeds man myself, now sorry I'm digressing you're here to talk about poor Chris not me take a seat" they took a seat on the settee

Dai started with the questions "Mr Collins I believe Mr Barker was here last night playing cards with you"

"Yes he was it's a thing we've done through the pandemic we use to play at Chris's pub but when he lost it we started playing here"

"About what time did he leave"?

"It Most have been about midnight it's only a short walk home for him from here" his wife came in with the drinks

"Sorry Graham it was about one o'clock don't you remember I sat up and watched that film on channel five that finished at one o'clock just as Chris was leaving"

"that's right I remember Chris looked at his phone to see the time but it was dead he asked me the time and said his goodbyes he wanted to get back to Chloe because of the baby being due any time now"

"So, he had his phone on him, what about his wallet"?

"He had both in fact his wallet had a few quid in it he fleeced me last night"

Patsy spoke "Fleeced you like hell he did, you let him win"

"Yes alright I let him win I felt sorry for him what with the baby coming and him not having a job"

"You're saying that Mr Barker never had a job, what about the driving job he had delivering for one of the supermarkets his family are under the impression that he worked for one of them"

"No that is my job I tried getting Chris in but they had no vacancies so he didn't get one that was about a month or so ago" Dave phone was ringing

"Sorry I've got to take this he went out into the hall "Vicky What you got for us"?

"Right boss we thought we would check with the centre MK security staff first and we struck lucky"

"How"?

"It seems Mr Barker is known to them but not as Chris Barker but Chris Parker a homeless man that they have had to shift on for begging, he's also a bit of a card sharp they caught him a few times taking money off people by playing chase the lady he fleeced one man of a hundred pounds the other day"

"Vicky was it not reported to the police"

"yes it was but by the time our guys got there he had disappeared "

"Ok keep going see if you can dig up any more see if at any point he was seen with a priest"?

"Will do boss" Dave went back into the living room Dai was just finishing his coffee

"Mr Collins you say you let Mr Barker win"?

"yes that's right"

"Now that was a colleague on the phone she has the impression from the staff at central MK that he was a bit of a card sharp"

"I'm not sure what you mean I wouldn't say he was a card sharp he could do a few tricks with cards and he was good with them but when it came to playing he was terrible and what's this about the centre MK"?

Dai took the copies of the photos from a folder he had "Mr Collins would you be able to explain these to us"? He handed them to him

"Well, that's Chris but who's the other guy"?

"It's a gentleman who Centre MK security staff know as Chris Parker a beggar they have had to move on a few times in the city"

"So, what's this got to do with Chris other than he's got a similar name Barker Parker"?

"If you look closely Mr Collins at the left hand and the ring on the middle finger"

He took a close look "That's the same ring" he went white "oh no you're telling me he went ahead and did it"?

Dave asked the question "Did what Mr Collins"?

"A few months ago, me and Chris were out I forget where but we saw someone begging, he turned to me and said that that would be the next thing for him if he didn't find a job I didn't take him seriously but it looks like he went ahead and did it"

"So, if you didn't know he was doing this, where did you think he was getting his money from"?

"The Social like everyone else"

"What about the clothes and all that you've never seen him in them before"?

Patsy spoke up "I have, remember that night at the pub Graham when he caught us all out"?

"Oh Yes that was so funny" they both stopped to think

"Sorry go on what happened"? Dave asked

Patsy continued the story "Well I was a barmaid at Chris and Chloe's pub that's how we came to meet, one day Chris said he and Chloe would be out for the day would I mind looking after the pub that evening I said ok, any way later in the night Graham had come in to check if everything was ok he didn't like it when there wasn't a barman at the pub you always felt that I needed protection didn't you?" Graham went red "Anyway this old man came in ordered a whiskey and went and sat at one of the tables in a corner he stayed there quite a while calling me over to get him another drink sometimes I would take it to him or Graham would, he sat there drinking then he started singing songs telling jokes he had the whole pub in hysterics but then he all of a sudden made a pass at me Graham saw red the poor old chap was well gone by this time but Graham was willing to show him the door"

"Then what a fight or what"?

Graham took up the story "No I grabbed at what I thought was the dirty old sod's jacket neck and was about to throw him out when his wig came off in my hand I stood there in shock when Chris turned round and revelled it was him all a long he wasn't even drunk no one of had noticed him switching the whiskey for a soft drink of the same colour"

"I always said he should have been an actor in film or telly I'm going to miss his funny sense of humour"

"Ok just one more thing we need to ask have either of you seen a priest or a vicar hanging round the area at all"? they both shook their heads "Ok that's all for now we may like to talk to you some more but in the meantime here's my card in case you think of anything"

Patsy spoke "Sorry but how is Chloe we've not heard a thing I hope she's not blaming us for this"?

"Oh, you've not heard she's had the baby one of my officers delivered her while she was giving her the news of Mr Barker"

"oh, she's had the baby was it the shock of being told about Chris"

"No, she was in pain during the night but could not get hold of Mr Barker on his mobile but as we've now ascertained his phone was dead"

"Why did she not ring here"

"I'm not sure I think she did ring your home number but could not get throw"

Graham went to one of the corners "That bloody dog he's chewed throug the cables again" he picked up the two halves of cable "and she wouldn't get us on our mobiles we turn them off at night poor Chloe do you think it would be alright to give her and the boys a call"?

"I shouldn't see why not she maybe needs to talk to someone she knows, but if you do call a family liaison officer may answer tell them who you are and I said you could call"

"Ok Thank you"

Dai and Dave said their goodbyes and headed for the car Dai's phone began to ring he looked at the caller number it was not one he recognised "DCI Rees"
"DCI Rees it's Holly Long"

"Miss Long if you're calling about the case I've already told you, you have to get have to contact the press office" he went to hang up

"No wait it's not about the case it's your dad"

Dave saw Dai go white "What is it"?

"It's my dad, Holly what's happened"

"I'm in Fenny covering another story as I came to the crossing by the pub in Aylesbury street I saw a man I now know as your dad crossing one car had stopped for him when another sped up behind it didn't stop and shunted the first car into your dad"

"His he hurt and how did you know he's my dad"

"the ambulance men seem to think he has a broken leg and maybe a cracked rib and a few cuts and bruises, I found out while I was sat with him who he was he mentioned you and when I said I know you he asked me to ring and let you know"

"Thanks for that Holly but how did it happen again I haven't quiet taken it in"?

"Right your dad was crossing from the side of the café to the pub side, one car had stopped for him it was a good way from him but as he got almost to the other side I heard the screech of brakes and this other car seemed to try and steer round the stopped car but instead it hit in the back and side sending it forward and to the left hitting you dad and sending him flying the traffic officer here as said if the car had not hit the crossing pole and the horse trough it would have gone over your dad"

"Thank you for that Holly can I speak to him"?

"sorry they've just left with him in the ambulance I did ask if I could go with him but as I'm not a relative they wouldn't let me" Dai heard a voice in the background "is that DCI Rees" "Yes it is would you like a word with him" "yes please" the phone was handed over

"DCI Rees, TC Oliver here traffic I'm sorry about your dad but it's just to let you know we have arrested a young male for dangerous driving, driving while under the influence of drink and drugs, no insurance, MOT, or licence"

"You've got him on the lot I see, what about the other driver is he or she ok"?

"Yes she's not a fault at all in fact this the lady was stopped totally we have seen dash cam footage of it she has a camera front and back so we have a clear picture of what happened, both the driver and passenger have whip lash they've been taken to
hospital for checks and so as the driver in the other car, I'll keep you up to date with everything I'll put you back to Miss Long now"

The line was quite for a moment "Holly are you there"?

"Yes I'm here just a little bit shaken but I'll be ok"

"Holly thanks again for looking after my dad I owe you one, now if you're not ok talk to TC Oliver and say I have asked for someone to run you home"

"No, I'm ok I've got my car here and I've spoken to my dad he doesn't want me to drive so he's coming with my mum to pick up me and my car, but thank you anyway bye"

With that she was gone Dai turned to Dave "Listen butty I'll have to drop you back at the station then head off to the hospital dad's been in an accident"

"What happened"?

Dai explained it all to Dave

"Listen Dai bugger taking me back to the station you head straight to the hospital I'll get control to send me a car out now go"

"You sure"?

"yes go now before I change my mind"

Dai headed straight to the hospital and parked up in what now seemed to be his normal place he headed for A and E as normal the reception was packed he waited for his turn to get to the counter

"Yes sir can I help you"? a rather snooty woman said

"Oh, Hi my father's been brought in after an accident"

"What's his name"

"Rees, Dafydd Rees"

She didn't look up just sat typing things into the computer "And you are"?

"I've just said I'm his son" Dai could feel his blood pressure rising

"Oh yes sorry, ah here we are he's just being checked in now if you'd like to take a seat I'll let them know you're here"

Dai took a seat he hated hospitals and he hated the waiting areas he looked around at all the people there some you could see what was wrong with them others you could not, if ever he was in there he would play a game with himself trying to guess what was wrong or if they were just wasting a doctor or nurses valuable time or not after what seemed a age a nurse came through "Mr Rees" Dai looked up "Your father can see you now" she handed him PPE to put on then She lead him through the double doors as Dai arrived he saw his dad laying in a bed "How be da"

"Oh, how be Dai bach as you see I've had a little accident"

"A little accident according to the traffic officer you are lucky to be alive"

"Oh, don't exaggerate it's nothing"

"Da Holly told me she was told by our traffic officer if it hadn't been for the light post and the horse trough the car would have gone straight over you"

"yes there is that but I didn't want to worry you"

"Da I am worried where was you going"

"I thought I would go for a walk down to the canal and also see if there was any rugby on at the fields but as you see I never made it"

"have the doctors looked at you yet"?

"No not yet as you can see they are rather busy what with this covid thing I'm surprised they let you in, the ambulance guy thinks I may have a broken leg but I'm not too sure" Dai pulled back the covers that were covering his dads leg

"Da you can see you have a broken leg the bone is sticking out of that gash there, you know that's the trouble with you, you never make a fuss even at a time like this"

"Oh boy that's nothing I saw worse when I was down the pit and what's to fuss about it's only a broken leg" He gave a cough and Dai saw him wince in pain

"And was you going to tell me about the possible broken ribs"?

"As I said what is there to fuss about it's nothing I'll soon mend" he winced again

"have they given you anything for the pain"?

"They gave me a shot in the leg to kill the pain before they put me in the ambulance, then in the ambulance they gave me what I think was gas and air, I thought they only gave that to women that were having babies and that helped"

"No, It's called Entonox and it used in other things now"

"Woo listen to you using the medical name, any way lets change the subject Holly's a nice girl isn't she"

"She is from what I can make of her I never really met her I've only spoken on the phone and seen her once at a press conference"

"Is she a reporter then"

"Yes she works for the local radio and press round MK"

"There's tidy, you should ask her to dinner"

"Da don't start this again she way too young for me"

"Not like that you silly bugger, As a thank you from me for looking after me, she did well I could see she was shaken how was she when you spoke to her"?

"Ok her mum and dad were coming to collect her as I think she was still shaken up a bit to drive home I did offer for a squad car to take her but she had already made the arrangements and we'll see how things go we may have to wait till this is all over before we can arrange a dinner" Dai felt his phone vibrate in his pocket he knew he should have switched it off in the hospital but he needed contact with the team he took it out and looked at it

"Duw (god) boy you just can't leave work behind can you turn the bloody phone off"

"Da you know I can't do that I'm the senior investigating officer on the case, any way it wasn't work as such it was Lisa asking after you"

"Tell I'm ok, she is a nice woman you know"

"Dad don't start that again" with that a voice came from behind Dai

"Good afternoon sir is everything ok"?

"Yes fine, just dad here trying to play match maker"

"Mr Rees is it I didn't realise that they did arranged marriages in Wales" She smiled at Dai "Any way I'm Doctor Banajee I understand you had a bit of a mishap with a car" by now a nurse had joined them in the cubical "Nurse could you help pull back the bandages and split please"

With that they began to remove the them Dai could see the full extent of the wound it was worse than he thought

"See it's not that bad, making a fuss of nothing"

"Not that bad Mr Rees I can see without an x ray that you have a compound fracture of the Tibia and that it's going to need some surgery, now let me look at your chest" his dad opened his shirt he saw the doctor pull a face as she looked at the blue-black scars on his body.

"Oh, take no notice of them doctor one of the hazards of getting a cut while down the pit coal dust gets into it and this is how they end up looking"

"The pit"?

"Sorry coal mine I was a miner, man and boy before they closed them all and" Dai interrupted

"Da they don't need your life story just let the good doctor here look at your chest" Dai saw his dad wince as the doctor felt his chest and rib cage

"Well Mr Rees I think you are lucky I can't feel any broken ribs but I think we'll send you for a x ray just in case, now let's have a look at that gash on the back of your head" Dai hadn't noticed the gash he was more concerned with his dad's leg he leaned in as his dad leaned forward "

"Bloody hell Dai give the doctor room to look" Dai leaned back it was a nasty cut but he could see that there was nothing else to it.

"Oh yes that a nice clean-cut Mr Rees not too much to worry about but we'll x ray that too just in case"

"X ray my head love you never know what you will find in there" Dai saw his dad wince again as he laughed

"Good well I'll leave you in the capable hands of Nurse Lee here she's going to glue your head for you"

"What no stiches to show off"?

"No, Mr Rees we try not to use stiches if we don't have to, but you may have a few to show off with your leg, bye for now" Dai followed her out.

"Doctor, thank you for that he's always making light of things I don't think he realised just how bad his leg is"

"That's ok they are made of tough stuff miners" she looked at Dai "Have we met before"?

"No, I don't think so"

"I could have sworn we had met" she looked at him again "Sorry I've got it now you're detective looking for that killer I saw you on the news the other day"

"Yes that's me"

"Right DCI Rees you have enough on your plate at the moment so why don't you go and leave your dad in the capable hands of the doctors and nurses of University Collage Hospital M K"

"Thank you doctor have you any idea how long things will take"

"I'm not sure at the moment we're snowed under with this pandemic but the way things are with your dads leg there's no concern about blood loss etc it just a matter of resetting the bone and putting a few screws in to hold it so they may take their time to operate"

"So, he'll be in here a while"?

"Oh yes that's for certain he will be"

"Right thanks again Doctor I'll go and give him the good news" as he turned he heard a loud crash from behind him and raised voices "Get away from me you bastard I'll stick you I promise" he turned and saw a young lad dart out from one of the cubicles followed by PC Joe Clarke he saw Dai "Oh come on sonny put down the scalpel you're in enough trouble as it is"

"No stay away I promise come any nearer I'll cut you I'm not afraid of any copper"

PC Clarke moved forward just as Dai came in from behind and tackled the lad to the ground Joe moved in and cuffed him "afternoon sir thanks for that, right up you get matey" the lad turned to Dai "Who the hell do you think you are I'll have you" before Dai said anything Joe turned the lad to him

"Now before you go mouthing off to this gent you should know this is DCI Rees he's a police officer too, now the reason he is here is because it's his dad you have put in hospital with your dangerous driving so I would keep your mouth shut before he really loses his temper now I can tell you that is something you don't want to see" the lad just smirked, another officer turned up and took him back to the cubicle still in cuffs Joe turned to Dai

"Thank you for that sir little bugger somehow got out of one pair of cuffs but I've made sure this pair are on good and tight, how's your dad"?

"He's ok thanks Joe he'll be in here for a while though they will have to reset and pin the leg, he's a cocky sod isn't he"

"To cocky he's only fifteen god knows what he'll be like in his twenty's, your dad is lucky I saw the state of the cars both a right mess"

"So, I understand are the ladies that where in the other car here"

"Yes, sir just over there they are not too bad both got a whiplash but nothing broken, it looks like your dad came off worse"

"It would seem that way, the lad doesn't seem to have much of an injury from the crash whys he here and what of his passengers"

"Oh, he didn't get injured in the crash sir it seems that after the crash he and his mates tried making a run for it, now according to a witness he jumped out of the driver's seat his mate in the back on his side jumped out at the same time he went to run to the back of the car his mate went to run to the front of the car and they both crashed into each other sending them flying, matey boy smacked his head on to the road all most knocked him out cold we have to get him checked out it's now procedure with head's, mind you it did help at least the witnesses were able to catch them both and hold them till we got there"

"What about the others"?

"They got away sir last seen legging it towards Water Eaton"

"Ok Thanks Joe I better go and tell dad the news he'll be in here for a while"

Dai turned and went back to his dad

"How be da I've just been talking to the doctor and I'm sorry to say it looks like you'll be in here for a while"

"I had a feeling I would be, was that commotion anything to do with you"?

"Yes it was the lad that crashed the car managed to slip his cuffs and pulled a scalpel on one of our PC's I just took him down"

"Gobby little shite I'd have given him the back of my hand if I wasn't in the state I'm in I may still do it"

"No, you wouldn't just keep you're self away from him, listen da I'll have to be making a move I'll pop by later with some p j's and cleaning stuff for you and I'll have to let Bethan and Bronwen know what has happened"

"Oh no Dai bach don't go worrying them I'm ok they'll only want to come up here"

"And what type of brother and father would they think I am if I didn't inform them and if they do come they can stay at mine, any way I'll catch up later bye da"

"Ok bye I'll catch you later"

Dai made his way out through the A and E main door his phone began to vibrate he took it out and looked at the screen Superintendent Wilcox "Sir"

"Dai I've just heard how's your father"?

"He's ok sir he'll be in for a while they are going to operate on his leg pin it back together but other than that he's fine"

"Right do you need any time with him take it Dave Parker can look after things till you come back"

"No that's ok thanks sir there's not much I can do while he's in there visiting hours are all up the shoot because of covid so I might as well keep myself busy"

"Ok but the offer is there if you need it"

"Thank you sir"

Dai hung up and rang Bethan and Bronwen both insisted that they came up and see to his dad while he was in hospital but Dai assured them all would be ok there was not much they could do while he was in the hospital, he made his way back to the office Lisa was the first to greet him putting her arms round him
" How be Dai how's your Da"? Dai looked up all the office was looking at him waiting for news on his dad.

"He's fine, he's got a broken leg that will need resetting with an operation and a few cuts and bruises, and the doctor thinks that his ribs are ok just bruising to them, he'll be in for a while"

"Oh, thank god for that I had visions of it being worse does he need anything"?

"No, he's ok for the time being but I will take him up some pyjamas and washing stuff later I have to find out where he will be the hospital is in full swing but with any luck he'll be on a ward" he changed the subject "right anything come up while I've been out"?

"Well sir I've looked into Mr Barkers Facebook etc makes interesting reading"

"Ok Mike fill us in with what you've found"

"Well sir Mr Barker was a nonbeliever in the pandemic he believes it's all down to the governments of the world coming together to cheat on the little men"

"His partner told us about that before she went into labour she believed in it and made sure he complied with the rules because of the baby" Lisa added

"He was a follower of Ukip believes in Britain for the British etc he's had many an argument on twitter and Facebook over it seems to have lost a few friends because of it"

"Seems a nice guy"

"yes but here's one thing he's put a post on about having an argument with a guy from a church who accused him of stealing from a food bank"

"Does he say where this was"?

"No sir just saying the bloke was a prat he's never stolen from food banks"

"Well, we have the note saying what he has done and the photos showing him dressed as though he was homeless so we can assume that that part of his post is a lie"

"Other than that sir there's not much on that side, but I could tell he loved his partner and sons there's loads of photos of them and scans of the baby"

"That's the impression I got from his sons boss when I spoke to them in the kitchen he loved his family and would do anything for them" added Taffy

"Boss I've had a look at his finances there are three accounts one that he shares with his partner, one for the pub they use to have then there's a separate account just for him, now when the pub was up and running every month money was taken from that account and put into the joint account under the heading wages the pub account was also used for paying the tax man VAT and all the breweries etc for the drinks and all the utility bills but then the first lockdown came and you could see it go down from there it looks like it closed in June last year the account then shows a large amount of money going in from a property company I assume that's when he sold up"

"So where has the money gone from the sale of the pub and how come he's taken to stealing food and begging Vicky does it say"?

"Well, some was used to pay off bills they still had over from when the pub was closed but most of it went into the third account for him"

"What just his not the joint account"?

"No boss it looks like his account mainly paid for online gambling he owed quite a bit of money to some sites so they were paid off but even after they were finished he still gambled the only thing that changed was if he had a big win all the money would go straight into the joint account and that's where it stayed he never took money out to pay for his gambling"

"So why the begging"

"Well in looks like the gambling was drying up he hadn't had a big win for a good while he wasn't in debt with it like before and he never let it go over his limit then every now and then he would pay some money into the account to cover his bets, also for the joint account they got payments from DWP so the money on that side was always in the green"

"So, he kept his family up to date with money and made sure they were ok but he just couldn't stop gambling"

"Looks that way sir"

"Right let's keep looking we now know the killer had contact with three of the victims Elena and Chris he spoke to, and he also sent the photo's direct to DJ family so he knew where they lived let's dig deeper see if he was known to the other three"

Paul and Paula arrived back from visiting the churches

"Hello, you two how did you get on with the churches"? enquired Dave

"Nothing as yet boss I never realised how many churches there is in Milton Keynes we've done about half so far in the south of the town but no show for our Mr Clements"

"Ok keep the rest till tomorrow someone most know this guy"

The team worked late but Dai left around seven thirty he went home and got his dads stuff and headed for the hospital, he found his dad in good spirits keeping the nurse's amused with his stories, he had been moved to a ward and with any luck his leg would be operated on in the morning, he stayed about half an hour then headed for home he needed sleep today had been a terrible day, he got home about nine, the house was cold he turned the heating on poured himself a drink and just sat there in the darkness of the living room he felt his eyes closing but he fought against it if he was going to sleep he needed his bed, he must have dozed off because the next thing he knew was his phone pinging to say he had a message he opened it up it was from young Holly saying she was sorry to bother him this late at night but she couldn't sleep and wondered how his dad was, he looked at his watch it had just gone twelve he must have crashed out he answered Holly and headed up stairs to bed. Dai woke at his usual time dressed and headed out for a run it had been almost a week since his last run and he felt it, he was back washed and changed by seven and headed out to the station,

Chapter Twenty-two

Saturday was spent taking photos of the wedding a lovely couple, it was a shame that their large families could not attend but he got some great photos of those who were there, then that night he taken his next sinner, Sunday morning he made his way to the church to clean up ready for that mornings service he put out candles, replaced the bible's into their places on the chair's he could never understand how people could be so untidy, before he knew it the vicar had arrived to take the service he sat and listened as he talked about the sinner who had committed those murders, he was no sinner he was the warrior of the lord the people who he had killed were the sinners the Reverend Mullen didn't know them like he did if he did he would understand why he was compelled to do the lords work, he went home just before one o'clock he took a frozen roast dinner and out and put it into the microwave, he had never bothered to learn to cook his mother had always done that for him, he had tried to learn while he lived in London but he could never master it plus there was so many good restaurants in London he was spoilt for choice he even took a liking to the fast food chains it was good and easy,

Sunday evening, he was back at the church for that evening service as he sat there his ears pricked up to the chatter of the ladies, the lady whose husband was a reporter stood out most he approached them "sorry ladies did I hear you right that the detectives who is in charge of the case father was in hospital"?

"Oh yes Stephen, young Holly rang my Brian to ask if it would be ok to run a story in the news tomorrow, but Brian said it would be better if she didn't DCI Rees has enough on his plate has it is"
"So what happened"?

"Well, it seems he was crossing the road down in Fenny on a pedestrian crossing when a car with a drunk driver hit one that had stopped to let him cross in the rear sending him flying"

"Was he injured"? asked one of the other ladies

"Yes he had a broken leg and bruises he was taken to hospital"

"Oh, that's terrible and you say it was a drunk driver"? his mind was already thinking could this be a new sinner he had been drunk driving and nearly killed someone so he could be a sinner he would have to see if he could find him

"Yes but they got him and one of his passengers they are in

police custody at the moment"

"That's great that they caught them hope they lock them up for a long time did you say one of his passengers"?

"Yes it seems there was four of them they got the driver and one of his passengers but two more got away, no regards for the poor man that had been knocked over"

His mind was racing these two were just as bad as the driver how could he find them? But the more he thought about it the more he realised that he could not he had to think what to do next. He would go home to think about it, then he had an idea maybe DCI Rees father would like a visit, yes that was it in the morning he would go and visit him, he could ask him questions about DCI Rees see if in the past he had been a sinner or was he always on the good side. He was just about to leave when one of the ladies caught him

"Oh, Stephen have you heard about George"?

"No wants happened to him"?

"He's only gone and got covid, he's pretty bad with it so it seems"

"Oh, that's a shame give his wife my regards when you next see her hope he's better soon" he had forgotten about Friday night but this explained why his sinners had not turned up, by the look of it, it could be a while before he could deal with those two but he would get them. As for tonight he would give it a miss these late nights sorting out sinner's was beginning to take its toll.

Chapter Twenty-Three

When Dai got to the office Lisa was already there and the kettle was on

"Bora da Dai, How be your da this morning"?

"I think he's ok I've not been able to get through to the ward this morning so I don't know, he was in fine sprits last night when I took his things in"

"That's good I've been thinking about him all night could hardly sleep, to think he comes all this way to see you and ends up in hospital"

"I know it was strange he was only here the one night but going home last night and him not being there just felt I don't know strange I know he's a cantankerous old sod but him being there when I got home that's something I've not had over the last few years"

"when are you going to see him next"?

"I'm not sure of visiting hours or if there is any because of covid I'll know when I get hold of the ward and it could be that he's having the operation on his leg"

"Well, when you do see him give him my love"

"I will do" the rest of the team began to arrive and all asked the same "How's your dad"?

Dave was last to arrive after asking after his dad he gave Dai a message "Ruth said she'll be doing the pm on Mr Barker at ten this morning do you wish to go along"?

"No, I better not could you go along I've a feeling I'm going to be tied up with the chief super and I think the sister of Elena is coming today"

"Oh, I thought that was tomorrow she is arriving in the country today"

"Yes you're right but I bet you that I have to meet up with the chief super"

"No thank you I lost a fiver to you already; I'll go to the pm as much as I don't like them"

"thanks for that Dave, right guys and girls what have we got anything"? the room looked blank at him "what we're still nowhere with finding this guy, how did we get on with door to door on Bancroft and Bradwell"?

"Boss we have one witness say's she saw Mr Barker at around one fifteen that night he was walking past her house she was letting her dog out when she saw him"

"Did she see anyone else"?

"No boss just him"

"Boss I've got CCTV from a house just across the road from where the lady said she saw him this fits in with the time frame but again no one else on it after he went past"

"OK that defiantly fits with time of death, the only thing is Mr Barker left his friend's house later than normal at around one am that means his killer must have been waiting for him from earlier in the night, right Vicky, Paula go back to the person who has the CCTV ask if you can look at an earlier time frame say from ten thirty eleven pm onwards it could be our killer went there earlier, Lisa, Taffy could you go back and see his partner and sons see if anything as come to mind, Steve can you and Alan contact the rest of the churches visit them if you can, Paul are you alright holding the fort here you look as if you had a hard night"

"Yes Sir, sorry sir I was chatting to the girlfriend last night I didn't notice what the time was, she was on her break at the hospital, she said it's a pleasure having your dad on the ward he's been cheering everyone up with his stories and singing"

"Oh god that means not much sleep in that ward if he started singing he never knows when to stop, any way if anyone needs me I'll be in my office"

Dai went into his office just as his mobile and office began to ring "How do they do that both ring at the same time"? he said to himself he looked at his mobile it was Bethan he cut he off and picked up the office phone "DCI Rees"

"Morning Dai" the unmistakeable voice of superintendent Wilcox "first things first how is your father this morning"?

"I'm not sure at the moment sir I've not been able to get hold of the ward to see how he is, but PC Stevens assures me he's in fine sprits his girlfriend is a nurse on the ward and he spoke to her last night"

"that's good the offer of time off still stands if you need it"

"No thank you sir I'm just fine"

"Good I hear also that DS Jones delivered a baby"!

"Yes sir the partner of the last victim went into labour while they were there giving them the news, it all happened so quick that the ambulance never arrived before the baby arrived"

"Oh, these things can happen so quick it happened with our last one I ended up delivering her on the bedroom floor, now do we have anything else to go on"?

Dai spent half an hour on the phone to the superintendent Wilcox he finished filling him in with the case then when he hung up he took out his mobile to phone Bethan back but before he could his office phone rang again "DCI Rees"

"Morning Dai" Maggie the Chief Superintendents secretary "The chief would like to see you at twelve thirty today is that ok"

"Yes that's fine I'll see him then"

Dai busied himself in his office with paperwork and ringing Bethan and Bronwen to let them know how his dad was, at eleven forty-five then headed out to see the Chief he had rang the hospital and got through to them he would visit his dad after seeing the chief. He parked up and was about to go in as DS Michael's came out.

"Afternoon sir how is your dad I heard he been in an accident"?

"Wow news travels fast around here, he's ok I'm going to see him after I've had my meeting with the chief"

"Oh, good luck with that sir, my DI as just been in to see him, he's in a foul mood"

"That's all I need what's upsetting him now"?

"the Met, the chief wants us to have the credit for nicking Gary Hackett, but the Met want to take the glory"

"Well, it was on our patch he was nicked so that must count"

"That's what he's saying but the Met said he was their man so it's down to them"

"Well, who are we to say let them fight it out between themselves"

Dai went in and made his way to the chiefs office; Maggie was sitting at her desk in the outer office

"Afternoon Dai you're nice and early"

"Yes got here a little quicker than expected"

"Would you like a coffee while you wait"? Dai could see her eyes giving him the once over

"Yes please" he took a seat, Maggie poured his drink and brought it over she leaned in close as she gave it to him he could smell her perfume it was so strong it nearly brought tears to his eyes. She leaned in closer and the top of her blouse fell so Dai got an eye full down it, he went red and turned away,

"Oh, silly me, sorry about that I keep forgetting how loose this top is, now I hear your dad has been in an accident how is he"?

"He's fine thanks Maggie I'm going to see him after I've finished here"

"Oh, that's good you know if you need any help I can come over and give you a hand"

Dai had to think quick "No that's ok thank you Maggie my sister will be coming up from Gloucester to take him home to her house after he's out of hospital"

"Well the offer is there if you want it" she put her hand on Dai's shoulder and as she took it away she let it brush his cheek, Dai hoped she didn't notice the cold shiver that went down his spine, as he sat waiting for the chief he couldn't help but look at Maggie as she sat behind her desk he had heard stories about her but he took no notice of them, and as asking her for help that was out the cold shiver hit him again this woman must be well into her sixties but the clothes she wore would be better on someone half her age, her phone buzzed "The Chief will see you now Dai" he spent about an hour with the chief he headed straight to the hospital he decided not to use the police parking as he was not on police business but use the multi-storey car park he was lucky to find a space on the lower floor as he pulled into it the car in front of the space pulled out he felt luck was on his side today he drove right through he was now even closer to the main doors of the car park, he took out a face mask and made his way to the ward his dad was on as he entered he bashed into a man coming out

"Oh, sorry my fault into much of a hurry" the man just smiled nodded his head and left without a word he found his dad sat up in bed looking a little drowsy "Afternoon da how be you"?

"Oh, ok boy I'm a little drowsy I'm going down soon for my op they've given he the preop. You just missed your friend he's just left"

"My friend da who was that I didn't see anyone I knew"

"The vicar said he knew you said he was a warrior of god"

"What da are you sure"?

"Yes boy he's just left you must have seen him black coat, black hair and a dog collar" Dai suddenly realized it was the man he had bumped into "Da sorry I've got to go I've a feeling you've just met our killer" Dai shot out of the ward into the corridor looking both ways he saw him off to the right heading for the main entrance he shouted "police stop that man" but no one seemed to take any notice he began to run nearly knocking an elderly person over no time to say sorry people moved to the side as he ran full pelt down the corridor he got to the main door to see the man by the crossing to the multi-storey "police stop" the man looked back and began to run he ran out in front of a car that nearly hit him it stopped with a great screech of brakes and a hand on the horn Dai sprinted after him and caught sight of him going up the main staircase he followed, this guy was quick Dai took the stairs two at a time he was gaining on him he was heading for the top floor has he got there he lost sight of him but has he got to the top of the stairs a figure came and side tackled him Dai felt himself being lifted into the air and over the rails he shot out an arm and managed to grab the rail at that point he heard a voice from below "Oh you stop" the man let go and Dai found himself dangling from the rail he heard the sound of feet heading up the stairs and a voice "Mr Rees sir hold on I've got you" before he knew it a hand came over the top and grabbed his and pulled and he came back up over the top "Mr Rees are you ok" Dai took a deep breath "Yes thank you Dwayne, thank god you came along"

"I saw what was going on, on the CCTV and thought you many need a hand"

"Thanks again" with that they heard the screech of tyres and horns blowing "Shit he's getting away"

"No, he's on the top floor if you get to the bottom now we should be able to cut him off"

Dai and Dwayne sprinted down the stairs Dai got to his car and opened it up just as a dark blue BMW came round the last line of cars Dai was not quick enough to get his car started it shot past him did a sharp turn and crashed through the barrier Dai followed him out hitting the two tones and blues and called control, "control I'm in pursuit dark blue BMW registration Golf Bravo 12 Alpha Bravo Charlie heading east on the Standing way he's now gone left, left onto the Marlborough street speed six zero"

"DCI Rees proceed with caution till we have other petrol's that can take up the pursuit"

"Control I am pursuit trained he is now approaching the roundabout for Marlborough street and Chaffron way he's taken the second exit still on the Marlborough street speed now seven five roads are clear still able to follow"

"DCI Rees we have a traffic officer heading towards you on the Childs way he should cut him off at the next roundabout" they got to the roundabout as the traffic car got there but the BMW managed to go round it the traffic car it fell in behind the BMW between that and Dai "Control the suspect has taken the third exit Childs way now heading east on the Childs way"

"DCI Rees Tango Charlie Five will now take over please stand down" Dai took no notice and kept up with Charlie tango five as they headed for the M1 at junction 14 an another patrol cars joined the chase to the motorway but dropped back as another traffic car joined them as the BMW took the left at the roundabout onto the M1 Dai stayed with them all along listening into Charlie Tangos Five running commentary The Triumph was screeching but it was doing well to keep up with them he heard Charlie Tango asking for another unit to come up to put on a TPAC (tactical pursuit and containment) but they were told another unit was about half an hour away Dai radioed through

"Control this is DCI Rees tell Charlie Tango Five to go for it I'm still with them and TPAC trained I'll bring up the rear"

"Dai this is Chief Superintendent Mackintosh you was told to stand down and let traffic take care of this"

"I know sir but I'm here now and I have the training and we need to catch this guy now before he gets into Northampton jurisdiction" Dai know this would get the chiefs attention after what happened with the Met

"Ok go for it but only if it's safe to do so"

"Yes Sir"

"Charlie Tango Five to DCI Rees are you ready to go on my mark"

"Roger that"

The TPAC went like clockwork with them bring the BMW to a stop on the hard shoulder, Dai shot out of his car and ran to the driver's door and pulled it open and dragged the guy out Dai looked in shock it wasn't the man he had chased it was a young man "Who the hell are you"?

"What's it to do with you"?

"Where's the vicar"?

"Who I don't know any vicar"

"Sir no one else is in the car just this guy who was you hoping to be here" asked TC Fitch the driver of Charlie tango Five

"The guy I was chasing at the hospital he was a vicar this car is the one we wanted to find in connection with the killings"

The face of the driver changed when he heard the word killings

"What do you mean Killings I've nothing to do with any killings"?

"Well, you're driving the car that was used by the killer so unless you start talking I think you are in trouble"

"Look all I know is some guy came up to me asked if I could drive when I said I could he offered me fifty quid to drive the car"

"And you never asked why"?

"Of, course I did he said it was a charity jail break in aid of the hospital he said if I was to see him running out of the door I was to gun it as a decoy"

"A jail break in a hospital, I think you're telling me porkies now what the true story"?

"That is the truth he never told me about no police cars chasing me when I saw the old car with blues following me I thought it was part of the jail break, it was only when the traffic cars joined in I realised it was for real"

"So why didn't you stop when you was signalled too, why carry on to the motorway"

"I knew I would be in trouble I'm a band driver I had my license taken away six months ago for two years driving without insurance"

TC Fitch spoke next "Well you're in a lot more trouble now mate no license, insurance driving without due care and I'm sorry but I need to give you a breath test"

"I haven't had a drink but I will confess to smoking some weed so you might as well add that"

"Ok, can I leave you to take him in and we'll need recovery for the car it needs to go to the forensic guys see if they can find anything"

"Yes sir I'll get into it straight away and thanks for your help"

"That's ok I quite enjoyed it brought back memories of when I was in traffic and I really wanted to catch the guy who is doing these killings, any way bye see you back at central"

"Yes sir" Dai wandered back to his car the traffic had almost come to a standstill as drivers slowed to look at what was going on, another traffic car had pulled up behind and the officer's from it where stood there waving the cars on and to speed up further down the motorway Dai could see a highways patrol was doing the same he got into his car and rang Dave

"Dai tell me you've got him"

"No such luck I lost him"

"But what about the chase we heard that the guy had been stopped by you and traffic"

"It was a red herring the guy was paid by our killer to make a run for it if he saw him running out of the hospital"

"Do you believe him"?

"I think he's telling the truth he didn't even put two and two together about the car, Dave I need you to go to the hospital see Dwayne see if he can give us any CCTV, and while you're at it thank him from me I never really got the chance what with the chase etc"

"What does he need thanking for"?

"I'll let him tell you I'll catch you back at the station, I'm just going to ring the hospital and find out how dad's op went, they were just taking him down and I had to run out on him"

"Ok mate, see you back at Bletchley"

Dai got into the car and joined the main flow of traffic he didn't fancy driving all the way to junction fifteen so he cut down the slip road used by highways and the traffic cars cut under the motorway and joined the south bound traffic, he'd only gone a few hundred yards when he saw blues in his mirror he turned on his to signal that he was police but the traffic car behind him still signalled for him to pull over Dai pulled off into a safety bay the traffic car followed and pulled in behind him the driver got out and approached Dai's driver's door Dai got out before he arrived

"Afternoon sir do you know why I pulled you over"

"Could it be that you saw me use the slip road that yourself and highways use"

"Spot on sir and now we have the fact that you have blues fitted to your car, now sir is this your car and do you have any id on you, driving licence anything like that"

Dai handed him his warrant card

"DCI Rees I'm sorry sir are you the one that has been involved with chasing down that BMW"?

"Yes I am, I'm just heading back to MK now I didn't fancy the twenty-five-mile round trip up to junction fifteen" Dai saw another traffic car pull in behind the Northampton traffic car TC Fitch got out

"Afternoon Rav you giving our DCI here a telling off"?

"Oh, hello Fitchy no not really I saw him do a u turn by cutting under the motorway and being an old car, I thought I'd give it a tug I was waiting on the details coming through when DCI Rees pulled over"

"Yes I must say DI Rees must have the oldest squad car in the Thames Valley fleet but I'll tell you what it kept up with us in the pursuit"

"Ag that's not down to the car it's down to my driving" Rav looked at him gone out "I was in traffic in South Wales before I came to Milton Keynes and I try as much as I can to train with the guys every now and again"

"You'll have to come up to us sometime maybe we can teach you a thing or two"

"I'll hold you to that, now can I get underway I have a killer to catch"?

"Yes of course you can, and sir I hope you catch him"

"So do I Rav so do I"

Dai got back onto the motorway and headed back to MK his mind was racing he really thought he had the guy but no he was one jump ahead of him this guy had planned everything and how did he know his dad was in hospital apart from the team and his family he had not told anyone he was so engrossed in his thoughts that he missed junction fourteen for MK he would have to go to thirteen and come back on himself. At the time

Dai was heading back Dave had got to the hospital and tracked down Dwayne in the security office,

"Hi Dave, how are you going did DCI Rees catch the guy"?
"I'm fine thanks Dwayne no he didn't he slipped through the net I'm here because we need to go through the CCTV"

"I thought you might I've got it set up over here on this machine If you come round I'll start it up" Dave went behind the counter and took a seat "I've got it set from the time I first saw Mr Rees chasing the guy, see here this is the guy entering the multi-story he then heads up the stairs followed by Mr Rees at this point I ran out to see if I could help" he switched to another camera "Now this is the guy on the top floor you can't see Mr Rees yet but this is the moment Mr Rees gets to the top and the guy lunges out at him pushing Mr Rees over the rails" Dave felt himself go white

"What the hell" he saw Dai grab at the rail and hold on then watched as Dwayne arrived to pull him back "This is why Dai asked me to say thank you, it's a good job you followed him up"

"All I saw was him flying over the rails I knew I had to get to him, by the time I got there the guy had disappeared from view I pulled Mr Rees back and we and heard the car come screeching round the parked cars so we ran down to the bottom floor"

"Have you got CCTV of where the car was parked and who was driving"?

"This is the car backing out of its space on the top floor now the top floor is normally used as staff parking it can't have been there long because I do rounds to make sure everyone is parked right and has a permit and I didn't notice it when I was up there"

"Have you the time it arrived"?

"Yes one thirty but I had finished my rounds by then" he put up a still photo of the car entering the car park Dave could just about see the driver "this is him arriving but you can see he has a passenger"

"That's more than likely the guy he had driving for him as the decoy, right have we any other shots of the top floor this guy just can't have vanished"?

"Right, this is the top floor as you can see there's no one on there at the time the car speeds off it just seems to back out for no reason" they followed the car on its way out of the carpark to the point where it crashed the barrier "now has you can see there are people all around but none of them match our guy" he left the video running

"This guy is getting to me we're nowhere near catching him and when we think we are no he vanishes again" all this time Dave was watching the video "Hold on Dwayne wind that a back a bit" Dwayne did as he was told "There what's that" Dwayne froze the frame "A guy on a bike" Dave took out his phone and rang the office Paul picked up "Paul I need you to ring Mr Bridesdale Mr Hanson's employer ask him what type of bike was it that the bloke crashed outside their unit a racing bike or mountain bike, is Vicky back yet from seeing the woman who had the CCTV of the last victim"?

"No Sir I've not seen her yet"

"Right don't bother ringing me back I'll be back in the office soon" he rang Vicky she picked up straight away

"Yes boss"

"Vicky are you still looking at the CCTV with the witness"

"No boss we left about ten minutes ago, there was no sign of anyone else on the video"

"What about someone on a bike a racing bike" Dave could hear Vicky thinking

"Hold on I'm not sure, yes Paula pointed out someone she remarked it was a funny time to be out on a bike, I didn't take any notice because I was looking for someone dressed as a vicar or priest why"

"I'll explain when we all get back to the office, thanks see you there" he hung up "Dwayne do you think" before he could finish his question Dwayne handed him a DVD disc "

"I'm one step ahead of you all the video you need is on their"

"Cheers Dwayne I owe you a pint and I'll make sure Dai buys you one to, now I've got to get back see you soon"

By the time Dave got back all the team was there "Dai I think I've got something team gather round he put the disc into a DVD player and pressed play he fast forwarded it he was going to stop it at the point he saw the guy on the bike but Lisa keen eye saw the bit of Dai going over the railings

"Whoa stop it there Dave go back a bit yes there" the whole team gasped as they saw the guy lunge at Dai and push him over the railings "Dai was you going to tell us about this or what"?

"It had slipped my mind, anyway I knew Dwayne was on his way up"

"It was a bloody good job you manged to catch the rail boss or that could have been it for you" added Steve

"I'm ok so Dave carry on what have you found" Dave played on to the point of the guy on the bike

"It's this Dai we've been wondering how we've not had the car on our radar it's because he's using a bike, Paul did you find out from Mr Bridesdale about the bike he saw"?

"Yes sir it was a racing bike"

"Vicky what was the bike you saw"?

"Sorry boss it was just a bike as far as I could tell" Paula spoke up

"It was a racing bike boss drop handlebar"

"Now when PC Rahman brought in the photos that where left on his patrol car the only person he saw was a guy on a bike he thought he had come from the firm that did bikes on the estate I think it was our man, I think he's using the redways and a bike to make his way round MK"

"Sir when you rang in about a bike I had a quick look at the photos the drug squad sent over and I found this" he stuck a photo of a guy on a bike on the white board "I also had a quick look at the CCTV from around central at the time of the press conference and I found this" he put up a still photo from the CCTV "This is round the side of the police station if I could use the DVD player"

"yes sure" he took out the DVD that Dave had put in and put his own in and pressed play

"Now this is from that day taken from a camera that overlooks the road at the side of the police station, and here we have a guy arriving on a bike he then disappears but then around twenty minutes later comes back he doesn't come out of the other end of the road so he must have stopped somewhere along there but we do have this guy coming and going into road from the opposite end to the bike guy"

Dai came over and studied the photo's "This could well be our guy he's around the same build, but I can't tell for definite because of the glasses he has on and the helmet right good work Paul, Dave it looks like we now have a lead, right let's get onto the CCTV guys see if we can trace this guy's movements he must show up somewhere else on the redways, Paul you and Alan go to that street see if there are any people in the buildings may have seen him on that day"

"Yes boss"

"Right folks let's get on Lisa, Taffy how did you get on with Mr Barkers partner and son's"

"Ok Dai, there's nothing more they could tell us that we didn't already know they're all shaken up still but the baby has stopped them from getting to down"

"Did you ask them about his work and what we found out"?

"No, the friend had already told them about it, one of the twins said he had a feeling that things were not right a mate of his had said he'd seen his dad in the city but he didn't believe him"

"Right let's keep working I'll be in my office if anyone needs me" he went to his office Lisa followed and closed the door behind them she then slapped him on the shoulder "You stupid bugger what was you thinking you could have been killed"

"Lisa what did you want me to do I was chasing a suspect I couldn't let him go"

"I know but seeing that on the video just shocked me I know you are ok but for a moment I thought what if you hadn't caught hold of that railing what if the security guard had not been there"

"Lisa to many what if's I'm ok and we have more leads" he saw a small tear form in her eyes "Look thank you for caring it means a lot now before everyone starts talking dry your eyes and let's get on with our work" he put his arms round her "there will a cwtsh (cuddle) put you mind at rest" she looked up at him and smiled

"Right, I'll get back but don't you go running into things like that without back up"

"I had back up Dwayne the rock Jonson was behind me"

"Dwayne the rock Jonson pull the other one"

"No, it's true the security guy that pulled me back his name is Dwayne Jonson"

"Well, I never, I almost forgot how's your da"

"He's ok I'm just waiting on a call to say how the operation went but when I spoke to the ward earlier they said he was fine"

"that's great I'll get back" she left and Dave Knocked and came in

"You alright mate, shame about the car driver not being our man"

"I know as I was chasing him I really thought I've got you now, but when we pulled him over and it wasn't him my blood boiled how could he outwit us again"

"He's crafty Dai he's had us looking for that car all along and he's not even been using it"

"The thing that gets me is the guy he got to drive it thought it was all a game, he told him that it was a charity jail break to raise funds for the hospital and that he was his decoy"

"if he thought it was game why did he crash the barrier"

"Do you know what I hadn't thought of that why did he crash the barrier, I'll have to ask him when I see him, anyway, how did the pm go on Mr Barker"

"Oh, as well as can be Ruth couldn't tell us much more than we know, she said she feels she's just going through the motions with them they are all very much the same, although she did find some black fibres under the victims finger nails she's sent them to forensics to see if they match the ones we already have, oh and she found what looks like puse on the back of his head she thinks it may have come from our killer"

"It well may be but unless we have a match to DNA we're still no further forward"

"It may match the blood found on the notes and photos"

"That's true but without a match on the DNA data base we're as I said no further forward"

"Oh, ye of little faith, we're going to get this guy Dai it's starting to come together bit by bit like a puzzle, a thousand-piece puzzle but it's coming together" Dai mobile began to ring "I'll let you take that" Dave turned and left.

"Bethan how be"?

"I'm ok dad just ring to see how grancha is"?

"He's fine he's in having operation and will be back on the ward soon, I was going to see him tonight but I think it best I leave it till tomorrow"

"Yes I think you're right he may still be groggy after the anastatic, best to let him sleep how are you any way any joy with catching your killer"?

"I'm fine I thought I had got the guy earlier on today but no joy"

"Oh, dad I'm so sorry this must be so frustrating for you are you sure you don't want me to come up I can take a few days leave"

"No, no don't you dare everything here is fine, anyway you're needed at the hospital you work at more than ever with pandemic, plus grancha is going to be in for a good few days, so there's not much you can do, listen there is one thing you can do for me ring your auntie Bronwen and the rest of the family and let them know how your grancha is"

"Ok dad I'll do that but if you need me there just ask"

"I will promise bye I'll keep you up to date"

"Bye dad"

Dai internal phone rang

"DCI Rees"

"Dai Colin here just to let you know we've had the car turn up but so far it's pretty clear two sets of prints one I think we'll match to the guy that was driving it when you stopped him, the other I've a feeling is going to be the owners, but we did find blood and it matches the blood found on the notes and photos"

"That's great at least it puts our killer in the car"

"It looks that way we've searched it for anything else but nothing that sheds any light on who it may be hold on a minute Dai one of the guys has just found something" Dai could hear talking in the background "Dai one of the guys has found a wallet under the front seat it's got cards in it in the name of Hanson there's cash to quite a lot and a note saying give this to his wife she needs it"

"Is the phone there"?

"No just the wallet I'm getting one of the guys to test it for prints, sometimes people don't realise that we can get prints off of soft stuff too not just hard surfaces"

"Cheers for that Colin let us know what you find"

"Will do bye" Dai went back into the main office

"Right folks this guy needs to be caught he's getting cocky now, that was Colin from forensics they have found Derek Hanson's wallet in the car with a note telling us to hand it to his wife, it's got the bank cards and cash in it" in the background a phone rang Steve picked up "Sir that was the Romanian embassy they will be here at ten in the morning" "Cheer's for that Steve"

Chapter Twenty-four

Has he sat having his evening meal he reflected on the day bumping into DCI Rees like that had not been in his plans, he should have not gone when he had but he needed to see the father he had hoped to find out things about DCI Rees but he hadn't all his dad had talked about was his accident he got nothing he was very sleepy the fact they had given him the pre-med, he had not expected DCI Rees to come after him and he was quick he had caught up with him in no time, he didn't expect him to go over the railings when he picked him up he had only wanted to push him to the floor but the momentum carried him it was lucky that he had grabbed the rail, he was going to stop and help him back but the security guard coming up the stairs like that had made him run, he knew he would safe him. He looked at his hand the cut had become infected and turned green with it he had tried to book a doctor's appointment but to no avail he had bathed it in salt water like his mother use to do whenever he had a cut but that had not helped at this rate he would have to go and see a doctor at the walk in centre but at the moment he felt it best to stay away from the hospital he may well bump into DCI Rees again, he took his dishes and washed up dried them and put them away then went into the living room he had put all the photos of his victims on the wall he looked at them who would be his next victim ? Could it be the lad he had seen with Diji? No there was still police around his house he had seen them when he rode past, what about that councillor he had seen with the girl? He was another who was cheating on his wife the others he had seen with her he didn't know but the councillor he had seen in the local papers he was easy to find but he had not seen him around since he had killed the girl so he would have to find out some more about hi, then there was this guy he had seen him at the flat the girl had used he had taken money of the girl could he be her what is it they call them pimp yes that's it pimp he would be worth finding out more about him he would have to think about it he had missed Friday night because of his victim having covid, he had decided to give tonight a miss too maybe that would lull the police inti a sense of false security thinking he had finished, so tonight he will give it a miss.

Chapter Twenty-Five

Tuesday morning came and Dai made his way up to central for the meeting with the people from the Romanian embassy and Elena's sister, he had spoken to Chief superintendent Mackintosh the night before and he had decided that he would like to be present at the meeting, he got to central a little early hoping to grab a coffee from the canteen his milk at home had gone off but as he walked in he was greeted by Sargent McGinty "Sorry to bother you sir but the chief said if I was to see you I was to say go straight up"

"Cheers Paddy are the vending machine's working I'm dying for a coffee"?

"Yes sir the one on the floor near the chiefs office, but I must say sir I thought you would have held on and let the lovely Maggie make you one"

"Cheers Paddy you're all heart I suppose I'll have to make do with one of hers"

"You're welcome sir"

Dai made his way up to the chief office Maggie was sitting at her desk "Morning Dai go straight in; do you want coffee I've just made the chief one"?

Dai felt a little relief that he didn't have to wait around in the office with Maggie "Yes Please Maggie" he knocked and went in.

"Morning Dai I trust everything is ok with you"

"Yes sir I'll just feel a lot better when we catch this guy"

"So, will I, how are we getting on with tracing him"?

"Well sir as you know we thought we had him after chasing the BMW but that turned out to be a decoy but DI Parker came up with something" Maggie entered with his coffee" thank you Maggie"

"Yes you said something about a bike last night when we spoke"

Dai had so much going on in his head he had forgotten what he told the chef "Yes sir Di Parker noticed a guy on a bike coming out of the multi-storey carpark soon after I had set out to chase the car, it made him put two and two together because a guy on a bike had been seen outside Derek Hanson's work place and the PC who brought the photos and notes to us saw a guy on a bike too, now after looking at more CCTV we are almost certain the guy on the bike is our man"

"That's great at least we will have something to tell the Romanians when they arrive, what time will they be here"

"Any time now sir I said ten"

"Right, it's almost that now, by the way how is your dad"

"He's doing well sir he had the operation on his leg yesterday and when I spoke to the ward this morning they said he was doing fine and that all went well"

"That's great Dai" with that there was a knock at the door Maggie entered "yes Maggie"

"Sir the people from the embassy are here Sargent McGinty showing them up now"

"Thank you for Maggie, right Dai I'll let you take lead on this of you don't mind you have more of the facts than me"

"Yes that's fine sir" it wasn't but Dai could not say that me had never had to deal with embassies before he had delt with the relatives of dead people but this may be different the door knocked again and Maggie lead in three people two men and a young woman Dai could tell straight away that she was Elena's sister, the lead man held out his hand to the chief, the chief took it "Good morning sir I'm chief superintendent Leroy Mackintosh and this is Detective Chief Inspector Dafydd Rees he's in charge of the investigation"

"Good morning gentlemen I'm Ambassador Baicu of the Romanian embassy this is inspector de politie Caragaile of the Bucharest police he has accompanied Miss Adamacha her to recover her sister's body and child" Dai saw he chief look at him and knew it was his turn to speak

"Good morning Miss Adamancha may I first offer our condolences to you and your family on the death of your sister and assure you we are doing everting in our power to catch the person who has done this" "thank you sir but I just need to take my sister and her child home to the family I thought that is where we were going now"

"Yes of course, but first if you don't mind I have some question I would like to ask you"

She looked at both men and spoke to them in Romanian it was the Police officer that answered in good English "Crina you have nothing to fear DCI Rees only needs you to answer some background questions about Elena isn't that so DCI Rees"?

"Yes of course, I understand how upsetting this is for you but it would help us if you could fill us in with some things"

"Yes of course I will, go on ask your questions"

"Miss Adamanacha when the was the last time you spoke to your sister"?

"Over two years ago I haven't spoken to her since I left to go home"

"I see and why was that"

"We had a falling out I wanted to go home to our mother she is not in good health I wanted Elena to come with me but she wouldn't"

"What about your mother was she in contact with her, we know she was sending money home to her"

"My mother cut her off the money she sent is still in a bank account in Budapest it's never been touched"

"I see"

"No, you don't my mother wanted us back has a family it broke her heart when Elena would not come home and it's broke her heart even more to find out she as a grandson"

"Miss Adamanacha I can understand that this is hard for you so I think we will call it a day and we'll go and collect your sister and Daniel, he is with Mr and Mrs Comea I believe he was your old landlord"?

"Yes he was, Daniel is that the little boys name"?

"Yes he's two years old Mr and Mrs Comea use to look after him while Elena was at work so social services allowed him to stay with them until you arrived to take him home, right shall we make a move do you need us to supply a car or do you have transport"?

The ambassador spoke "We have transport if you have a post code we can give to our driver we will meet you there"?

"Yes by all means where do you want to go first"?

"We will collect Elena first we have our own undertaker to ship her body then we will go and collect Daniel"

"Yes that's fine"

"DCI Rees do you mind if I travel with you" asked inspector Caragiale "I have some questions I would like to ask" Before Dai could answer the chief spoke up

"Of course, and I will travel with ambassador Baicu and Crina, right shall we go"?

While Dai was with the chief Dave Parker had taken a call from Mary he headed out and arrived at the house at around ten fifteen he rang the bell Mary answered

"Oh, Dave sorry to bother you but I think you should hear what Tommy as just told me" Dave followed Mary into the living room where Tommy sat. "Mr Parker sir it's him sir I've seen him" Tommy was getting excited

"Tommy calm down please who is it you've seen"

"The man the one that killed the wee lassie I've seen him Mary showed him to me, show him Mary"

Dave turned to Mary "What is it Mary"

"Well Dave I was going through some of my old photos we do it sometimes as a social thing, when Tommy saw this one" Mary showed him a photo of herself with a young man

"Who is this Mary"

"He's an old boyfriend of mine I dated him back in the late nineties until his mother put a stop to it, Tommy here is insistent that he is your killer"

"He is Mr Parker it's him I no forget that face"

"Mary have you a name for this man"

"Yes Stephen Muller his father was German and Mother English the last I heard his parents had passed away and he was working as a rector at the church his parents looked after"

"Mary are you sure it's Muller"?

"Yes Muller as I said he was from German ancestry" Dave could see her thinking

"Mary do you know his Mother's maiden name"

"Yes it's Clements, no wait Stephen told me once he was going to change his name by deed poll yes I remember now someone telling me he changed it just after his father died"

"Mary do you have an address for him I'm sorry to say but I think Tommy is right we have been looking for Stephen Clements"

"Well last I heard he was living in his parents old house I think I still have the address somewhere"

"Cheers Mary and Tommy if this is right I owe you a drink"

As Mary was looking up the address Dave phone began to ring in his pocket "DI Parker"

"Boss It's Mike I think I've found him the guy has changed his name by deed poll It's Stephen" before he could finish Dave finished it for him "Yes boss how did you know that"

"Tommy McClintock saw a photo of him it's an old one but Tommy knew him straight away, have you informed Dai and what about warrants"?

"I've not been able to get hold of the boss he's with the chief, and Lisa's on to the magistrate for the warrants now"

"Great let me know when she has them and I'll get hold of Dai" he rang off and dial the chiefs office Maggie answered "Maggie its DI Parker is DCI Rees still there I need to talk to him it's urgent"

"They are just heading out hold I'll catch them" the line went quite then picked up "Dave what have you got"

"Dai we've got him Lisa is getting the warrants now"

"What how" Dave explained all to Dai

"Right give me the address we'll meet up there"

"Ok boss, see you there"

Dai came off the phone "Sir sorry can I leave you to look after these good people, we have had a breakthrough in the case and I need to be there"

"Yes go I'll sort everything here" Dai turned to leave but was stopped by Inspector Caragiale

"Sorry Detective Rees but I couldn't help but overhear are you making an arrest"?

"With any luck yes"

"Would you mind if I tag along I will not get in the way, I just feel it would help the family if an officer from their own country was there to confirm the arrest" Dai turned to the chief who in turn turned to the ambassador who gave him the nod "I shouldn't see why not but only as an observer"

"Thank you sir"

Dai and inspector Caragiala headed out and got into Dai's car for once nothing was said about the car the inspector was first to speak "DCI Rees I thank you for this, Carina has not shown it but I can tell you It has hit her family badly"

"The name is Dafydd but everyone calls me Dai and It's a pleasure it would be great if you can go back to them and tell them we have the killer, we need him off the streets so far he has killed five people and from the notes he has left he isn't intending to stop there, he even nearly killed me"

"My name is Florin, sorry you say he almost killed you how"?

"My father is in hospital I went to see him and our killer had been into see him I gave chase and as I got to the top of some stairs he throw me over the top if it wasn't for me managing to grab a rail and the security guard I wouldn't be here now so I'm determined to get this guy"

"So, this is personal you have every reason to catch him"

"Every case is personal until the killer is caught"

"Yes I see what you mean I've quite a few cases like that back home" Dai's phone rang

"Dave speak to me"

"Right Dai Lisa has got the warrants and is heading there now I'm on my way too, we have uniform standing buy with the big red key so we're already to go when you get there"

"Righty we're under five minutes out see you soon" he hung up Florin gave him a look

"Big red key what is that"?

"It's the nick name we have for a battering ram we use to gain entry to a home it's handheld by one person and for some reason it's painted red"

"I will stand back when we get there I don't want to be in your way"

"That's ok so will myself and team until the uniform lads have gained entry and succoured the site you can follow me in when I go" Dai glanced to his left he could see Florin swaying from side to side as he took the roundabouts "you said you have questions for me what where they"

"It doesn't matter now I was going to ask you to fill me in on the case but now we are going to possibly catch the killer, but I still have one question"

"Well, what's that"

"Why does this town have so many roundabouts I've never seen so many in my life"

Dai smiled "That Florin you will have to ask the planers, ah here we are" Dai pulled in behind a riot van and got out Lisa and the rest of the team pulled in behind him "Lisa you got those warrants"?

"Yes here's the entry warrant and I have the arrest warrant" Dave arrived

"Ay up boss I see the gangs all here plus one" Dave said straight to the point,

"Yes everyone this is inspector Caragiala of the Bucharest police he is over with Elena's sister and will be observing the search and arrest, right we're good to go where's the sergeant in charge of the uniform guys"

"I'm here sir" Dai turned to see sergeant McGinty "we're all ready to go when you are I have pc's front and back just say the word"

"Right lets go for it" sergeant McGinty give the word and the uniform guys moved in the lead knocking loudly on the door and shouting, "Police open up" Florin turned to Dai

"Dai you have no firearms"

"No, we don't use firearms in this country if we don't have to, the first officers at the front and rear doors have a taser if they need it but I don't think we'll need them"

The door opened and Dai saw the face he had seen at the hospital he took the warrant from Lisa and went forward "Stephen Clements I'm arresting you on suspicion of the murders of Diji Okore, Ryan Carter, Elena Adamacha, Derek Hanson and Christopher Barker you do not have to say anything but may harm your defence if you do not mention when questioned something which you later rely on in court, Anything you do say may be given in evidence do you understand"

"Yes I do DI Rees and may I ask how your father is"?

Dai just looked at him and then said to the uniform Pc "Take him away"

By now officers had filled the house Dave called Dai from the living room "Dai you better look at this" Dai went into the living room followed by Lisa and Florin one whole wall was covered with photos Lisa spoke first

"Boss these are all his victims there's DJ, Ryan, Elena, Derek and Chris but who are all these others"

"I'm not sure I just hope that there are no more bodies out there that we haven't found" Dave shuck his head.

"I don't think so Dai look here the victims that he has killed so far have a red cross in the corner none of these have"

Florin was stood there beside them "this man he was mad, did he think he could kill all these people and get away with it, I have seen some bad things in my country but nothing like this"

"Boss, look at this it's young Andy and this here is the councillor who we know was with Elena the night she died" pointed out Lisa, a voice came from behind them

"And that's William Morris, Elena's pimp or as he likes to call himself boss" Paul said. Florin had been studying the photos

"Excuse me Dai but I have just noticed this photo, it looks like your man and there is a woman with him and next to the woman there is a red cross"

"Right, we need to find out who this is, it looks like we have another body we don't know about" a pc came in from the back of the house "Sir I think you should see this" Dai and the others followed him through to the back of the house and the shed that held his dark room "it looks like he had more victims lined up sir"

Dai looked in amazement there in the dark room was more photos hanging up on lines like washing

Lisa let out a whistle "how many people was this man planning to kill there must be upwards of a hundred"

"He's a mad man Lisa who knows what goes on in the mind of a mad man, the day they work that out will be the day the world becomes a better place. Right, I think we need to be having words with Mr Clements or Muller whatever name he likes to use, Lisa you with me Dave are you ok to take charge of things here"

"Yes by all means Dai I'll see you back at the station later"

"Florin can I leave you with one of our PC's he can take you to meet the ambassador"?

"Yes of course you have a lot to do I am just glad that you gave me the opportunity to see this guy arrested I can now tell the Elena's family justice will be done thank you" he held out his hand to Dai

"Our government advise us not to have close contact because of covid but what the heck we're both wearing gloves and masks" with a shake of a hand both went there ways.

Dai and Lisa made their way back to central went in and found the duty sergeant

"Morning sergeant Foote I trust you have our man safely locked away"?

"And good morning to you sir and you Lisa I've not seen you in a while, now your man has been booked in and we've given him a nice comfy cell, he's made a call to his lawyer, it's one that is just around the corner so he should be here soon"

"That's great when he arrives give him time to have a chat then show them into an interview room and give us a call, we'll be in the canteen I need a cuppa" as Dai and Lisa made their way to the canteen Chief superintendent Mackintosh was coming the other way

"Dai, sergeant Jones I hear we have our man"

"Yes sir we're waiting on his lawyer to arrive then we'll interview him" explained Dai

"You are sure it's him"?

"Yes sir we have all the evidence we need at his house, photos the rope and cross the lot"

"So, we have enough to charge him with the five murders"

"Yes sir but we think we may have a sixth victim, he had photos on his wall of all our victims and beside them was a red cross but we also have a photo of him with a woman and next to the woman is a red cross"

"Right keep me up to date I'm just going to ring superintendent Wilcox give him the news"

It was a good fifteen minutes till the lawyer turned up another fifteen while he talked things over with Stephen Clements, Dai and Lisa made their way to the interview room as they entered Stephen stood to greet them.

"DCI Rees how are you; you never answered my question at the house how is your father"?

Dai ignored the question "Take a seat Mr Clements please"

"Stephen call me Stephen please"

Lisa placed a disc in the recorder and pressed record "The time and date are sixteen hundred hours on Tuesday Thirtieth March 2021 and this is an interview with Mr Stephen Clements also known as Stephen Muller in the presence of myself DS Lisa Jones, DCI Dafydd Rees and Mr Clements Lawyer Mr Giles Harrington, for the recording can you just confirm your name and date of birth please Mr Clements"

"Stephen Clements twenty first July nineteen seventy-seven"

Dai now spoke "Mr Clements we need to ask you questions about the murders of five people"

Before Dai could finish Stephen spoke up "DCI Rees I admit I killed those people but I did not murder them I punished them they had sinned and god gave me the right to punish them" Mr Harrington was trying to stop him speaking "no don't stop me as I said I admit to it those five people deserved to die you surely can't lock me up for doing the lords work"

"Mr Clements we need to ask you one more thing in the photos on your wall all of your victims are marked with a Red cross, five we know but there is a photo of yourself and a woman beside the woman is a red cross who is she"?

"Oh, that is my first sinner, my mother the cow that she was, she sinned against my father I found out after he died my mother was not the saint I thought she was, she had been carrying on with a man from the church, so I punished her she stopped me seeing Mary said she was no good for me but she was no better"

"Mr Clements where is your mother's body" asked Lisa

"Oh, she's buried at the church we use, you see everyone thought mums death was an accident she fell down the stairs, but no I pushed her, I then rang for an ambulance and told them that I had found her at the bottom of the stairs no suspected a thing she was old, you see my parents were old when they had me in their forties they called me their miracle child" Mr Harrington spoke

"Stephen I think you have said enough for now, DCI Rees, DS Jones my client has admitted to the murders but I would like to put in a plea of diminished responsibility" with that Stephen got upset

"I have not got diminished responsibility are you saying I'm mad, I'm not mad I was doing the lords work I knew what I was doing"

"Look Stephen claim down I'm only trying to help you"

"I don't need your help, you can go, go on go I'm firing you the lord will help me with my defence" Mr Harrington tried to claim Stephen down more but it only made it worse "DCI Rees sir make him go I don't want him here anymore"

Dai had Lisa terminate the interview and Stephen lead back to the cells, he then escorted Mr Harrington out "I'm sorry about that Giles but I think you're right he may get away with diminished responsibility"

"Don't worry about it Dai, now he has sacked me I can say it I think he's a mad man and Milton Keynes is safer with him locked up, but I think the cps is going to ask for his mental state to be looked at before the trial"

"Well, we agree on something but I think he's going to be locked away for a very long time no matter what"

"Ok see you Dai" he turned to walk away but then turned back "Oh Dai there is one thing he asked me did I know how you got on to him"

"Well, you remember him talking about Mary that his mother stopped him seeing" "yes I do" "well it was her she was showing photos to a witness we have and he recognised him from a one of them"

"Well, I never ok Dai be seeing you some time. You on for the match on Saturday"

"I'll be there, see you then"

Dai took out his phone and dialled it pick up straight away "Holly Long"

"Holly DCI Rees, thank you again for looking after my dad and now it's time for me to do you a favour but you never got this from me" Dai explained all to Holly then headed back inside Lisa was heading out "Ah there you are, Dave's been on he's handed the house over to Colin and the forensics guys and he's heading over to give Tommy the news that we have caught or killer"

"Right lets head back to Bletchley and I think via supermarket, drinks are in hand being as we can't go to the pub"

They got back to Bletchley as most of the team did he carried in a few crates of beer and put them on a table "Right team just to say a big thank you I know we still have a lot to do before we can get him to court, but I think we all deserve a drink and remember most of you are driving so I'm sorry to say it's one drink each" everyone came up and took a drink and mingled, Dave arrived back with Ruth

"By heck I hope you left some for me"

"Help yourself, how did you get on with Tommy"?

"Ok it was Mary was shocked about him, she said she had lost touch with Clements back in the early nineties after his mother stopped them seeing each other" Dave called the team together "right folk as you now know myself and Ruth are a couple and now as we are having a celebration we'd like to announce that we are getting married, it's not yet it will be sometime in the future but we'll keep you up to date"

Dai stayed for about an hour before he made a move for home he needed to phone the hospital and Bethan, he had made all his calls when the doorbell went he answered and there stood Lisa with her arms full of bags "Lisa what are you doing here"

"Well, I promised you a meal when this was all over so here I am, spag bol do you"?

Dai stood there in shock for a few seconds "yes by all means come in here let me help you"

It turned out right Lisa was a good cook the meal went down well then they spent the rest of the evening drinking and talking.

Dai rolled in his bed his head was thumping and there was a ringing going on had he drank that much he realised the ringing was his phone "DCI Rees"

"DCI Rees Nigel Fosdyke" Dai's mind was racing "Sorry I've not been in touch before but I've been stuck in a Brazilian rain forest for the last few weeks with no contact, I believe you want to know where my car is" a smile came on Dai's face oh Mr Fosdyke if only you had contacted us earlier we could have saved someone's live,

"Yes Mr Fosdyke thank you for calling" he spent a while explaining to Mr Fosdyke what had happened and where his car was now, he put his phone down and felt an arm come round his waist he rolled over and pulled Lisa in close, he had a feeling thing where on the up.

Printed in Great Britain
by Amazon